Galaxy's Edge: SWORD OF THE LEGION
By Jason Anspach & Nick Cole

Hardcover ISBN: 978-1-949731-35-4
Paperback ISBN: 978-1-949731-34-7

Edited by David Gatewood
Published by Galaxy's Edge, LLC

Cover Art: Fabian Saravia
Cover Design: Ryan Bubion
Interior Design: Kevin G. Summers

For more information:

Website: GalacticOutlaws.com
Facebook: facebook.com/atgalaxysedge
Newsletter: InTheLegion.com

JOIN THE LEGION

FOR UPDATES ABOUT NEW RELEASES, EXCLUSIVE PROMOTIONS, AND SALES, VISIT INTHELEGION.COM AND SIGN UP FOR OUR VIP MAILING LIST. GRAB A SPOT IN THE NEAREST COMBAT SLED AND GET OVER THERE TO RECEIVE YOUR FREE COPY OF "TIN MAN", A GALAXY'S EDGE SHORT STORY AVAILABLE ONLY TO MAILNG LIST SUBSCRIBERS.

FREE SHORT STORY 'TIN MAN' WHEN YOU SIGN UP FOR OUR VIP MAILING LIST

INTHELEGION.COM

DARK OPS KILL TEAM VICTORY SQUAD

01

The planet Rawl Kima.

Captain Chhun lay on his side, using the almost-meter-high wall at the edge of the roof to shield him from the barrage of blaster fire raking up from the street below. "Booker!" he shouted to the Repub Navy attaché. "Find out what the hell is holding up the *Illustrious*."

Positioned in an attack orbit, visible overhead, the *Illustrious* was the sub-destroyer-class capital ship that had jumped the Victory kill team into Rawl Kima. Another of the endless missions to capture Mid-Core Rebellion VIPs. This had been the familiar pattern for Chhun's kill team over the past several cycles: identify VIP, abduct. Repeat ad nauseum. It had gotten to the point where Chhun would go out of his way to get his kill team attached to a Legion company and set up sniper overwatch, advance recon, and short force penetrations just to change things up.

This mission looked to be another success. The target, a rotund dwahser, sat in the middle of the roof. A plus-sized isolation hood, large enough to contain her trunk, had been fit firmly over her head, and her portly gray arms were ener-chained behind her back.

Now the mission was in jeopardy. *Illustrious* needed to hurry up and send down fighter support. Or at the very least, an evac shuttle to extract the team and target. The shuttle that should have been waiting for them in the first place. The closer one got to the core, the more the Republic military seemed incapable of basic military procedures.

Swarms of MCRs spanning the biological spectrum were surrounding the building that, prior to the kill team's op, had served as the local MCR militia headquarters. But Chhun and his kill team had the high ground, controlling the roof of that building, the tallest building in the modest urban sprawl that populated whatever town this was. *Kahl*, Chhun thought it was called. Not that it mattered. They just needed to get out of there—either that, or get some help killing bad guys.

There were a lot of bad guys.

Booker, the navy liaison, looked at Chhun from deep beneath his helmet, his eyes draped in shadows. If the thing were pulled down over his head any tighter, you'd think he was a war tortoise. "Holding up what, Captain?" he asked. "The evac or the bombing run?"

A spray of blaster fire chewed into the building's façade, with some shots streaking up so close that Chhun could hear the sizzle through his bucket. "Both or either, Booker. I don't care! Just get some—"

A fragger arced overhead, thrown from the street below. Whoever tossed it had quite an arm. Or trunk.

As the Dark Ops legionnaires watched the grenade fall, their buckets mapped its trajectory and probable landing spot, accounting for any bouncing rebounds on the surface of the rooftop. Through some kind of Republic coder magic, the bucket HUDs also identified the amount of time left on the fuse. A newer feature the kill team was happy to have.

"I'm on it," Masters called, running toward the fragger as it landed and setting up a mobile containment bubble around it. They called it a bubbler—a thick blue energy shield capable of withstanding physical trauma as effectively as two feet of impervisteel. It formed a dome around the fragger with seconds to spare.

Chhun watched the grenade as his HUD ticked down the final second. The primary and secondary explosions gave a muffled *bamf* beneath the containment bubble. "Nice work, Masters."

"Thanks, Cap." Masters powered down the bubbler, allowing a thick cloud of smoke to rise heavenward. Where the bubbler had been, the roof was scorched and piled with a layer of now harmless shrapnel. A number of other similar scorch marks and shrapnel piles already dotted the roof. "But at some point these mids are gonna get one that explodes before I can reach it. Can't keep this up forever." Masters shrugged. "At least they're too dumb to throw 'em all at once."

More likely, the ill-equipped rebels—they'd never recovered from the loss of Scarpia—didn't want to part with their fraggers unless they were sure it might save their lives.

"We need to re-take the initiative," Chhun said. "Pin *them* down. Fish!"

A leej in the black armor of Dark Ops hustled to Chhun's position from his station on the opposite side of the roof. A poorly aimed rocket streaked over their heads and landed a kilometer away with a faint *crump*.

Sergeant Andrevel Fisher threw himself against the roof wall beside Captain Chhun, his rapid-fire SAB at the ready. "Sir?"

"I need you and Averill to keep those mids pinned down and quiet for a while. I'm gonna try and convince our target to call off her dogs, for whatever that's worth."

"We should just throw her over the edge and get out by foot," offered Fish.

"Today, Fish," Chhun said, his voice betraying a smile.

"On it," Fisher answered. He waited for Sergeant Averill—Sticks—to join him on the side of the roof where the blaster fire was thickest, counted to three over L-comm, then sprang up, unleashing fury through the barrel of his SAB while Averill picked off targets with his N-4.

With the rest of the squad keeping the MCR honest from all four sides of the building, Chhun approached the dwahser, who sat oblivious to the firefight, thanks to her isolation hood. Chhun had just reached out to remove the hood when Sticks shouted an urgent heads-up.

"Three mids made it inside the front doors!"

A rumbling boom erupted from below, shaking the foundations of the building.

"And they found the A-P mines," Masters quipped over L-comm. He replenished a charge pack, leaned over the edge, and continued firing on the rebels below.

"Right where I left 'em," answered Bear, a two-meter leej who looked like he could do more damage with his hands than his N-6.

Chhun grabbed the top of the target's isolation hood and pulled it off like the lid to a covered dish dinner. The sudden transition from absolute stillness, devoid of all light or sound, to the bright sunshine and brilliant noises of combat caused the dwahser's eyes to grow wide in panic. The MCR cell leader spouted a nasal alarm through her trunk, then began to frantically slap at Chhun's chest and bucket.

"Hey—stop!—knock it off!" Chhun grabbed the nose-like appendage and drew the Kublaren tomahawk Masters had bought for him years before. "I'll cut that thing clean off if you don't stay still."

The dwahser stopped fighting. She fixed a hateful gaze at the legionnaire. *"Urah trah trah."*

"Where's the stupid translator bot?" Chhun called out. His bucket could translate the dwahser's insults just fine, but it was painfully slow. A bot was still the better option.

A cylindrical robot hovered over from a hiding spot somewhere on the roof. "I am here, Captain Chhun," the bot said, flashing blue lights accenting each syllable.

Chhun was thankful his team had been given a bot with repulsor functionality. Most beings of the galaxy might be more comfortable with bipedal machines, but taking stairs was a hell of a lot simpler with this model. "What'd the target just say?"

"Death to tyrants," the bot answered.

Good, it was translating the same as Chhun's bucket. The kill team had run into a situation a few months back where a translator bot wasn't calibrated for the proper regional dialect—and as a result, Chhun accidentally spent ten minutes making romantic overtures to a zhee cell leader. Worse yet, the zhee seemed to be into it. It looked like its little donk heart was broken when the bot's software updated.

Heart-breakers and life-takers.

Chhun gritted his teeth. He had hoped for a more compliant captive, but this sort of resistance wasn't uncommon from the MCR. Well, not from the alien ranks anyway. The humans tended to roll over the moment Republic pressure was applied.

"Today might be your lucky day," Chhun mumbled to himself. To the translator bot he said, "Tell her the blaster fire coming our way is just as likely to get *her* killed, and she needs to order—"

"'Nother fragger coming in!" shouted Fish.

"I can't get to this one!" called Masters.

The fragger bounded onto the rooftop. Legionnaires dove onto their stomachs in an attempt to avoid as much shrapnel as possible.

Boom!

A shower of debris tinked against Chhun's armor. The shrapnel blast of the fragger had missed him, and fortunately this model of grenade only exploded once, unlike the Legion's standard ordnance.

"Everyone all right?" Chhun asked his team, allowing his voice to transmit over both L-comm and externals.

One by one, the kill team called out affirmatives and went back to their firing stations. Masters was the last to reply. "I mean, nobody *important* got dusted," he said.

Uh-oh, thought Chhun, scanning the rooftop for the naval liaison. "Is Booker—?"

"He's fine," Masters said. "It's the target who took the brunt of it."

Chhun looked down beside him. The dwahser was severely perforated and bleeding heavily. He nudged her with his foot, and the MCR leader rolled onto her back. Clearly dead.

Chhun whistled at his luck. The rebel's girth had absorbed almost the entirety of the blast, and had probably saved his life.

Booker was still lying prone, covering his head with his hands. "Hey!" Chhun shouted at the liaison, snapping him out of the concussive daze caused by the fragger. "Really could use some support from your friends up in the *Illustrious* right about now!"

Booker nodded and keyed open his comm, covering one ear to better hear above the din of blaster fire. "Agro Seven to Virtue One, come in."

Chhun's Dark Ops–enhanced L-comm ported the comm transmission into his bucket's receivers.

"We hear you, Agro Seven."

Booker shouted into the comm. The fragger must have damaged his hearing. "Requesting immediate orbital support and exfiltration. Transmitting current location."

"Where's our ride out of here?" called out Bear, his voice every bit as large as his physical size.

There was a pause, as though the comm station officer aboard *Illustrious* was considering. Then: "Request is denied, Agro Seven."

Chhun didn't wait for Booker to plead his case. He broke in over the comm. "This is Captain Cohen Chhun—what the hell are you talking about, 'Request denied'?"

"Don't take that tone with me, Legionnaire."

Unbelievable.

"Listen, whoever you are," Chhun began, fuming with anger, "you get support down here right now or the first thing I'll do when I reach the ship again is hunt you down so we can talk about 'my tone' in person. You got that?"

No one in their right mind wanted an angry leej gunning for them. Especially not a Dark Ops leej. When the comm officer spoke again, his voice sounded much more charitable. "Sir, I have orders that outrank yours. We are not to send any craft into the region. No exceptions. Sorry, Captain."

"Unreal," Chhun muttered to himself. He opened up his squad comm. "Wrinkle in the op, Victory Squad. We're gonna have to get ourselves out of this. *Illustrious* says they can't send down fire support or an exfil shuttle."

"Are they thinking that would be too easy?" Masters said. "Because I don't mind the easy way. Really."

"So we kill 'em all," said Bear, jamming home a new charge pack into his weapon. "Would have been nice if they let us do that in the first place instead of that smash, grab, and

9

dash crap. Could have set up a nice ambush, have these mids all dead in the street by now."

"Typical point garbage," Fish responded, switching out his own charge packs. "Hey, I'm chewing through these. Booker! Bring me that satchel with my extras. And keep your head down."

Booker grabbed the pack carrying the extra charge packs for Fish's SAB and sprinted toward the legionnaire, keeping low, but still clearly above the roof line.

"Keep your head down!" warned Fish a second time.

An MCR blaster bolt struck the navy trooper in the temple, killing him instantly.

Fish hissed in anger and crawled to reach the satchel of ammunition.

"Move it, Fish!" called Sticks, his firing partner, as he cut down an MCR peeking from around the corner of an alley with a shoulder-mounted rocket launcher. "We need that SAB to keep them back!"

"I know, I know!" Fish shouted. He scrambled rapidly in monkey crawl. "Any of you guys notice that the closer to the core we operate, the worse trained our attachments are? I mean, I feel bad for the kid, but..."

"Stay focused," Chhun said. "We've got enough charges to keep what's in the streets busy well into the day."

So long as MCR reinforcements don't show up. Chhun resisted the urge to shake his head. His team had been in tighter scrapes than this—the runaway corvette-of-death came to mind—but knowing that didn't make the situation he was in look any better. This was bad, and it didn't promise to grow any better with time. So far, the MCR didn't seem to have a mortarbot or any repulsor vehicles at their command, but it hadn't been all that long since his kill team drove into the city in an unmarked repulsor sled to apprehend the dwahser target. Resistance could still be scrambling for a counteroffensive.

Chhun ran through scenarios. The best bet would be to forget the capital support ship and go directly to Dark Ops. No way they'd let a team hang out to die. They might already be scrambling. L-comm should be able to reach the deep space orbital platform hosting the Dark Ops command center for this section.

"Major Owens," Chhun called into his command L-comm, trusting the message would get through. "*Illustrious* doesn't want us tracking our muddy boots back on her decks. We need some relief up here."

"I know," came the Dark Ops controller's voice. It sounded crystal clear. Modern technology was a beautiful thing. "I'm watching the whole thing via remote peeper. And trust me, I chewed enough point ass to make 'em need a rabies shot. But they aren't budging. Damn fool captain agreed to a cease-fire designed by the MCR to get you guys isolated and killed, and he ain't breakin' it. Good news is that a contingency plan is already inbound. Can you hold off another fifteen minutes for an updated status report?"

"Gonna have to."

"Roger," Owens answered. "KTF."

02

Deep Space Supply Station 9
Dark Ops Headquarters, Galaxy's Edge
90 Minutes Earlier

Major Ellek Owens fumbled his cup of caff on the way to the conference room. It was hot, but not enough to elicit anything beyond a disgusted frown from the Dark Ops sector commander. He switched his mug into a dry hand and shook the drink from his fingers. Six cups this morning and he still didn't quite feel awake.

"Weak," he mumbled to himself.

The station's beverage dispensers seemed incapable of delivering caff that was either hot enough or strong enough. Owens dreamed about past rotations on super-destroyers and the first-rate meals those ships provided. At least the Republic Navy got that much right. Then again, there were leejes in the field who didn't even have time to drop a caff tab into a water unit. Owens knew he shouldn't grumble about the station's weak coffee, cold showers, or rickety hull structures. Embrace the suck and remember that Dark Ops never promised a life of ease. Owens had it better than most in his role as a sector commander, essentially tactical field commander for this section of the edge. Though he had finagled his way into remaining the team controller for Victory Squad, which kept him from feeling completely isolated from the action.

He put his dripping mug on the conference table. He did not use a coaster. Flopping into a chair, he leaned back and looked down his nose, acting as though he had only now noticed the woman already seated at the table. He hooked a finger on his sunglasses and pulled them down to reveal his dark eyes. "Thought you were off station?"

Andien Broxin, the lone Nether Ops agent Owens had ever liked or found helpful, offered an unapologetic smile. "That was the plan. But so many field reports have chimed in the last few hours that it seemed like a good idea to stay in one place a little while longer."

Owens examined the stained ceiling, still showing the wear from some contaminant leak who knows how long ago. "Picked a pretty lousy place."

Andien shrugged. "Our line of work doesn't lead us to the galaxy's nicer places."

With a half smile, Owens said, "Forty-eight hours ago I forward Wraith's report. Now you're here. Legion Commander Keller schedules a private-band meeting... I'm guessing our very first Dark Ops agent found the goods?"

"Time will tell..."

The conference comm light flashed, indicating that the time was now. Owens leaned forward and opened the channel, and a holographic image of Legion Commander Keller was rendered at the head of the table in a seated position.

"Commander," Owens said.

"Major Owens," Keller replied. He turned to face Andien. "Agent Broxin."

"Commander," answered Andien.

The three of them shared a history—one that dated back to the aftermath of the Battle of Kublar. The trio had worked together in forming the Victory kill team, which had become the most successful team Dark Ops had ever known. They shared information, with Andien confirming intelligence through her

Nether Ops contacts—at personal risk—while Owens's kill teams and Keller's control over the Legion allowed Andien to strike at the bad guys even when her political handlers wanted Nether Ops to look the other way.

And now the culmination of years of collaboration was at hand.

"Goth Sullus," Keller said, as if speaking the name itself was the story.

And in a way, it was. The whispered storm at galaxy's edge, the link that connected the failing MCR, numerous crime syndicates, and who knew what else... was named Goth Sullus. It was a name none of them had ever heard of prior to the transmission by Captain Ford—call sign Wraith, alias Aeson Keel—a scant two days prior.

"If you'll allow me the use of an archaic expression," Keller continued, "Goth Sullus is our white whale. And he's made the first move."

Owens shifted in his seat. This was the first he'd heard of any action. By the way Andien straightened her posture and cleared her throat, Owens imagined this was news to her as well.

"How do you mean, Commander?" Andien asked, leaning toward the holoprojection.

"It's unconfirmed," said Keller. "but with the intelligence sent in by Major Owens's agent in the field... it's him. That is, assuming we can still trust Captain Ford. I spent the morning reading up on 'Captain Keel' and the bounty hunter Wraith's actions. Clever trick, that. Using his armor to create a secondary persona. He certainly took to heart the directives to blend in and become part of the fringe of the galaxy."

"Ford's the only one who could have pulled off this job," Owens offered. But he knew the legion commander's observation was true, and it troubled him. Captain Ford, as Aeson Keel, had made a reputation for himself that rivaled that of the notorious Tyrus Rechs—who was, apparently, now dead.

Andien offered her support. "There's no disputing his effectiveness. He also disrupted multiple MCR operations and provided tips that helped the Republic clamp down on pirate activity throughout the galaxy."

Keller nodded. "We can discuss Captain Ford another time. I don't disagree with either of you."

The room fell silent. Owens and Andien both waited for Keller to drop the bombshell they knew was coming.

"At zero-one hundred hours, local time, Tarrago Prime and its moon were attacked. We are not receiving any communication from Fortress Omicron and suspect saboteurs may have shut down base communications. The Tarrago defense fleet is engaging with three Republic destroyers, and citizens on Tarrago Prime are transmitting grainy holocam images of what appear to be legionnaires in black-gloss armor. Not our boys. Now that all matches up exactly with the intelligence we received from Wraith, reporting what he saw on Tusca, which is now a nuclear disaster zone according to a Legion recon team."

"So Goth Sullus is attacking Tarrago," Andien said.

"The shipyards," Owens added. "He wants to destroy them. Or..." He considered. "More likely he wants to control them."

"That's my assessment as well, Major," Keller said. "My belief is that he's looking to build an armada that would threaten the Republic itself." He rubbed his chin. "And if he *does* take Fortress Omicron, he's more than capable of taking the shipyards. The defense fleet is ill trained and not suited for anything beyond scaring off pirates or smugglers. Omicron's orbital defense gun is the only thing capable of defending Tarrago. Once Sullus is in control of that gun... we won't be in a position to win it back."

"What's Utopion's take on all of this?" Owens asked.

Keller gave a brief look of contempt at the name. "The Security Council is under the impression this is a hit-and-fade by the MCR. They aren't meeting, though I've been asked to stand by all the same. That the House and Senate... *dislike* the Legion is known. Given the information we have, what we've done to obtain it, and who's involved, I'm not inclined to tell those armchair generals any more than I have to."

Andien nodded grimly. "The report by Captain Ford mentioned Admiral Devers attempting to make contact with Sullus. Do we know why?"

Owens let out a grunt of a laugh. "Knowing that point SOB, I doubt it's good."

"Well," Keller said, shifting and pulling his uniform taut. "His fleet is right where it ought to be, based on comm relay reports. And though I can't disagree with your assessment of the Republic's favorite admiral, we don't have time to worry much about him at the moment. Let me cut to the chase. Sullus wants the shipyards. We need to deny him that. Now, I can't unilaterally organize a full-scale counter assault with the Legion without starting a civil war. The House and Senate have been trying for decades to assume control of the Legion, and something like that would give them precisely the pretext they need to do so. I'll be ordered to stand down, and stand down I would. For the sake of the galaxy."

"But they can't stop a kill team," Owens offered.

Keller smiled. "They can't stop a kill team. But it needs to be our best."

"Victory is near the region, on Rawl Kima, dealing with some MCR warlord-flavor-of-the-month." Owens consulted his datapad. "Op shouldn't be more than forty-five minutes to completion. I can get them back in the field and on their way to Tarrago within two hours."

Andien shook her head. "Rawl Kima might be a problem. I read an intel report that a cease-fire and no-fly order was negotiated between the MCR government and the *Illustrious*'s captain. I'll bet you your Legion crest that your team is denied exfiltration."

Owens stood up abruptly. "If that's true, I need to work on some contingency plans to get them out."

Keller looked down at his own datapad. "It doesn't look to me like there are any Legion resources in position to get your team off Rawl Kima. What do you have in mind?"

Owens gave a grin. "Don't worry, I've got a resource that doesn't even show up in the battlenet. The *Illustrious*'s captain won't even know his no-fly order has been disregarded until it's too late."

Captain Aeson Keel looked away from the swirling layers of hyperspace to examine the message once more.

Wraith. LS-33. Return to shell.

P-1.

It was a clarion call. A message that communicated volumes while saying nothing in and of itself. At least, nothing to anyone other than him. Keel had expected this transmission since the day he'd left the stolen corvette, *Pride of Ankalore*.

How far would they have him go before they called him back in?

How would he know when he'd found whatever it was that he was sent to discover?

This call was the culmination of years of work all across galaxy's edge. Work that had seen him become rich beyond his wildest imagination.

Not that I've had any time to enjoy it, Keel mused to himself. He'd only been a galactic multi-millionaire for a few days.

But it wasn't credits that had led to him leaving his brothers on the kill team, Victory. The Republic had enemies out beyond the edge. Foes who had made the machinations of malcontents on Kublar possible. Murderers who had caused the destruction of the *Chiasm*. Terrorists who had nearly destroyed the House of Reason, warts and all.

Keel was a new man, forged by the threats of the past and the promised dangers of the future. His was an identity formed thanks to a wealth of credits funneled through Dark Ops. Enough to buy a ship. Clothes. Contacts.

Enough to disappear.

So why come back now? Had he finally found what Dark Ops had sent him looking for?

Even as layers of hyperspace unfolded outside of the *Six*'s canopy windows, possibilities swirled in Keel's head.

Was it Rechs? Keel had seen the infamous bounty hunter die aboard his ship in a nuclear explosion. Was that really something that would require a recall and debrief?

Maybe it was whatever Admiral Devers was up to with this Goth Sullus player? Or something to do with the mysterious dark legionnaires?

Or was it him, Keel?

Had he gone too far in... everything? There was an unspoken expectation that this job would leave his hands dirty. But had they become too filthy to clean off?

Too much theft and smuggling. Too many contracted kills. And, yes, real legionnaires dead—not that the crop of legionnaires the Republic put out these days was anything like the Legion Keel had served in. The Legion was now overflowing with points at almost every level. The Republic's goal of assuming control was practically a *fait accompli.*

But no, this shouldn't be about that. Keel had been careful around the kill teams. Around any leej he felt to be the real deal. He had made sure those leejes survived.

But... who could say?

"Do what needs doing." That's what Captain Owens had said to him as he prepared to depart aboard the newly acquired *Indelible VI.*

"Don't lose yourself out there." That's what Lieutenant Chhun had said next.

Even then, when the trappings of a commission as a Legion captain were still fresh, Keel knew he couldn't do both. He couldn't do what needed doing without losing himself. He had chosen the former. And now he would accept the consequences of his actions. Dark Ops and the Legion commanders would determine whether he had fulfilled his mission. And whatever their determination was... he would live with it.

He was already living with it. The legionnaires, basics, marines, and navy troopers he had dusted along the way... these were acceptable losses. That's what he told himself. They had to be.

Leenah was watching him. The pink-skinned Endurian former rebel—the genius mechanic who had spent as much time in Ravi's old navigator chair as she'd spent in the maintenance hatches—had read the message. And now she was waiting for a response. Patiently.

Keel took a deep breath and turned to face her. "We all have a past, right?"

Leenah nodded. Delicately. Eager to agree, it seemed to Keel.

He pointed at the display, letting his hand linger for a moment before speaking. "This message is the exact point where my past catches up to my present."

"So you were a legionnaire," observed Leenah. "I figured as much. When you put on the armor—became Wraith—you had that... bearing, I guess. I'm not sure what else to call it."

Keel shifted in his chair. "Technically I'm still in the Legion."

Leenah's face betrayed surprise... which soon gave way to skepticism. "I... but I've seen you... fight. *Kill* Republic legionnaires and soldiers and..." She bobbed her head, causing her pink, hair-like tendrils to sway. "I guess I've seen you shoot a *lot* of people."

"Nothing to be confused about," Keel said with a slight frown. "It was them or me. Always has been."

"So this whole time you've been—what?—undercover? Working for the Republic?"

"For the Legion." Keel flipped a few switches above the console, readying the ship to dump out of hyperspace. "There's a difference. At least, there used to be."

Leenah clenched her jaw, but didn't pursue the issue further. Keel felt an urge to provide an explanation, but what would he say? He brushed the urge aside. For now, he needed to make contact.

Keel looked over his shoulder, trying to read the nav display in front of Leenah, without success. "Hey, uh, do you mind telling me where we are?"

The mechanic-turned-navigator paused, as though weighing an objection, then studied the display. "Looks like nowhere. Deep space, nowhere near... anything."

"Good."

Keel squeezed the hyperdrive's gear control, disengaging the safety, and slowly reduced the ship's speed. The swirling layers of space receded into the elongated lines of each individual star, and, finally, the vastness of space. Billions of distant, twinkling lights winked through the darkness, mere pinpoints visible through the ship's canopy.

Leenah stood. "The rest of the crew will wonder why we've dropped out of hyperspace. I'll go and tell them you received an urgent message."

Keel grabbed Leenah by the arm as she attempted to move past his pilot's seat. "No, hey... why don't you sit down? You want to know what's going on, who I am? This is your ticket."

Leenah considered, and for a moment it seemed that she could go either way. Stay or leave.

"Stay," Keel said gently. "I don't know exactly what's coming, but I know I want you to stay aboard."

"As a crewmember?"

Keel swallowed. "Sure."

As she sat back down, the comm chimed. Keel nodded for her to answer it. She missed what he meant entirely, sitting still in her chair with a confused look.

Ravi would have brought up the comm.

"Never mind. I'll get it." Keel reached forward and switched the comm to audio only. "This is the freighter *Frisky Landshark*." He gave a slight grin. He'd wanted to use that false registry for ages, but Ravi had always nixed it. "Go for—"

The cabin lights dimmed, and a projected holodisplay splashed before Keel. The larger-than-life image of his old Dark Ops team leader, Ellek Owens, appeared before him. Keel's eyes darted down to verify that he had indeed selected audio only.

He had.

"Go for Captain Keel," he said, a wry tone of exasperation in his voice. "And be thankful you didn't catch me in the shower."

"Yeah, we can force your visuals. Badass, huh, Captain Ford?" Owens said, his voice booming over the comms. He looked the same, thick beard, muscles. If he'd developed crow's-feet, his perpetually worn shades covered the evidence. "Got your message and decided the time has come to bring you back in. Trouble's here."

03

Keel leaned back in the pilot's seat, rubbing the stubble on his chin. "Bring me in how?"

Owens worked over a piece of gum before saying, "Assigning you to an op. Well, two of them, technically. If you're feeling rusty, don't worry. All you have to do is pick up Chhun's kill team and fly them to a target."

"I didn't let myself get rusty," Keel said, giving Leenah a sidelong glance.

"Relax. Giving you a hard time. I've read the reports filed by all the people you've"—Owens made air quotes with his fingers—"*done business* with. Trust me, I know you're still capable of some KTF."

Keel swallowed, wondering how often those reports included his treatment of the new class of legionnaires. Moral questions long buried were scratching their way to the surface of his conscience like undead monsters. Would it all be seen as 'whatever is necessary'? Had he made the right decisions? These were the issues that deep down, he had hoped he would never have to deal with. His role in Dark Ops had been dangerous enough. Throw in working out on the edge as a smuggler and bounty hunter, and Keel had been banking on getting killed before he ever had to sort all this out. But no matter how hard the other guys tried... they never seemed able to snuff him out.

Owens looked over at Leenah in the navigator's chair. "Who's the Endurian?"

"I'm Leenah," the princess said.

There was a certain impetuousness in her voice that led Keel to believe that, deep down, perhaps she truly *did* identify as a princess. He made a mental note to keep using the titles. "Her Majesty is a member of my crew. Mechanic."

Leenah blushed, her pink skin growing scarlet at her cheeks.

The Dark Ops commander surveyed her, then gave a fractional, approving nod. "Right. Endurian princesses." He gave a two-finger wave. "Hey, Leenah."

Leenah gave an awkward, half-wave of her own. "Hi."

Owens returned his attention to Keel. "I'm beaming jump coordinates. Victory Squad will be awaiting extraction from a Naseen light freighter. Expect the situation to be hot. And no more shooting leejes. You're back in."

Keel shut his eyes, seeking to temporarily black out the universe. "What comes after I make the pickup?"

"After that," Owens said, a grim smile on his face, "you're headed to Tarrago Prime. More details once Victory is on board."

"This about what I reported? About Devers?"

From the corner of his eye, Keel saw Leenah react to the word "reported." She hadn't expected him to have been actively reporting to the Legion all this time. His mind drifted for a moment. He wanted to stand up and soliloquize about the Legion, the Republic, liberty. To just... explain. For his own benefit as much as hers. To remind Owens that he'd been a true legionnaire. A son of freedom in a galaxy diseased beyond repair.

And when he saw them, he wanted to tell Chhun and the kill team the same.

Owens's reply came before the rushing patterns of Keel's thoughts could form into articulated ideas. "Is this about your report?" Owens repeated. "Yes and no. You found the big bad wolf, I'm sure of that. This Sullus guy is exactly who Andien was hunting. We just didn't have a name until you provided it. We believe he's leading some sort of evolved rendition of the MCR."

"How about Devers?" Keel asked, aching to hear that justice was coming for the worthless point. Confirmation of what he already knew in his heart—that whatever Devers was doing there, it wasn't good.

Tell me that a kill team—that someone—is picking up where I failed, he thought to himself, as if willing Owens to speak the words.

Owens shook his head. "Let it go, Ford—"

"Call me Keel," the captain interrupted. "I'm not... I'm not quite ready to be Ford again. Y'know?"

"Well *that* doesn't give me the warm fuzzies," Owens replied. "But sure, Keel. Look, hardly anyone in the chain of command even knows what we're doing. I ran it by Legion Commander Keller—who's in charge of the whole show now, if you hadn't heard. And there's nothing we can do. We've got no proof of anything beyond a meeting between Devers and Sullus, and with the House of Reason giving their points the authority to negotiate with the MCR, that won't go far."

"I should have let Exo put him down on Kublar."

"Hindsight," said Owens. "But look, even if you had holos of him going over plans to load up his super-destroyer with koobs and zhee to take over Utopion, nothing would come of it. And you know why. He's the Republic's golden boy. The handsome, smiling face of the Republic military-industrial complex. The right people won't believe us, or won't *admit* to believing us. Then they'll send in their favorite pet Nether Ops agent to find out how we found out, and they'll shut our little Dark Ops cell down. And you can believe me on that. The Republic wants to shut down or bring the Legion under its full control as soon as they get the chance. Whatever Devers is up to, just gotta let it happen. He's not the big sol-fish, anyway."

Everything Owens said made sense. But they both knew that a man like Devers, a man out only for himself, was up to no good. And somehow, he was again free of consequences. So what if the Republic gave its points authority to negotiate? Keel was sure that what he had seen in the crosshairs before Tyrus Rechs committed suicide in his starship was a Republic parlaying with a murderous warlord who'd attacked the Republic without provocation or warning.

And your blaster bolts weren't real? Keel asked himself. *You weren't participating in open hostilities against the Republic, MCR, and anyone else who got in your way?*

But that was different. It had to be.

"Young miss, the ship has changed its course."

Prisma rolled over in her bunk aboard the *Indelible VI* and blinked at the inky darkness. She found KRS-88's glowing optics in the same corner she'd last seen him before turning off the lights and going to sleep. She didn't need a night-light. Not anymore. And that made her feel grown up. Grown up in a way that somehow seemed more noteworthy than losing her parents and then Rechs and surviving conflicts that she had no business being involved in.

Captain Keel had said that the galaxy was full of orphans. He'd told Leenah that. Skrizz had told Prisma that children always died in wars, and she was lucky to be alive. Or at least, that's what she thought Skrizz said. It was what Crash translated, anyway. But her daddy had programmed Crash to lie if that might protect Prisma or her feelings—because her daddy had wanted Crash to make her feel safe. That's what Garret, the code-slicer, told her.

Everyone on the ship knew everything, and Prisma was just a kid, a little girl. That's how they treated her. Especially Leenah. Leenah was nice and tried to be motherly. She didn't seem to know what it meant to really be a mother, but being nice helped. Prisma liked Leenah.

But Prisma was not a kid. Kids could lose their parents. Prisma knew that. And kids could live or die in battles. Prisma knew that too. But kids were also afraid of the dark—and Prisma was not... so long as Crash stayed with her. As long as she wasn't alone.

"Crash," mumbled Prisma, "what?"

"I said that the ship changed course, young miss." The bot's servos whined in the darkness as it moved its head. "I do wish you would listen better."

Pushing herself up on her elbows, Prisma said, "So?"

"Oh." The bot's servos moved again, and it seemed to think about this. "I thought that was interesting. Captain Keel dropped the ship from hyperspace, sat in open space for some time, and then jumped in a different direction. I debated, and decided you would like to know."

Prisma flopped back down onto her pillow. "No, I don't care, Crash. I said wake me up if we get wherever we're going."

"I see."

"I'm going back to sleep," Prisma said. Feeling brave, she added, "Why don't you power down? Your optical lights might keep me awake. I like to sleep in the dark."

"Yes, I've noticed, young miss." Crash dimmed its eyes. "I would rather not power down at the moment. A diagnostic and recharge would be inefficient given the time of last cycle."

"Okay, whatever," Prisma managed, already drifting into sleep as the ship thrummed through hyperspace.

"I *could* power down for a few hours," observed Crash, "if it would please you for me to do so. I did not wish to be difficult if—"

"Fine," Prisma said, annoyed that her drift into sleep was interrupted. "Shut down."

"Shutting down, young miss."

Prisma lay in silence. She looked in the corner, but didn't see the comforting glow of Crash's eyes. She pulled her blanket up to her chin and rubbed her heels against the rough sheets of her bunk. Her eyes grew heavy again.

"Prisma."

The girl jumped as if woken from a dream. "Crash?"

"No, not Crash."

"Ravi?"

The familiar voice of the hologram answered in the affirmative. "Prisma, you must listen to me. Do not let anyone know we have spoken. Not yet."

"Why?"

"For your safety, Prisma."

"How?"

"We are all heading toward unimaginable danger. And unavoidable. Captain Keel and Leenah will want you to stay with the ship, and you must listen to them. You must not let anyone see you."

Prisma peered into the darkness. "Why can't I see you?"

"Because I am not projecting myself in your room. You are not afraid of the dark."

Prisma leaned against her headboard. "I'm not," she said in small voice.

"Do you understand what I have told you?"

"Not really."

"But you do understand what I've instructed you. Stay hidden. Keep our discussion private."

"Yes."

"Good. Pay attention, Prisma, I will keep you safe."

"Ravi, they're looking for you, you know…"

No reply came from the darkness.

"Ravi?"

Nothing, and then… servos whined, and Crash's optical lights came alive again. "Did you say something, young miss?"

Prisma slid her arm under her pillow and lay back down. "No. Go back to sleep, Crash."

04

The *Indelible VI* roared in low over the planet Rawl Kima. Coniferous forests covered most of the planetary surface, their canopies a green blur streaking beneath the heavily modified starship. The kill team Captain Keel was sent to pick up was still several hundred kilometers away.

Leenah monitored passive sensors from the navigator's seat. She felt inadequate reading the displays, worried that she was missing something obvious. She'd always felt more comfortable fixing things than using them. "The ship's not detecting any other starcraft—Republic or otherwise," she said.

"Good," Keel acknowledged. He pointed to a blinking yellow light to Leenah's left. "When that light turns blue, tell me. It means we can contact the kill team on L-comm without a listening station picking up the burst. The navy won't know what we're saying, but they'll know we're coming. And according to Owens, they'll try and stop us for violating a no-fly order."

"How long?"

Keel glanced at the HUD projected over the *Six*'s cockpit window. "At current speed, shouldn't be more than a few minutes. Say seven, tops."

Nodding in understanding, Leenah began watching the light like a mother monitoring her sleeping child. She wanted to let Keel know the moment it changed color. But seven minutes of silence was a long time. "You sure you don't want me to get Skrizz up here? I'm sure he'd do a better job than me."

"No," Keel said. "You're doing fine. I don't exactly trust the wobanki. Especially without Ravi around to watch my back. Don't tell him I said that though."

"I won't." Leenah puffed out a breath of air. She wanted to check in on Prisma, but there wasn't time. So she attempted polite conversation. "Would have been nice to enter atmosphere on a better trajectory. Why do you think the Republic established a blockade here?"

Keel adjusted the throttle controls. "Could be any number of reasons, from smart to stupid. But you can bet how it would impact the legionnaires on the ground didn't factor much in the decision."

Leenah pressed her lips together. "It's odd. Hearing you talk about legionnaires as if they're the good guys."

"*These* are the good guys. Dark Ops is what the entire Legion used to be like. Other than a few appointees, it's how the Legion was when I was on tour."

"And now things are different?"

Keel sighed, and Leenah got the impression he didn't much want to discuss it. But she didn't understand the man. And she wanted to.

"Keep in mind," she said, "you're talking to a former rebel. You've got a few years of Endurian propaganda to overcome."

"The Legion's purpose is to protect the Republic from all its enemies—inside and out. A lot of us are still doing just that—but from what I've seen in the past years..." Keel paused to lick his lips. "A lot of people wearing the Legion crest are more interested in doing the Republic's bidding than upholding the ideals the Ancients built."

The trees and wilderness began to give way to hamlets and agricultural grids. Bots attended to the harvest, undeterred by the low-flying freighter roaring above their heads.

Leenah watched the orchards and fields of grain pitch and sway in the wake of the *Six*'s atmospheric thrusters.

The light continued to blink yellow. Keel seemed like he was finished talking. Leenah was not. "Even with a blockade though, I can't remember the last planet I was on with this little air traffic."

"Oh, there's traffic out this way," Keel said, visually scanning his airspace. "Just not the kind that shows up on most sensors. Drag the blue reticule into your scanning array."

Leenah placed two fingers on the holoprojected screen and shifted a blue circle with a black dot over to the scanner's readout. Immediately a swarm of blue triangles appeared at all ranges. She gasped. "What are those?"

"Lymars," Keel answered, a smile on his face. "Winged mammals native to the planet. The local population uses them instead of speeders, sort of a cultural distinction. If you look down, you can probably see some skimming between the trees."

Leenah tried to peer down out of her window to spy the creatures. Keel tilted the ship, allowing her to see straight down.

"Oh!" Leenah exclaimed. "I see one. It looks like... do you know the borash from Enduria?"

Keel shook his head. "I, uh, I'm not quite as familiar with Endurian customs and culture as Ravi was."

"Well these look a lot like them. Only without feathers." Leenah glanced back at the display. The light was blue. She cursed her inattentiveness. "Light's blue," she said.

"Good. Bring up L-comms."

"Umm..." Leenah searched through the comm keys, not seeing what she was looking for.

"You have to toggle crypto and then Legion, Dark Ops," Keel said, not taking his eyes away from the flight displays projected over the forward canopy. The buildings were coming faster now, and staying low no doubt took additional concentration.

After punching in the necessary commkeys, Leenah held her finger above the transmission button. "Okay, ready?"

Keel nodded. A soft chime sounded to announce a secure patch into the L-comm network.

"Legion kill team Victory," Keel said, his eyes glancing up at a velocity display. "This is Rescue One. Be advised, we're coming in weapons hot for exfiltration. Naseen light freighter, ETA eight minutes."

"Copy, Rescue One," a voice answered over L-comm. "Major Owens said you were coming. We'll hold out until you arrive. Vic One out."

The calmness in the legionnaire's voice was reassuring. Leenah had been worried that the legionnaires would start shooting at them the moment they showed up. The idea of being part of a *legitimate* freighter crew—not to mention one that had apparently been given carte blanche to operate outside of Republic law—was surreal. But it was also welcome. It had been the promise of freedom that had most influenced Leenah to join the Mid-Core Rebellion. And now—somehow—she had it.

The comm chirped again, and another legionnaire's voice came online. "Holy strokes—is that really you, Captain Ford?"

Keel smiled. "Never heard of him. KTF."

Chhun risked another peek over the wall. The Mid-Core Rebels were packed thick in the streets, and the atmosphere was that of a city-wide celebration. The crowd included a mix of dwahser, human, and kimbrin, mingled with the typical galactic diaspora of species found at galaxy's edge. But the celebration had nothing to do with Unity Day. These revelers were on hand in the hopes of witnessing the death of a Legion kill team.

And they weren't shy about helping to make that hope a reality.

Blaster fire continued to strike against the half-walls providing rooftop cover. "Peeper is showing another group massing by the west entrance," Chhun announced over L-comm.

Bear moved in a low crawl to a potential vantage point. The fusillade of MCR blaster fire was thick enough that the legionnaires had very little time to deliver return fire. They would pop over the wall, lay down a burst of viciously accurate blaster fire, then pop back into cover before they were picked off. All the leejes had scorch marks on their armor from glancing blaster bolts, but thankfully they'd been struck by nothing powerful enough to cause any real damage. The MCR just didn't have the weaponry it once did—a testament to how effective Republic blockades and crackdowns on smuggling and piracy had truly been.

"Goin' up," Bear announced. The burly soldier popped up and sprayed a few rounds into the oncoming soldiers before cursing and dropping back below cover to avoid a stinging retort of enemy blaster bolts. "I got like... maybe two guys."

"Throw a fragger at them," suggested Masters.

"Looks like there's civs mixed in with the mids," Fish said.

"Then they made a bad decision," said Chhun. He mirrored the observation bot's feed into the HUDs of his men, and fed them trajectory lines for tossing grenades into the massing rebels. "And if we don't keep this crowd back, we're going to get a real push to get inside the building instead of just a couple of brave—"

"Stupid," corrected Masters.

"—ones," Chhun concluded. "The auto-turret can only do so much."

He knew that Pike, who usually carried a Mark 950 repeater but had had the thing shot and disabled by a storming MCR, was now running around inside the building, replacing anti-personnel mines as needed and making sure the turret had adequate charge-cans. The team was almost out of both of those. Ammo was running close to black as well. If the mids down below came at them in a wave, Pike would be hard pressed to keep them at bay. It was paramount that the rooftop defenders kept the rebels back, even if that meant fragging civilians who, let's face it, weren't standing in a crowd and yelling "Die, Legion!" to encourage Dark Ops morale.

"On my throw," Chhun told his team. He set his fragger to smart-det, allowing the grenade's destructive little AI to decide the optimal time to detonate. Not all of the grenades were "smart," but now seemed like the time to use the ones that were. "Fragger out!"

The grenade sailed over the roof wall, followed by four more. The observation bot made them glow blue on the HUD relay, along with a comet-like tail to indicate their course into the enemy. The fraggers' dual detonations wreaked havoc in the crowd, sending the combatants into a panicked stampede. It was enough of a distraction to allow the legionnaires to get back on the wall and resume firing.

"They're already re-forming," Sticks said between bursts of his N-6.

Chhun saw the same thing. The fraggers had had the same effect as tossing a large rock into a stream. It dispersed the flow for a brief second before the rushing water came right back. "Don't stop shooting! Make them pay for every step!"

The legionnaires dished it out every bit as good as they took it, and rebels dropped in every direction. Even the non-fatal shots proved deadly, as the crowd trampled over their own fallen. The fraggers had apparently made them mad.

"They're gonna breach the building," Fish said, stating what was now obvious to everyone.

"Then we stack the bodies so high in the doorway that they need a pulsor dozer to get through," Bear growled. His N-6-dry fired. "I'm out of charge packs!" He laid down his rifle and begin firing careful shots with his service pistol.

"I'm almost done, too," Masters announced.

"One fresh pack left," added Sticks.

Chhun had the same.

"Still good with the SAB," Fish shouted between bursts.

That was a relief.

"Pike!" Chhun called to the legionnaire manning the stories below. "Gimme a sit-rep."

"Turret is chewing them up, getting pretty hot. But enough are getting through. First one that's packing an ion grenade is going to be able to shut it down."

"Let's hope they don't have 'em!"

"They'll have 'em," Pike replied. "We've got that Dark Ops luck today, Captain."

Wasn't that the truth? This mission should be finished. And while Chhun didn't dwell on how much had gone wrong or the amount of fault the Republic Navy had in *causing* so much to go wrong, he did think that it sure would be nice to not have to do this alone.

"How are we on mines?"

"No reserves. I've got them set up behind the turret. I'm hoping if they get past that, they'll rush as a group and we'll get a few multi-kills."

"Roger," Chhun said. He checked the countdown chrono on his HUD. "Better fall back to the roof, then. Our ride should be on its way."

"On my way."

Chhun looked to the leejes sending plunging fire down onto the rebels below. "How we doing?"

"Mids are pretty good at dying," Masters answered, "but enough of them are squirting through and sheltering at the base of the building. They just keep coming."

The L-comm chimed to indicate a non-squad communication. "Victory Squad," came the voice of Wraith. "I'm positioned for an attack run to clear the area before landing. You might want to curl up into little balls and say your prayers. This is gonna be a little rough…"

"Grab some cover!" Chhun commanded.

The roar of an incoming ship softened into the hum of repulsors, and a Naseen freighter slowed and moved above the main avenue, its nose pointed slightly down toward the streets. Its heavy blaster cannons opened up, sending concussive explosions rippling through the crowd—impacts that Chhun could feel in the cavity of his chest. That ship was packing some serious, and technically illegal, firepower.

Fish's voice was shaking from the impact of the blaster cannons. "Is that pilot shooting anti-vehicle blasters into the mids? Holy hell!"

"Sure sounds like it!" Bear shouted. "That'll clear 'em out. Ooah!"

"Oh, nasty!" Masters said. "It's raining rebel pieces."

Chhun saw the carnage Masters was referring to. Some of the MCR had made it to the roof—in fragmented pieces—blown apart and upward by the ship's tremendous firepower.

Pike's voice came over L-comms. He still hadn't reached the roof. "Oba! Sounds like the whole building is going to come down!"

"What's it look like downstairs?" Chhun asked.

"They're coming in. We'll know when to get guns on the door when we hear the—"

He was cut off by the booming explosion of the mines, their last line of defense.

"Okay, so now," Masters said, swinging his N-4 around to cover the rooftop door.

"Wraith," Chhun called over the L-comm. "We'd really love to get off this roof right about now."

"Sorry," Wraith replied. "They're setting up a crew-served anti-air battery. Shields won't stop the ray-shielded missile that thing fires, and I'll be a sitting groose hovering over the rooftop. Gotta take one more pass. You really ticked the mids off today."

05

Keel made a wide, rolling arc, frowning at the small-arms blaster fire that extinguished itself in harmless flashes against the *Indelible VI*'s shields. "One more pass," he announced to the cockpit.

Skrizz popped his feline head inside and yammered a question.

"Nothing much you can do up here," Keel said. "But thanks for the offer. Oh, and are you staying on or getting off this stop?"

The wobanki yowled a negative, and pointed out that his desire to move on in the galaxy on his own didn't mean he wanted to get dropped in among a mob of rebels. The catman would be staying. For now.

"Can't say I blame you," Keel said, leveling the craft for its next strafing maneuver. "Word of advice: don't mess with the legionnaires that come on board. They'll drop you before you can twitch your whiskers." He felt that Skrizz was the only one on board who might think it was a good idea to test the oncoming Dark Ops team. The message was his fair warning.

With a parting yowl, Skrizz left Keel to vector in his weapon systems.

"Here we go," Keel said, arming his forward cannons.

Leenah, still in the navigator's seat, covered her eyes. "Oh, I can't watch this again."

The *Six*'s blaster cannons ripped into what remained of the MCR, cutting a path to the mobile A-A emplacement and reducing it to little more than melted slag and broken parts.

"Why not?" asked Keel.

Leenah dropped her hands from her eyes, but didn't look outside. Instead she fixed a hot-take stare at Keel. "Because they're getting ripped apart and blown to pieces!"

"So?"

"So, that's an *awful* thing to see!"

Keel shrugged. "They'd do the same to us."

Leenah folded her arms and leaned back in her seat. "That doesn't mean I have to like it. *Or* watch it happening."

"Suit yourself, princess," Keel said with a smile. The ship finished its attack run, leaving the streets around the target building virtually clear—except for the smoldering dead. "Let's pick up our new crew. It's gonna be crowded for a few hours."

He maneuvered the ship on repulsor power so that it hovered above the roof. The building didn't look like it could handle the weight of a landing, and besides, the legionnaires were in the middle of a firefight with MCR that were attempting to make it through the rooftop door. Keel eased the ship off to one side, just off the edge of the building, and dropped the ramp. His spacing was perfect, and the ramp lowered onto the wall like a gangplank.

"Deploy the belly turret," he said to Leenah.

The Endurian pressed the requisite areas of the touch console.

"Aim it at the doorway where all the MCR are trying to spill out."

Leenah complied, though somewhat more hesitantly. She touched the console as if it were covered in a muddy slime and all she really wanted was to keep her hands clean.

"Victory Squad," Keel called into the L-comm, "I've got you covered. Fall back into the ship. And don't get in the way of my cannon."

"Copy, Wraith," answered Chhun.

Keel held the craft in place rather than trusting the ship-board AI to keep it steady. He wanted to depart with full thrust-ers on the moment the door closed, and waiting for the AI to allow the dangerous maneuver would cost him precious seconds. So, manual it was. "Okay," he said softly to Leenah. "Open fire and dust those mids."

"Oh..." Leenah's hand hovered over the button. "Aeson... I can't!"

"Whaddaya mean you can't?" Keel said, incredulous. "Shoot them, or our reason for coming gets killed, and *we* probably get a grenade or rocket sent inside the ship for our trouble!"

Leenah gritted her teeth, still hesitating. "I just... I just don't want to be *responsible* for ripping people apart like earlier. I—"

There was no time to argue. Keel leaned over to press the button on Leenah's screen himself, keeping one hand on the flight controls in an attempt to hold the *Six* steady. He thought this would be faster than dragging things over his way, but the simple task proved difficult. The distance was enough that he stretched himself to his limits, and when his neck craned upward for a glimpse of the screen, the side of his face was pressed against Leenah's chest. He swatted his hand around blindly in an attempt to hit the fire control, feeling as though his cheeks might be as pink as Leenah's skin.

Under different circumstances, he would have made a joke about their position and predicament, given that Leenah wasn't exactly trying to push him off of her. But now wasn't the time. The ship listed as Keel kept swiping for the fire control.

"You gonna open up anytime soon?" Chhun asked over L-comm.

"Yeah!" Keel shouted back. To Leenah, his voice somewhat muffled by her coveralls, he said, "A little help to get me in the right direction?"

Leenah grabbed Keel's wrist and slapped his hand down onto the fire control. The high-pitched rapid fire of the belly turret sounded, and Keel sprang back into his own seat, righting the ship so the kill team could run aboard.

"Thanks," Keel said.

The Endurian straightened her coveralls. "That doesn't count. Technically it was still you who shot all those people."

"Seems fair," Keel replied with a nod.

The turret's ready fire laid waste to the rebels who had reached the doorway, and prevented any more from trying. The constant stream of blaster bolts made it suicidal for them to press the attack.

"We're all on board and secure," Chhun announced.

Keel raised the ramp and switched over fire controls to himself. He retracted the belly turret and turned the ship so that its rear thrusters faced the rooftop door. A few MCR took advantage of the lull to spring out onto the roof and shoot without effect at the Naseen freighter. They were promptly incinerated when Keel punched up the ship's main thrusters and the *Indelible VI* rocketed away on a planetary exit trajectory.

"Unidentified starship, you have violated a Republic no-fly zone! Power down and await immediate impound."

The stern rebuke was broadcast from the Republic destroyer looming in the distance.

"Must've missed the sign," Keel mumbled to himself. He signaled for Leenah to activate the comm. "Republic destroyer, this is the freighter *Probable Horseshoe*. Transmitting authorization credentials."

Keel burst his kill team credentials and waited.

And waited.

Chhun came into the cockpit, his helmet off. For a moment the two men just stared at one another, as if unsure how to proceed. Then Chhun extended a hand to the seated Keel. "Thanks for the rescue."

Keel shook Chhun's hand. "Don't mention it." He nodded toward his navigator. "This is Leenah."

Chhun shook Leenah's hand as well. "A pleasure to meet you."

"Thank you," Leenah answered.

"She used to be MCR," Keel said offhandedly, hiding a grin behind his hand.

Leenah's eyes went wide. She looked up at Chhun as if expecting him to lock her in ener-chains or point a blaster pistol at her head. But the legionnaire didn't pay the comment any mind.

"We can catch up later," Chhun said. "I just wanted to pop in and see where to put my guys. See if you need anything."

"There's a storage locker in the—" Keel began before he was interrupted by an incoming comm transmission from the destroyer.

"Freighter... *Probable Horseshoe*?" the comm officer said, as if in disbelief at what he was reading. This was a new voice. The comm transmission had probably been sent up the chain of command, given Keel's use of the kill team credentials. "This is Chief Comm Officer Pillman. Am I to understand that you have a Republic kill team on board?"

Keel leaned toward the comm. "That's correct. They're all here. They seem pretty mad that you didn't send down a shuttle. I wouldn't bother them if I were you."

"*Horseshoe,* you are to await fighter escort and follow to *Illustrious* docking bay two."

Keel leaned in to speak in the comm. "Uh, negative, *Illustrious.* Kill team has orders to move on."

"Await Raptor escort," the comm officer repeated.

"*Illustrious,* this is Captain Chhun. We have orders from Legion Command to move directly to another target."

Leenah looked up from her sensors. "Two Raptors have left the destroyer and are on an intercept course."

"Not my problem, Legionnaire," said Pillman. "You all can go wherever you want after you dock, but this ship is a private register, and it is being impounded for violation of a duly mandated no-fly zone."

"Fat chance of that," Keel muttered. He looked up at Chhun. "Better get strapped in."

"What for?"

"Even if we had time to deal with these Repub rules and regs—which I didn't get the impression we did—you can forget it. This is how you lose your ship. Trust me."

"So you're going to, what? Outrun a Republic destroyer and two Raptors?"

Keel waited until he heard the click of Chhun's safety harness. "Pretty much."

The *Indelible VI* rolled vertical and dramatically increased its speed, shooting between the two Republic Raptors as they lazily drifted in place to assume an escort formation.

"*Probable Horseshoe!*"

Keel laughed at the protestations of the comm officer. He loved when the outraged or bewildered voices on the other side of the comm were forced to use one of the ridiculous false names and registries Keel had manufactured. The only thing missing from this moment was a slow head shake from Ravi.

"Ford," Chhun said, and Keel could tell that the legionnaire was gripping the back of his chair. "What're you doing? We're going to run into the *Illustrious*."

"*Probable Horseshoe!* Decelerate and adjust course or we will be forced to disable you!"

"The Raptors are getting within firing range," Leenah warned.

"Relax," Keel said calmly. "I've done this a hundred times. They won't catch us."

A blaster cannon burst sizzled in front of the canopy before it was snuffed out by the *Indelible*'s shields.

Keel nosed his ship down abruptly, his sublight engines whining as he sent more power to them. "Hang on," he called out before squeezing the light speed controls.

Star lines filled the cockpit. The ship picked up speed—and then just as quickly slowed.

"Did you just do a micro-jump?" Leenah asked.

"Yeah. We're a good thousand kilometers away."

"I thought those were dangerous," Chhun said.

Keel shrugged. "Incredibly so. But with enough practice..."

Leenah unbuckled from her chair. "Those are *murder* on a ship's engine. I'd better go and make sure everything is all right."

"I'm sure it'll be okay," Keel said, watching her go. "Ravi and I used to make those jumps all the time."

"Doesn't mean that this time you won't have fused the drive couplers," Leenah grumbled on her way out the door.

Keel smiled. Leenah was too much a mechanic to not use any excuse to pore over the engines, just to make sure the ship was still operating in peak condition.

"So..." Chhun began.

Keel stood and stretched, then clapped Chhun's armored shoulder. "C'mon. You can introduce me to your team before we get a brief from Owens."

"Sure," Chhun said, getting up himself. "Only, I need to know where we are, where we're going... I didn't realize we were getting picked up just to go on another op. My team's not set. We've gone dry on ammo, maybe a pair of fraggers and ear-poppers between us all."

Keel gave him a devilish grin. "I've got that covered, too."

Prisma wasn't sure if she liked the black-armored legion-naires that commingled with Skrizz and Garret in the ship's common lounge. She peered out from her quarters, watching them down the hall.

"Why is their armor black?" she asked Crash. "They look different from those black soldiers on Tarrago. The ones who killed..."

She stopped, not wanting the cursed image of her father's final moments to rush back into her mind's eye.

"They are a Republic Dark Ops kill team, young miss," Crash answered, sounding pleased at being able to provide the answer. "They are the most capable soldiers in the Legion. Highly trained and deadly."

"Could you kill them if you had to?"

Crash seemed to consider. "Some of them, though I believe they would terminate me before I could dispense of the entire team. It would be better to do whatever they say, as lawful representatives of the Republic. And perhaps they are friendly."

"Do you think they're here for me?"

"Based on what the *Indelible VI*'s AI has told me, we picked them up in some sort of rescue mission. They may be friends of Captain Keel."

Prisma scrunched up her face. "Who would want to be friends with *him*?"

A legionnaire looked down the hall and saw Prisma staring. She gasped and ducked back inside her quarters. He looked dangerous in his armor. And scary. And that made her upset. Because she was done being afraid.

She willed herself to step out into the hall. She would not let this... Dark Ops person know that she was afraid. Even if he wanted to capture her or do terrible things to her and take her away from Crash, he would say, "That girl sure is brave."

The legionnaire took a step toward her, and Prisma reflexively took a step back. She wanted to retake the ground she'd given up, but her muscles seemed frozen in place. But the black armored soldier didn't advance any further. Instead, he lowered himself to one knee, pulled off his helmet, and placed it gently on the floor. He smiled at Prisma and gave her a wink.

"Hey," he said. "I'm not going to hurt you."

Prisma felt less afraid. And she thought the man underneath the helmet was handsome. She liked the way his face looked. But it was strange. She'd always imagined that the men beneath the armor were all ugly and frightening—that their helmets covered grotesque scars and colorless eyes, twisted teeth and snarling curled lips.

"My name's Aaldon," the legionnaire said. "But everyone calls me Masters. What's your name?"

Prisma felt the urge to run into her quarters and lock the door. But she was brave now. "Prisma," she said.

"It's nice to meet you, Prisma. Do you like candy? I have..." Masters began to rummage through his belt pouches. He produced an empty chocolate bar wrapper. "Oh. I guess I ate it."

Prisma giggled, and that made the legionnaire named Masters smile.

"Oh, very funny," Masters said. "But you didn't answer my question. Do you like candy?"

Prisma nodded. It had been so long since anyone had given her anything like that. Her daddy used to bring her sweets. But only sometimes, and Prisma was never allowed to tell her mother, because then Daddy would get into trouble for spoiling her appetite. Hogus and Skrizz had never offered her sweets; they just grunted over bowls of white reprocessed slop and expected her to do the same. And Crash didn't even eat food. It felt good for someone to offer her something nice. Even if she didn't actually *get* a candy bar.

"Okay, hold on," Masters said. "I'm going to use my special legionnaire skills. Watch."

Prisma stood transfixed as the handsome young legionnaire stealthily moved back down the corridor as though he were infiltrating some dangerous enemy base. He snuck up right behind a very tall legionnaire and opened a pouch on the man's belt. He pulled out a brand new chocolate bar, turned to face Prisma, and gave her a thumbs-up.

She gave a thumbs-up in reply, and felt a wide smile break out across her face.

The legionnaire began to move back toward her, candy bar in hand.

"Excuse me, young miss," Crash said from inside the room. "But what is happening outside?"

Prisma turned to face her bot. "You were right. He's nice."

"This is very welcome news, young miss. I have grown tired of so much *roughness* in our travels. It will be refreshing to meet someone friendly."

Masters was still maintaining his stealthy squat-walk. "Who're you talking to in there, Prisma? Is it a friend? I only have the one candy bar..."

"It's Crash," Prisma answered cheerfully. "But don't worry. He doesn't eat."

The war bot stepped out into the hallway, towering behind Prisma.

"Holy strokes!" Masters said, taking an awkward step backward and falling on his bottom. "Your friend is a war bot?"

"Only when Captain Keel makes him one," Prisma said, looking up fondly at her bot companion. "Normally he's just Crash."

"It is my deep pleasure to meet you. I am KRS-88," the bot said.

Masters stood up and handed Prisma the candy bar. She marveled at it, turning it over in her hands as if it were a priceless treasure. She removed its wrapper carefully, ceremoniously.

"It's uh, nice to meet you too," the legionnaire said to Crash. "You can call me—"

"Masters!" bellowed the voice of the tall legionnaire. "Did you swipe my choc-ration *again*?"

"I don't know what you're talking about," Master shouted back without turning. He looked down at Prisma and smiled. "Quick! Eat it fast!"

Prisma didn't need much encouragement. She chewed rapidly, taking bite after bite. It was delicious.

06

Captain Keel followed Chhun from the cockpit, through the corridor, and into the ship's common area. He felt apprehensive the entire walk. It had been years since he'd last seen Chhun, Exo, Masters... and he didn't know what to say or how to act. He had been Keel for so long, the thought of resuming the stiff, military posture he'd held as a Legion officer felt alien and oppressive.

He entered the common room to see that most of his erstwhile crew was already mixing with the legionnaires. All except Leenah, who must still be poring over every circuit, housing, and detail in the engine room. He didn't recognize these men, though—except for Masters, who was sitting next to Prisma. Whatever he was saying to her, it was making the girl smile.

Closer by, Skrizz was chatting with a particularly large legionnaire. "Yeah, I wrestled a wobanki once," the legionnaire was saying. "They're pretty tough customers." The man, who wore a beard that rivaled Major Owens and slicked his hair back, the sides shaved, looked over to Keel. "Pretty badass to have one as a co-pilot, though."

"He's not my co-pilot," corrected Keel. "Ravi... ah, forget it."

The large legionnaire and the wobanki returned to their discussion. Skrizz confidently asked the big legionnaire to continue his tale of fighting a wobanki. The catman's posture carried a feline swagger of excessive pride.

"Well," the leej said, "this one was MCR, so I had to break his neck." The legionnaire held up two massive hands as if to demonstrate how he'd done it. "But the wobanki was a mean one, nearly twice as thick as you. Almost got through my armor with his claws until I snapped the life out of him."

The big legionnaire broke out into a hearty laugh while Skrizz tucked his tail and shot a look at Keel. If Keel read that look correctly, it suggested he was both ashamed of what happened to his kinsman and hoping for an opportunity to try his own luck against the towering soldier. That's all the wobanki really were—evolved hunters, always looking for the kill. It came naturally to them.

"Everybody," Chhun said, raising his voice to get everyone's attention. "This is Captain Ford, the original lead of Victory Kill Team, and a survivor of the Battle of Kublar. Call sign: Wraith. Wraith, this is Fish, Bear, Sticks, and you already know Masters."

The legionnaires gave their greetings. Keel felt sheepish at being called by his real name. He felt exposed—the full reality of his past story was being revealed to people who had only ever known him as Captain Aeson Keel of the *Indelible VI*.

"Wait," said Garret. "Your name is *Ford*? And you fought at freaking Kublar?"

"It's... complicated," Keel answered.

Skrizz purred out an intricate question.

"Yeah," answered Keel, "that's why I have the armor. I just modified it a bit."

"You look older," Masters said. "Hey, is this wobanki your co-pilot?"

"No!" Keel answered. "Why does everyone keep saying that? He was Rechs's co-pilot. Not mine. He sheds."

Skrizz shrugged and yowled in agreement.

Keel was still thinking about Masters's comment. Of course he looked older. It had been years. The odd thing was, Masters or Chhun hadn't aged a day. He decided to ask about it. "So how come you and Chhun look the same as the day I left?"

Masters stood up and came to Keel's side, assuming the posture of a father ready to impart a lesson to his son. "One of the benefits of working on the Republic's bleeding edge," he said, sweeping his arm wide as if showing Keel the panoramic view of all the Republic had to offer. "About six months after you disappeared, all the kill teams started getting these twice-yearly shots. Regenerative tech. 'Cause as you know, being on a kill team is hard work, and too many guys were going down with injury and getting all cybernetic just to stay in the field. So we get these shots, and it's like you don't age. Maybe when you get back to *Mercutio* you can have the docs inject, like, forty at once and see if you can catch up."

Keel shook his head. "Well, *youngsters*, make yourselves at home until Major Owens tells us where we're going. Seems like you've already met everyone, but I suppose as captain I should offer some introductions. This is..." Keel looked at Garret and snapped his fingers as if trying to remember the name.

"Garret," Prisma said, unhelpfully.

"I know," Keel said. He pointed to the others. "And these are Skrizz, war bot—"

"Crash," corrected Prisma.

Keel frowned and held a hand toward Prisma. "... and annoying little girl."

"I like Prisma!" Masters said.

This made Prisma blush.

Masters looked down the hall that led to the engine rooms. "Who was the Endurian who came running through? Holy strokes was she hot!"

This comment seemed to make Prisma jealous, and Keel had to hide his smile behind his hand. "That was Leenah, the ship's mechanic and temporary navigator."

Masters gave a whistle. "Are you hooking up with her, Wraith? Because if you are," he put his thumbs up, "nicely done. Really. I mean, if I knew that going into deep cover meant that I could go under *the* covers with a girl like that I'd—"

"Ahem." Chhun cleared his throat and tilted his head toward Prisma.

"Oh," Masters said, ducking his head sheepishly. "Right. Sorry, Prisma. Forget those last fifteen seconds."

"Leenah is nice," Prisma said. She gave Keel the evil eye. "She wouldn't want to kiss someone like *him*!"

The legionnaires all broke out in laughter, and Prisma gave a satisfied smile.

Keel placed both hands on his chest. "I'm *nice*."

"No, you're not."

"Yes, I am."

"No you're not!"

"Yes I am, I—" Keel looked up at the ceiling, frustrated with himself. "Why am I arguing with this kid again?"

The big legionnaire, the one Chhun had introduced as Bear, said, "So is Prisma your kid, or...?"

"No!" Keel and Prisma answered in unison.

"My father was named Kael Maydoon," Prisma said, an affectation of dignity in her voice. "He was a hero, and he was *murdered* by Goth Sullus. I hired Tyrus Rechs to kill Goth Sullus and—"

"Whoa!" shouted one of the legionnaires. Pike. "What do you mean you *hired* Tyrus Rechs?"

Prisma smiled, happy at the attention this had gotten. "I paid a stinky old smuggler named Hogus to take me to

Ackabar, and then I found Tyrus Rechs and told him what happened, and he agreed to kill Goth Sullus for me."

The legionnaires looked at each other in wonder.

"Rechs has been the Republic's top non-MCR target for years," Chhun marveled. "Are you serious?"

"She's not lying," Keel said. "I was hunting Rechs down for a job, and that's how Little Miss Sunshine came into my life."

"Holy strokes, Ford," Masters said, returning to his seat next to Prisma. "This is the most kick-ass—sorry—*cool* girl in the universe."

Keel pinched the bridge of his nose. "She's really not."

"So you tracked Rechs down?" Chhun asked Keel. "Did you call it in? I mean, I know it's more the House and Senate that had it in for the guy than the Legion, but that's a really big fish!"

"Didn't have time. We ended up sort of... teaming up."

Prisma stood up defiantly. "That's not how it happened. Tyrus Rechs *hired* you. You were his *servant*."

Keel put his hands on his hips. "Pipe down or I'll order your war bot to hold your mouth closed." He turned back to Chhun. "Yeah, I was ready to leave him there and collect the bounty, call it in to Owens later on. But he made an offer that I had to take."

"No. Way." The words came from Fish.

Keel rubbed the back of his head. "Yeah. Rechs and I went after this Sullus guy together. Turns out Sullus is a pretty big warlord, even has his own little Legion, if you can believe it. We got into it on Tusca. Rechs didn't make it out."

"So he's dead?" Chhun's tone was that of an officer looking to file the proper reports. "Confirmed?"

Keel shrugged. "I saw him blow up in his own ship. Nuked the thing to help us escape, I guess. In reality the old codger almost killed us."

"Man," Masters said, shaking his head. "I can't believe you hung out with the guy."

Keel gave a lopsided grin. "Didn't just hang out with him. I trapped him, got the draw on him, and then agreed to work with him on this Sullus problem for enough credits to allow us all to retire to an island somewhere."

"You got the draw on Rechs?" Masters asked, his mouth agape. "Stop lying to me."

Skrizz yammered that he had been there and saw it happen.

Keel found himself enjoying the conversation with his two old friends. And the three new faces, too. He didn't really know them, but he liked them. They were all leejes—true leejes—and Keel felt comfortable around them. It was obvious that none of them had read the report he'd sent in to Owens. But then, why would they? They probably hadn't seen any of his reports.

Which also meant they didn't know the other things.

The lengths Keel had been forced to undertake—the people he'd had to get out of his way—in order to reach mission success. It had been them or him. That was how it had to be.

Chhun leaned against a bulkhead, his arms crossed and a smile on his face. "Never imagined either of us would see something crazier than Kublar and *Pride of Ankalore*, but you managed to do it, Wraith."

"You don't know the half of it." Keel pursed his lips. He wanted to tell his friend more. Lao Pak and pirates. Bounties, corrupt Republic officials, legionnaire brute squads under the thumb of points to collect taxes. And Devers. He wanted to tell them about Devers. What he'd seen. What he'd almost done with Twenties's own blaster rifle.

A sense of shame at his failure momentarily put a knot in his stomach. But then... would these leejes even have approved? Would they have welcomed the news that he, a Dark Ops agent, had assassinated a Republic admiral? That he would have executed the man after serving as his judge and jury? Keel couldn't be sure. Maybe Chhun, and probably Masters. He couldn't say about the other three. They weren't there. On Kublar.

But there was one Dark Ops agent who Keel knew would have been glad to hear of it, had he been successful. And it occurred to Keel that he was nowhere to be seen. His stomach dropped again. "Hey, where's Exo?"

"Gonna have to answer that one later," Chhun said, motioning for his squad to form up. "Got an incoming comm chime from Major Owens."

"He's not dead, is he?"

Chhun shook his head. "Not that I've heard, no. Where's that armory you said we could have a private briefing?"

Keel motioned for them to follow. "This way."

Prisma got up to join the party.

"No, you stay *here*," Keel said, taking the girl by the shoulders and pushing her back in her seat. He received a kick in the leg for his troubles.

"That kid is so awesome," Masters said as the kill team departed down the corridor.

07

The kill team looked approvingly at the room Keel had led them into. It had once been one of the *Indelible VI*'s crew quarters, but had long ago been converted into an armory that rivaled—no, surpassed—what the legionnaires had at their disposal while on Republic destroyers. Blaster rifles, pistols, shotguns... all hung neatly on the walls, held in place by a localized electromagnetic field. The makes and manufacturers were from throughout the galaxy. Military-issue, planetary police, hunting rifles, Republic-approved home defense weapons modified to still be able to punch through legionnaire armor... it seemed as though Keel had squirreled away something for just about any situation.

Fish opened a storage locker stocked full of charge packs. "Man, I was expecting something like this. You could fully arm a few squads with what's in here. Where are the SAB charge packs?"

Keel pointed to an impervisteel cabinet on the opposite wall. "Over there. Aeroprecision missiles are stored under this deck plate, if anyone needs those."

"We didn't bring a heavy loadout for this op," Pike said. He paused to look at his partner. "Except for Bear, I mean."

"Grab a launcher from the wall," Keel said. "I have a feeling you're gonna need it."

Chhun silenced the others with a gesture. "Let's load out later on. Major Owens is on comm to brief us on what's coming. Ford, can you link the L-comm into the holos for this room?"

Keel nodded. "Yeah, Ravi—" He stopped himself, remembering that Ravi was still gone.

"Who's Ravi?"

Keel shook his head. "Never mind." He opened a central control panel and keyed in the relay to display in the armory, then stepped back to lean against a display case full of blaster pistols as the lights dimmed.

A holoprojected image of Major Owens appeared. "Gentlemen," he said to the gathered legionnaires. "By now you've met or been reacquainted with Captain Ford. For those of you who weren't on this kill team when we stopped the *Pride of Ankalore* from jumping straight into the House of Reason, Captain Ford—Wraith—was my team leader, the same position Captain Chhun holds now. We realized something in the aftermath of that mission: the standard procedure of the Legion sending in Dark Ops to clean up messes could only do so much. The ops just kept coming, and the opportunities to actually put a stop to something, instead of just bringing in payback, were growing fewer and farther between. Meanwhile the threats were getting bigger, as seen with the destruction of the *Chiasm*."

The kill team stood still and waited for more. They'd heard this story from the team veterans plenty of times.

"I can tell you're thinking you've heard all of this before," Owens said. "Well here's what you don't know. That mission to blow up the House of Reason was made possible by Nether Ops. In fact, it was a Nether Ops scumsack who blew up the *Chiasm* and Camp Forge. I'm sure the schlep they convinced to murder thousands of Republic soldiers felt he was doing it for the greater good. But look around you. Things ain't good. In fact, we're on the brink of a galactic meltdown."

Keel chewed the inside of his lip and wondered if something similar would ever be said about him. But... he'd found the dark thing at the edge of the galaxy. He'd given the intel that had provided the Legion with a chance to get a leg up. His choices—and they were always life or death—his choices were different.

They had to be.

"So what's the target?" Chhun asked.

"Yeah," Bear added, cracking his knuckles. "We gonna nab this Goth Sullus guy?"

Owens chewed a piece of gum loudly enough that the smacking could be heard over the comm. He looked to Keel. "I see you've been getting advance intelligence from Captain Ford. *No.* You are *not* going after Goth Sullus. Because you can't. Because we don't know exactly where he is, and because I have hope that you'll make it through this mission alive. The odds of that go down if Sullus becomes our objective. Although, trust me, I'd love to have him. Dead or—scratch that—just dead."

A small planet and even smaller moon appeared on the holodisplay.

"This," Owens said, as the holoprojection rotated to give a full view of the system, "is Tarrago Prime and its moon."

"Where the Kesselverks Shipyards are?" Fish said.

"Affirmative. A little after midnight, local system time, Goth Sullus launched a surprise attack on the system. They're using tech very similar to Republic, right down to their own legionnaires. Similar, but different. We don't know if it's better, worse, or the same. But we do know that they attacked the moon and Fortress Omicron with small attack craft, and Republic-style destroyers opened fire on the Tarragon defense fleet."

"And this is Sullus?" Keel asked. "Not—"

Owens cut him off before he could mention Admiral Devers's name. "We know it's Sullus from the troops reported on the ground on Tarrago Prime. They match the description you provided of the dark legionnaires encountered on Tusca. Unfortunately, that's all we know. Comm relays to the Tarrago system are offline. So this is all the intelligence you'll get."

"So what's the plan?" Keel asked, crossing his legs at the ankle as he leaned back. "I'm having a hard time figuring out what Victory and the *Six* can do against a full-scale invasion. Does the Legion still have control of the orbital defense gun?"

"We don't know."

Chhun nodded gravely. "So our job is to go to Tarrago and make sure the gun platform is secure. Hold it until relief can come. With that thing in Republic hands, the best an opposing force can do is send troops in from long range via shuttle and hope they aren't shot down. Maybe harass with starfighters and bombers—and that would be costly. Any invading force would need that gun down in order to get their capital ships close enough for a full wave assault."

Owens pinched the bridge of his nose and let out a sigh. "Ordinarily I'd agree with you. That's a sound plan, and it's what needs doing if relief were coming. But... it ain't coming."

"What do you mean?"

"The House of Reason security council believes this is a hit-and-fade attack by MCR. They're attempting to reach Admiral Landoo should she need to be brought in, but as of right now, they don't view this attack as a threat. We know better. These guys are armed, numerous, and legit. That's all based on Wraith's intelligence reports."

"Don't tell me we get to storm the House of Reason and talk some sense into the council," Masters said. "Because that would be amazing. So actually, *do* tell me that."

Keel set his jaw. Among this group, only he had seen exactly what Goth Sullus had at his disposal. The mechs, the training of his soldiers... the funding. The fact that Sullus had hired virtually all of the Brotherhood to serve as mercenaries told Keel that Sullus had credits to burn. If he could afford all of that, there was no doubt in Keel's mind that he also could afford to raise an army on par with what the MCR was able to put together before they'd taken down Scarpia. That had been enough to wipe out a company on Kublar, and a company of legionnaires was all that defended the Tarrago moon. And there were no leejes at all down on the planet—only Republic marines and local security forces.

Tactically, it made sense for Sullus to attack Tarrago Prime. The planet was a mid-core world, but close enough to the core that it would be defended with the Seventh Fleet in a time of emergency—and that fleet was soft. Full of points. The non-legionnaire defense of the world would be the same. If Sullus had even a basic understanding of Republic military capabilities, he'd know the fighting wouldn't be hard, except for on the moon.

But what was his objective? Striking Tarrago Prime wasn't going to get the people of the core worlds shaking. It would take a hit on a major core planet like Utopion, Persus, or Melaine to get noticed. That was how the MCR had gotten its start—a surprise attack launched simultaneously on several core worlds, followed by a quick retreat before they could be exposed in a prolonged fight. But ever since then, they'd fought mainly in the mid-core and edge, and the populous center of the galaxy had slowly stopped paying attention—because, hey, they didn't live where all the shooting took place.

So this wasn't some terrorist attack in order to get noticed. It was a military strike. The obvious objective—because it was the only thing of value on Tarrago Prime—was the shipyards. But destroying them wouldn't be a major achievement. It would mean a headache for the Republic, sure, but not a huge one. The House and Senate would simply prioritize a rebuild and get them operating again within two weeks.

But... if someone were to take those shipyards and *hold* them, they could start pumping out their own fleet. And with the resources and recruitment power Sullus had...

"We're going to blow up the shipyards, aren't we?" Keel blurted out.

The room fell silent, all eyes turned to Keel.

"Pretty much, yeah," Owens answered, his face unreadable. If he was surprised that Keel had guessed the mission, he didn't show it. But then, Owens rarely showed any emotion. "As I said, we have limited intel. Nevertheless, our assessment is that Tarrago Prime and its moon are going to fall. Keller is attempting to organize a force to jump in in relief, but we assume the navy won't go for it. And the Seventh Fleet can't be reached, not that it matters—let's be honest, it's a core fleet. Landoo has no real experience and will perform like every other point we've ever come across. The only good navy is in the edge."

Chunn pushed his palms down flat on a display case full of banned weaponry—slug throwers and disintegrators. "So what you're saying is, it's up to us to make sure that even in victory, Sullus is denied the shipyards."

"Right. So here's our plan." Owens transmitted a holo showing the *Indelible VI* entering the system. "Captain Ford will deliver the team to Tarrago Prime. This boat of his has the capability to outrun whatever it comes up against and land undetected by scanners. Expect things to be hot when you arrive. The defense fleet shouldn't be knocked out before you get there. They're still destroyer-class, after all. Those don't go down without taking a beating."

"Unless Sullus takes the orbital gun," Pike interjected.

Owens nodded. "True. But if there's one element of our defenses that will give 'em hell, it's the legionnaires defending that gun."

"I can get everyone on planet," Keel said, studying the proposed advance vectors. "But once we land... then what?"

"Legion Commander Keller spoke with Captain Deynolds of the *Intrepid*," Owens answered. "Some of you have served on that ship. Good captain, competent crew. You'll have thirty minutes to get into position and guide pulse-home bots into the shipyard's three central reactors. Here, here, and here."

The holodisplay panned to the shipyard superstructure, cast in red, with yellow indicating three large sections where energy for the massive shipyard was generated.

"You keep the targets painted. *Intrepid* will do a quick jump in, launch a payload of MAROs, one for each reactor, along with a synced fire of all blaster batteries, and then jump back out. Engineering believes we'll disable the shipyards even if only one MARO hits its target, but we're Legion, so we go all out. Any questions on the op?"

Silence.

"Okay," Owens said, scanning the room. "Captain Ford will get you out and then rendezvous with *Intrepid*—I'm going to have you operate from there after the stunt pulled by *Illustrious*. Ford, we'll figure out what's next for you down the road. Plan on meeting with me and Legion Commander Keller aboard the *Mercutio*."

Keel nodded. This was happening fast. Too fast. He didn't know if he *wanted* to get back to life in Dark Ops. Serving aboard a destroyer, jumping from hellhole to hellhole. The thought of leaving behind the ability to do as he pleased and go where he wanted made him feel like he was dying inside. He wanted to complete this mission with the kill team—and then run.

"Let's talk supplies," Owens said. "I'm sure you guys are all black on ammo, and your kit isn't optimized for the op. There's an orbital depot along the way. I can get you command clearance. Should limit the delay to ninety minutes."

Bear picked up a two-man-served plasma grenade launcher and wielded it at the hip, as though the ninety-pound weapon didn't require a tripod. "No need, Major. We've got more than enough goodies here in Captain Ford's secret stash."

Owens smiled from behind his bushy red beard. "Good. KTF, men."

08

Hyperspace unfurled outside the cockpit windows of the *Indelible VI*. While Captain Keel read over systems reports, Leenah monitored the finer details, watching for the slightest hint that the ship was operating sub-optimally. Things broke on every ship, but she never let them stay that way long. And what she considered "broken," most other beings would look at as working just fine.

"All systems are reading optimal," she informed Keel.

The captain gave her an appreciative grin, which she returned with a blushing smile of her own. This kind of work would have taken three hours in dock with anyone else working the wrench—but it had taken Leenah only twenty minutes to get the engine's drive couplers where they needed to be. Where *she* needed them to be. They hadn't fused, but another couple of micro jumps and they *could* have fused, rendering the ship incapable of anything faster than sublight speed. And in Leenah's mind, the potential was every bit as bad as the reality.

By the time she'd returned from the engine room, her coveralls sporting fresh smears of grease, it seemed as if everyone had become fast friends. Prisma was recounting tales of near-death experiences for the benefit of the legionnaires, who appeared enthralled. They kept asking her to fill in technical details about equipment, positioning, and tactics—questions the girl didn't know the answers to. It troubled Leenah, the things that Prisma had been forced to live through. And it troubled her even more to see this kill team so taken with her, and the young girl's face lighting up in response.

This was Prisma's chance to be a girl again. To be a child. These professional soldiers couldn't see that, or didn't care.

Leenah disliked the kill team. Perhaps "dislike" was too strong a word; she just didn't trust them. She worried that, when this was over, they'd lead her off the ship in ener-chains. And if they did, would Keel try to stop them?

The legionnaires were polite enough with her. The team leader, Captain Chhun, had treated her respectfully. Kindly, to be honest. And that seemed to be the squad standard. The only exception was Bear, the big one, who only seemed to have a mind for weapons and fighting. But all of that could be misdirection. A way to get Leenah to lower her guard. She vowed not to let that happen.

"The *Six* is ready for whatever comes her way," she said, checking for a fourth time to make sure the sublight repulsors showed an adequate charge level.

99.8%. That would do.

"Nice work with the ship," Keel said, swiveling in his chair to look directly at her. "But tell me, princess. Are *you* ready for whatever comes your way?"

Leenah swallowed. "What do you mean?"

"I mean that you've been in the middle of war zone after war zone since the moment I picked you up back on Jarvis Rho." He rubbed his jaw and looked up at the cabin ceiling as if contemplating. "I just worry about your royal sensibilities, is all."

Leenah looked straight ahead, steeling herself. "Don't be. I can handle jumping into a fight."

"It's not the jump I'm worried about," Keel insisted. He leaned against the armrest, invading her space. He had a...

disarming look. Eyes that seemed to ask forgiveness for the bad things he only thought of. "It's what happens when we land. We'll probably have to shoot more people. And the best way to do it is in a way that keeps them from getting back up. Using the *Six*'s big guns."

"I'll be fine, Keel. Or should I call you Ford? Or Wraith?" Leenah batted pink eyelashes over doe eyes. "Or is there another secret identity you'd rather I use... Captain?"

"Keel is fine." The captain sat back in his chair and brought up the payload and inventory status of the ship's missile launchers. He sounded bothered. Annoyed. Hurt?

Leenah's first instinct was to apologize. But she squelched that urge. Did she *really* have anything to apologize about? Keel had been dishonest—well, disingenuous at least—ever since she'd met him. And all *she* had done...

Leenah sighed. All she had done was go along with a plan by an inexperienced MCR "general" to pretend that her royalty meant she held a high place in the rebellion—when she was really just a grease dunker with no appreciable MCR time of service to speak of.

If this partnership, serving on the same ship together, was going to work, it would require that she and Keel be honest with one another. He had come clean before they'd picked up the Dark Ops team; she needed to do the same.

"Listen," she said. "I want you to know... just because I don't like watching this ship rain mayhem down on organics, doesn't mean that I'm not willing to do what it takes to keep the *Six* and its crew safe, if that's what you need from me. Especially Prisma. Give me a blaster and tell me where to be, and I'll be there. But I'm never going to be good with switching on remote weapons systems and—I just don't like it, okay?"

"Sure, Leenah." Keel paused. He seemed to be considering what to do next. Leenah's stomach fluttered as he again leaned toward her. "We'll figure something out."

Leenah moved her face toward him. "Like what?"

"Something," Keel repeated, leaning in closer and closing his eyes.

The cockpit door behind them whooshed open, and Captain Chhun walked in. Keel and Leenah jumped back into their seats, both red-faced.

Chhun slowed, then stood behind the two of them. "I'm not interrupting anything, am I?"

Keel's fingers were dancing over the *Indelible*'s console. "Nope. Uh, no. We, uh, we just... we were checking the ship's latency sys—uh, no."

"Captain Ford," Chhun said, his voice even and professional. "I'm not an idiot. I understand that dramatic and stressful events like what you and your crew just went through together can accelerate bonding. I get that. But if my bucket is right, we're about thirty minutes to Tarrago. Not the time. Not the place."

The military bearing of the legionnaire had a sobering effect. Leenah could see it in the way Keel handled himself. He looked embarrassed, like he knew better and was upset with himself.

And then something seemed to... click inside the man. He softened his posture, leaned back into his chair, and looked up at Chhun nonchalantly. "Relax, Cohen," he said, waving his hand lazily. "Don't get excited. We can fly an op like this in our sleep. Just make sure you have your crew ready to go once the ramp drops.'

"They are," Chhun said, a hint of frustration in his voice. "Listen, I get that it's been a while since you've been in an op, but—"

Keel interrupted. "You've got your way of doing things, and I have mine. Only *my* way tracked down Sullus, Rechs, and got the death mark bounty on Cal Camp. And that was just from one job. Multiply those results over *years*. Don't worry. I'll get you taken care of."

"Ford, this op—"

"Don't worry about it," Keel answered, sounding every bit the brash smuggler.

"It's my job to worry about it," Chhun said. "Used to be yours, too."

"Ah, c'mon."

Leenah cleared her throat "We really were just... checking out systems."

"Reproductive systems," Chhun said just loud enough to be heard. In a louder voice, he added, "I'll have my guys take up spots on your turrets. I'll still take a leej firing over target AI any day I can."

"Good idea," Keel said, turning back to his console. "And hey, KTF."

"Yeah," Chhun said before exiting the cockpit.

The door slid shut.

Keel looked over at Leenah. "To be continued?"

The Endurian princess nodded, then giggled inwardly when she saw Keel blush.

Major Owens leaned back in a repulsor seat on board Deep Space Supply Station Nine. The seat wasn't designed to recline, but the repulsors were so weak and dilapidated, they didn't have the energy to send him shooting across the room with the change in trajectory. They only whined and made the chair sort of bob in place, which Owens liked. It made him feel as though he were aboard a boat sailing some planetary sea. He'd done a few ops like that. A few vacations, too. He'd always liked them. Both types.

In the corner of the room was a holoprojection of Captain Deynolds of the *Intrepid*. Like Owens, she was waiting for Legion Commander Keller to enter the private comm meeting. Behind her projection, there looked to be several piles of space rat droppings. Owens briefly considered chewing out whoever was in charge of station sanitation—who would in turn chew out whoever was keeping the maintenance bots, who would just deal with it—but decided it wouldn't matter. This space station was a crap-hole, plain and simple, and no amount of cleaning would change that. If it weren't for its proximity to where the kill teams seemed to be most needed, Owens would have requested a change of location for his Dark Ops HQ long ago. Maybe if he waited long enough, the House would pass a spending bill to get these edge and mid-core stations retrofitted and upgraded.

He held back an urge to laugh out loud at the thought.

"I'm glad to hear your family is doing well," Captain Deynolds said. Apparently waiting for Keller meant they had to continue to engage in small talk.

"Thanks," Owens replied, stroking his beard. "How 'bout you? Still married to the stars, or has one of those points the House keeps sending your way swept you off your feet?"

"No," Deynolds said, only a hint of mirth in her voice. "I have a hard enough time keeping those appointees from ordering my ship too close to a star. The idea of..." She shook visible as if a sudden case of the chills had come over her.

"So, how do you like the plan?" Owens asked.

"Risky," Deynolds admitted. "But I don't have a better one. Still, your team needs to have that target lit up the moment *Intrepid* hits subspace. I doubt my gunnery team will have time for manual target and fire. For all I know, we could be the only friendly craft left in the system."

"They'll be ready for you."

"I know."

The comm chimed, and the holo-image of Legion Commander Keller materialized before the two of them. He looked irate.

"I'm just going to come out and say it," Keller began, not bothering with pleasantries. "I'm pissed the hell off beyond belief. By order of the House of Reason Security Council, the operation to destroy the Kesselverks Shipyards is now off the table. That's an order. That's official."

"Commander," Deynolds said, her voice measured, "did they give a reason why? I don't see the advantage to this decision."

"Isn't it clear, Captain?" Keller said sardonically. "The Republic *needs* those shipyards. And if they lose them—which they will—it will be the Legion's job to take them back, the cost of lives be damned."

"No one on Utopion ever cried for a leej," Owens said. "There's a small problem with those orders, though."

"What might that be, Major Owens?"

"My team's already too close to Tarrago. I can't reach them."

A smile began to form in the corners of the commander's eyes. "They'll want you to check again."

"Yes, sir." Owens pinched his nose and sniffed, but otherwise remained motionless. "Just checked. Still can't reach them."

"A shame." Keller's face went sober. "But even so, this is a suboptimal situation. I want to make sure to clarify the severity of this situation. Your kill team will be on its own."

Owens snapped his gum. "Understood."

"They won't be on their own," Captain Deynolds said. "I can still bring the *Intrepid* in at the pre-appointed time."

Keller shook his head. "No, I'm sorry, Captain. You're not in Tarrago, and the Republic knows it. You make the jump after the House has spoken, and you'll be replaced by whatever appointee on your ship currently holds the highest rank. We can't afford to lose officers like you in the navy. Not with what's coming."

"All due respect, Commander," insisted Deynolds, "that's a risk I'm willing to take."

"And I appreciate that. *All* of the Legion appreciates an officer such as yourself. But I have to think of the bigger picture. We're at the bleeding edge of what will be a bloody conflict. I'm willing to risk a kill team to slow down this attack from the shadows of the edge—but I'm *not* willing to lose an entire destroyer with the know-how and will to fight."

"Dumpster fire," Owens muttered to himself.

"How's that?"

"Dumpster fire," Owens repeated. "It's something Chhun says. Means a bad situation—beyond control. Something his dad used to say. Ancients talk, you know."

"Never heard that one before," Keller said. "But it sounds accurate. So Captain Deynolds, the answer remains negative. If the galaxy is on fire, you're a key part of the Legion's plan to put out the flames."

Deynolds nodded begrudgingly. "And just how much planning does the Legion have in place?"

"We've got a plan for everything."

"The House? The Senate Council?"

"Everything." A chime sounded in Keller's office. "That's the security council again. They'll *love* the news I'm about to give them. Owens, be ready to deal with some blowback. They'll be looking to point fingers once the team accomplishes its objective. I'll protect you and your leejes, you know that, but it may be a little uncomfortable for a while."

"Understood."

"Oh, and Owens," Keller said, as if just remembering. "I see Miss Broxin left the station. Did she give you any indication of what she was up to?"

"No, sir."

"All right. Probably best not to know. Keller out."

As soon as Keller was off channel, Captain Deynolds said, "I'll still go."

Owens shook his head. "No. The commander is right. We need officers who are truly loyal to the Republic first. But... if you can keep your ship close enough to Tarrago to pick up my team once they make their way out, I'd appreciate it."

"Consider it done."

"I will." Owens ended the transmission.

Alone in the filthy meeting room aboard the deep space supply station, he keyed in the comm frequency to communicate with Chhun.

No answer.

He tried a separate channel.

No answer.

"Huh," Owens said to himself. "Guess I was telling the truth after all." He leaned back in his seat, chewing his thumb. The Victory kill team truly *was* alone.

09

"Less than a minute to subspace," Keel announced to Chhun over L-comm.

Keel flipped switches and arranged displays over his tactical HUD. Leenah, at his side, was watching the navicomputer count down to the end of their trip through hyperspace. They were sixty seconds to Tarrago space, set to arrive just beyond the moon.

"We're in position at your manual turret emplacements," Chhun replied. "Give us targets, we'll shoot 'em down."

"Copy," Keel said. He switched off the comm and shook his head once. "Shouldn't be any shortage of those..."

Leenah turned to him. "*Six* is reporting that everyone is in their quarters—even Skrizz, finally. Wait. Scratch that. Garret made the ship *say* he was in his quarters, but he's still at his workstation. I can see him on the holocam."

"Doing what?" Keel asked, venturing a glance at Leenah's displays. "Ravi?"

"Could be." Leenah shook her head doubtfully. "I can't tell."

"Well, let him work. If he's on to something, I don't want to break his concentration. He should be safe enough where he is."

The navicomputer gave a two-note warning of the impending dump from hyperspace. Keel wrapped his hand around the manual lever. "Switch hyperspace controls over to me," he told Leenah.

"All set," the princess replied.

Keel liked to end the jump just a split second *after* the navicomputer told him he should. It was dangerous, but it often got him deeper into a system and in a position to surprise whoever might be waiting for him. Of course, he knew of some smugglers and spacers who had blown themselves into atoms trying this maneuver—by not dumping fast enough and travelling directly into the hyperspace shadow of a planet. But Keel was too good for that.

Probably.

"Now!" he shouted, to himself more than anyone else. The stars stretched and then became stationary, and the canopy windows of the *Indelible VI* were filled with pitched blaster fire from desperate dogfights. In the distance, between the moon and the planet, Keel saw what looked like two Republic fleets hammering on each other.

The passive and active scanners shrieked wild alarms.

"There are fighters and capital ships everywhere!" Leenah shouted.

"I know! I know!"

Keel rolled his ship to get a broader visual of the space battle raging around him. He found that he was flying belly to belly with one of the largest ships he'd ever seen. Bigger than a super-destroyer. A battleship class of some new make he didn't recognize. It was black, and gave him a sense of dread. He threw power into the *Six*'s accelerators, hoping to move past it before whoever controlled the battleship decided to take an interest in him.

"Hey," came the voice of Sticks over the comm. "We need some help identifying the targets. They all look like Republic models. Tri-fighters, bombers, Raptors... everyone's shooting at everyone else."

Keel had noticed the same thing. "Goth Sullus has a thing for black. If you see a black starfighter that looks like an updated design, it's probably his."

"Probably?" Chhun said.

"Yeah, sorry, pal. I must've dozed off during the part of the briefing that identified all the new starships. It matches Sullus's style, I can tell you that much."

"Yeah," Masters agreed. "I'm watching these black tri-fighters and they're taking down what look like vanilla Repub Raptors..."

"Well there you have it then," Keel said. "Now keep your eyes open, but don't start shooting at targets of opportunity. The plan is get you down to the surface of Tarrago Prime, and that'll be a whole heck of a lot harder with an attack squadron on our tails."

An eruption of flaming gases light up the interior of the cockpit as a Republic tri-fighter was ripped apart by blaster cannon fire. As Keel banked the ship into a hard roll to avoid the debris, he watched a pair of Raptors streaking after a dark tri-fighter and sending it up flames. The dark tri-fighter ejected its escape pod—but unfortunately for its pilot, the pod ejected directly into the flight path of the *Indelible VI*. With a loud *clunk*, the pod's canopy windows shattered from the impact with the *Six*'s shields, leaving the helpless pilot exposed to the deep freeze of space.

"That was unlucky," Keel said to himself, before adjusting his course and nosing the ship toward the Tarrago moon. He clicked on L-comm. "Chhun, it's too hot up here to fly straight toward Tarrago Prime. Even if someone doesn't get it in their heads to chase us, there's too good a chance we catch an errant blaster bolt. I'm taking the ship down to the moon. We'll go in full speed and slingshot undetected over to Tarrago Prime."

"You sure about this?" Chhun asked.

"Of course I'm sure." Keel muted the comm and looked over at Leenah. "Mostly."

"That's not encouraging," Leenah said, as she began updating the navicomputer to provide the optimum entry path to maintain speed while not diving down straight into the moon's surface. She sent the path to Keel for him to follow on manual control.

"Not encouraging? It's me, princess," Keel said with a wink. "Don't you think if I was going to get us killed, I would have already done it?" He guided the ship onto the recommended entry path.

"One of those black ships is following us down," advised Sticks over the comm.

"Anyone have a clear shot?" Chhun asked. Chhun was the only member of the team not manning a turret. There were only so many turret ports, so Chhun had opted to monitor progress through his HUD from a central position in the ship's lounge, where he would keep things prepared for when the time came to leave the ship.

"Nothin'," answered Bear. Keel could hear the man's disgust and self-pity over missing a chance for a kill.

"Nothing here either," Fish said.

"No," Sticks added. "He drifted out of my field of vision coming around by Masters."

"Almost," Pike said, a hopeful strain in his voice, as if he were willing a target to line up.

"I will kill this man," Masters said. Keel recognized this as a quote from some century-old holo-film about a galactic crime syndicate family. "But you will owe me a debt of gratitude. And such a debt must be repaid."

The sound of blaster turrets firing carried throughout the ship, followed by the secondary noise of an exploding ship.

"Next time just shoot, Masters," Chhun ordered.

"Yes, sir. Requesting permission to just talk to myself. I shoot better when I'm quoting movies."

Chhun didn't respond.

"Should I take that as a yes?" Masters asked.

"Would it make a difference?" Fish retorted.

"Nah."

Keel leveled the *Six* and revved to a scorching speed. "Sensors?"

Leenah examined her scopes. "We're approaching the eastern wall of Fortress Omicron. Passives are picking up... five starfighters ahead."

"Friends?"

"I can't tell. I think—"

With a brilliant flash, an explosion erupted in front of them, and a cloud of smoke rose from the distant eastern wall.

"Bombing run," Keel said.

Leenah studied her console. "Active scanners showing Legion anti-starfighter batteries calibrating. Looks like... two waves? First one got its payload away. We're gaining on the second, though."

"Yeah, I see them," Keel said, throttling forward. "I think I can take them down, but those guns aren't going to bother differentiating between us and others. I don't want to see how the *Six* handles a pole-axe anti-starfighter missile."

"Can we peel away and go around?" Leenah asked.

"I'd rather not lose the speed. That, and there's no guarantee one of the other walls won't shoot at us all the same." Keel bit his lip for a brief second and made up his mind.

"Transmit our Dark Ops credentials to Fortress Omicron—to the wall. Hopefully they'll get the idea and let us through."

"And if they don't?"

Keel raised his eyebrows, inclined his head, and said, "Then you'd better hang on tight."

The *Indelible VI* raced behind the starfighters. They moved in an attack formation suggesting a bombing run—a single Republic tri-bomber flanked by a pair of the black, modified tri-fighters.

Judging by the active scanner displays Leenah had sent to his HUD, Keel figured the anti-air missiles would have a target just in time for his arrival. "Are they responding to the clearance code transmission?" he asked.

"I forgot to send it," Leenah said in a worried tone.

"You *what?*"

Leenah smiled. "No, I sent it. And the Legion gave us the green light. I just didn't want you to be the only one making light of the situation up here."

"Hilarious," Keel said. "I don't deserve this. It's not fair."

Bear spoke over the L-comm. "Are we dusting those ships you're chasing down?"

"Affirmative," Keel said, keeping his speed constant. "Aim for the bomber. It might take the fighters down with it."

"I'm all about that," Bear answered.

Keel flew within firing range, the moon's surface racing by below him. They were now streaking through the artificial atmosphere contained by shields all around the eastern defense wall. He hoped the legionnaire would be as fast with the butterfly triggers as Keel himself would be with the slave-fire control button in the cockpit.

The *Indelible* reverberated with a steady stream of outgoing blaster cannon fire. It ripped into the back of the tri-bomber, igniting its munitions and booming into a thunderous fireball. Atmospheric explosions were so much more impressive than their deep space counterparts.

The fireball engulfed both of the bomber's escort fighters, sending the cooked starships plunging downward. Keel pitched his ship to avoid the blast and residual heat, and heard his gunners fire again. The legionnaires blew apart the two plummeting starships before they had the chance to impact the hard deck in one piece.

KTF.

"Looks like I've got one for you," Keel said, spying what must have been the initial bomber from the first run, taking a wide circle in the high atmosphere. Checking his instruments, he determined that a sharp roll should give his belly turret a kill shot while keeping his speed constant. The maneuver was fluid and took only seconds, and the legionnaire manning the turret raked his target with blaster cannon fire, splintering it midair and sending it spiraling down.

Keel leveled out and accelerated.

"Hey," called out Masters. "One more behind us. Doing its best to catch up."

With a lopsided smile, Keel confirmed from his reading what he already felt to be true. He had more speed than he needed, and could afford to slow down, just a little. "Say hello to the pilot, huh?"

The *Six*'s tail turret sent several blaster rounds into the cockpit and pilot of the enemy craft. The pilot never registered the attack, never even flinched or attempted to dodge. The blackened wreckage of his ship smashed into a distant, gray and craggy hilltop outside of the shielded atmospheric zone.

"Sensors are saying that's all of them," Leenah reported. "That was... impressive."

Keel gave a big smile, showing his teeth. "It's like I said, princess: it's me."

"Nice flying, Ford," Chhun said over L-comm. "Not something they teach you in the Legion."

"No," Keel agreed. "You gotta go off the beaten path to pick up that trick."

Prisma was fuming. That stupid Captain Keel had ordered everyone but his legionnaire friends and Leenah to their quarters. Even Skrizz! It wasn't fair. She wasn't afraid of another battle. She should have at least been allowed to stay in the common lounge, so she could watch holocam feeds of what was going on. It sounded exciting. Instead, she had to while the hours away with Crash. Again. She liked her bot, but she was starting to resent him. Like maybe Keel still had him under control, and Crash was just a... a babysitter.

Prisma didn't *need* a babysitter. Though... she wouldn't mind spending some time talking to Leenah. She wanted to ask her something. Something she'd almost mustered the courage to ask the last time they'd sat together at the table, eating hardtack. But Skrizz and Garret were there, too, and there was never any telling when Keel might show up. So she'd lost her nerve.

But she'd *almost* asked.

How do you become pretty? How do I get beautiful, like you?

That's what Prisma wanted to ask Leenah. And she didn't even know why. Her daddy had always told her she was his "beautiful, sweet little girl." But... men looked at Leenah in a different way. And Prisma wondered what it would be like for a man to look at *her* that way. Just in case she ever wanted one to. In case it ever became important. For later. For someday.

Crash would probably answer her. The bot wouldn't laugh. But Prisma didn't think it'd be helpful, either. *"Young miss, beauty standards are exceptionally diverse throughout the galaxy, depending on custom, region, culture, species, and a host of other factors."* That's what Crash would say. And then it would list off some weird things people or aliens thought were pretty that might be interesting but wouldn't help her.

Maybe later she would ask Leenah if they could be alone to talk. The Endurian would do it. Maybe Leenah would take her into the engine room and show her how to recycle a shield phantom to tease out more power. Leenah liked to talk about things like that. Things other people pretended were interesting to them, too, because she was oh so beautiful. And then, when they were talking about shield phantoms, Prisma could ask her. When they were alone. And no one else could hear them.

The ship shuddered, making Prisma bounce up and down on her bed for a little bit before the inertial and gravity dampers caught up.

"I believe," Crash said in its most tutorial voice, "that Captain Keel has brought us into one of the four atmospheric sections artificially maintained on Tarrago Moon."

"That was the plan, right?"

Crash blinked its visual receptors. "The plan was to enter the atmosphere of Tarrago Prime. However, based on the time lapsed from our exiting hyperspace to now, he must have entered the atmosphere of the Tarrago moon instead. I do hope that he was not confused by the similarity of names."

"Probably he just—"

"Tarrago," Crash continued unabated, "is a common name used in reference to Tarrago Prime. But the moon is also named Tarrago. And so the moon is called Tarrago Moon, and the planet Tarrago Prime—"

"Crash..."

"But such naming allows for confusion. Tarrago, left without clarification, can mean the moon or the planet, or even the system itself—"

"Crash..."

"And so if Captain Keel was told to infiltrate Tarrago—"

"Crash!"

"Yes, young miss?"

"I don't care about any of this."

Crash pulled its head back, as if surprised. "I apologize, young miss."

The ship hummed as it fired blaster bolts at some unseen foe. Prisma pricked up her ears, straining to hear what became of the shots. She was rewarded with a distant explosion.

"I have analyzed the sound. It was at least three medium starfighters exploding in atmosphere, approximately two hundred meters in front the *Indelible VI*. That is to say: we were chasing them down."

Prisma smiled. *This* was something she could hear more of. "Tell me everything that's happening outside!"

The bot enhanced its audio receptors. As it processed each noise, it delivered details its best interpretation of the action outside. Prisma sat riveted.

"Prisma..."

"Prisma..."

It took several moments for Prisma to realize that someone other than Crash was speaking to her. "Ravi?" she asked.

"Yes, Prisma." Ravi seemed to materialize next to her in the room.

Crash stopped its narrative. "Who are you speaking to, young miss?"

"I—" began Prisma. "You can't see him?"

The bot blinked its visual receptors. "See whom?"

Ravi smiled and sat down next to Prisma. "I am... beyond the reach of this machine. It neither can see nor hear me. Though there may be a time when Crash achieves sufficient awareness to commune with me in my present state."

"If someone other than Crash came in... could *they* see you?" Prisma asked.

"Some of them could, yes."

"But not all?"

Crash looked around the room in apparent confusion. "Young miss, who are you—"

"Shh!" Prisma hissed. "Not now, Crash."

"Very well."

Ravi smiled. "We are flying near the eastern wall, and I am needing your assistance."

"For what?"

"Something very important. Something that will save lives." Ravi inclined his head. "Will you help me with this, Prisma?"

Prisma nodded.

Ravi held up his palms to face her. "I am wanting you to place your palms against mine."

Prisma obeyed... and, for reasons she couldn't articulate, closed her eyes.

It was black. Blacker than when she normally closed her eyes. Blacker than when she slept without the lights on. The sort of black that swallowed the light. Removed it.

It made her feel afraid.

"Do you feel this?" Ravi asked.

"Y-yes."

"I feel it too. It is... a way of death. A way of self and of destruction."

Prisma's lip quivered. She felt... sad. As if she'd known this feeling before. As if it was there when her daddy...

"What I am wanting you to help me with, is to push this darkness away." Ravi pressed his palms against Prisma's, and she could feel them. Feel the gentle warmth of his hands. "Even the most determined darkness cannot take away *all* of the light. We are to be pushing this darkness away. Bring forth the light, Prisma. You are being called to bring forth... the light."

Prisma imagined a sunrise. She imagined a sheet of blackness turning white as snow, the dark being pushed off the page from corner to corner. The light grew in intensity, until she found herself squeezing her eyes tight, as if *asking* for some darkness to protect her from being overwhelmed.

And then it was all gone. She felt as though she was simply sitting in a room with her eyes shut. She opened them, expecting no longer to see Ravi, but there he was.

"You have done very well, Prisma," Ravi said, his mustache curling up with his smile. "I am proud of you."

"What did I do?"

"As much as you were called to do. As much as you were capable."

Prisma tried to smile, but found that she couldn't. "Are you going to leave again?"

"Only for a time."

"Ravi," Prisma began. She hesitated, picking at her fingers. She picked at them whenever she felt nervous now.

There was no one left to tell her not to. "Am I... how do I become... *pretty*?"

Ravi placed a hand gently under Prisma's chin. "Oh, my dear child, you are beautiful right now."

"I don't feel like it. Not like Leenah."

"Hoo hoo hoo," laughed Ravi. "The pupatar always wishes for its wings, and the flutterer longs for the leaf. But I see beyond what is outside, dear Prisma. And *you* are filled with beauty."

Prisma smiled. Feeling a tear trying to escape her eyelids, she quickly wiped it away. "Thanks, Ravi."

"You are being very welcome." Ravi began to fade from sight. "Remember what I have told you. Now is the time. Stay hidden. Do as Captain Keel and Leenah tell you. Stay safe."

10

"That's *right*," Keel repeated into the comm as he juked and rolled the *Indelible VI* through a staggering minefield of debris hewn from the destroyers in their exchange of heavy turboblaster fire. "Don't shoot unless you pick up a tail. I don't care how fat of a target you see."

"Sorry," answered Sticks over the comm.

Leenah looked up briefly from her sensors. "Legionnaires aren't much for being subtle. Guess the kill teams really like to emphasize the *kill* part of their names." Keel liked that she understood the need to fly into Tarrago Prime without interceptors calling them in and making a big show of their arrival.

He gave the princess an almost leering grin. "That's not always such a bad thing, is it, Your Highness?"

"Look out!" Leenah pointed out the canopy window at the wreckage of a vanquished starfighter spinning like an asteroid amid a belt of ruined lives and machinery.

"I see it," Keel said, feeling unjustly scolded. He banked sharply upward, the belly of the *Six* coming within meters of a blasted-out cockpit unit from one of those new model tri-fighters. "See?" He smiled. "No problem. Besides, you know as well as anyone that the *Six*'s shields would have handled that."

The freighter shook from some unseen impact. Keel's eyes went wide.

"Something hit us," he said. "What hit us?" He was sure he'd cleared the starfighter graveyard that studded the open space between Tarrago's moon and Tarrago Prime.

"Wraith," Chhun called over the comm, "a black-painted tri-bomber just seeded this whole area with proximity mines. Looks like Sullus's pilots are conceding this sector and leaving some surprises for any Repub featherheads who come out this way."

"*Now* he tells me," Keel muttered, scanning his sensors and visuals for sign of the disc-shaped explosives.

"Are those dangerous?" Leenah asked.

Keel could tell from the look on her face that she felt embarrassed for asking the question as soon as it left her mouth. He gave his head a half shake. "Fly in too close to one of those babies and they'll detonate right inside our shield array. Make our mission real short."

Looking uneasily at her sensor display, Leenah said, "Well, they're *every*where." She sent over an isolation layer that made all the mines show as a bright yellow, whether seen out of the cockpit windows or on the HUD map display.

"How 'bout that," Keel mumbled to himself.

"I know," sighed Leenah. "I'll start plotting another route to planet."

"No," said Keel, "I mean, how 'bout that, there are no destroyers or starfighters between us and the planet. Just the mines."

Leenah's mouth hung open. "You're not actually going to try and take us through them? The shields won't do a lot of good if those things blow up *inside* them."

"Don't worry," Keel said. "It's me, remember?"

Leaning forward, he flipped on the ship-wide comm. "Everybody strap in. Captain's order. We're flying through the minefield to get to Tarrago Prime."

"What?" came a chorus of incredulous replies.

Keel overrode the incoming comm replies. "Shut up and let me concentrate!"

The comm fell silent.

But Leenah could still make her objections heard. "Aeson, this is suicide."

"Only if we *die*." Keel adjusted some settings on his console, and the cockpit dimmed to a soft, red light. "Putting all power to shield and thrusters. Weapon systems powered down, life support is—"

The cockpit door whooshed open, more slowly than usual, and Chhun entered. "What's going on?"

"Gonna run us through the minefield," Keel said evenly. "Strap in."

Chhun took a seat behind Leenah and fastened his restraints. "C'mon, Ford. Let's just circle around and run the blockade. The destroyers won't be able to catch up, and we can take care of any starfighters that pursue."

"Have a little faith, Chhun." Keel continued his adjustments. The *Indelible*'s engines whined with the influx of power being routed their way.

The cockpit door again opened, and Masters stepped inside. "This is a joke, right?"

"Sit down and strap in!" Keel shouted, giving Masters an angry look over his shoulder. "I'm about to hit the throttle, so unless you want to be a smear on the back of a bulkhead..."

Masters quickly sat behind Keel and locked his harness in place. The moment Keel heard the click, he throttled forward at full speed.

The burst of speed forced everyone to the backs of their seats. It felt almost as though the ship were making the jump into hyperspace, only without the padding provided by inertial dampers syncing with the jump.

As the yellow-highlighted mines drew nearer, Keel felt a halting sensation, as if someone were alternating between hard brakes and rapid acceleration. This was the ship's dampers attempting to counteract the inertia and give the cockpit a feeling of stationary stability. Ships the size of Keel's freighter simply didn't accelerate this fast—normally. He'd installed inertial dampers straight out of a Republic Raptor, two of them, but even they weren't enough to keep from feeling the thrust in so large a craft without sufficient notice. And Keel needed to fly in the moment. Maybe Leenah could figure something out. Still, the help of the twin dampers was enough to allow Keel to take hold of the flight controls and begin swooping in large, wide arcs through the field.

The first mine streaked by the cockpit, and Keel saw it flashing red from the proximity. It exploded in the *Six*'s wake, twenty meters behind it. The freighter streaked onward.

Keel afforded himself a satisfied grin. This would work. At least, it *could* work. He increased the ship's speed.

Apparently not everyone shared Keel's optimism. Leenah had grabbed hold of his shirt at the upper arm, constricting the garment so it pinched him like a half tourniquet. "Aeson..."

"Wraith..." Chhun warned, his voice exuding the caution of a parent trying to head a child off from some impending catastrophe of his own making.

"Oh, Oba!" shouted Masters, his eyes closed and face blanching white.

As the *Indelible VI* rocketed through the minefield, more mines exploded, but the anti-vehicle ordnances were unable to keep up with the starship's intense speed. The designers of these mines hadn't anticipated a ship as fast as the *Six* lacing its way through a field.

As the cacophony of explosions continued, Master's shouts turned into a sort of mantra-like prayer. "Oba-Oba-Oba-Oba-Oba-Oba!"

And then they were through, with open space between them and the planet.

"Ha ha!" Keel laughed triumphantly. Bright interior lights returned as he rerouted power to the ship's other systems. "I told you I'd do it," he said, mostly to Leenah.

The Endurian leaned over and planted a celebratory kiss on his cheek. "That's for my doubting you," she said with a smile.

Keel felt a rush of warmth to his face, swallowed, and stared straight ahead, hoping that Chhun and Masters wouldn't see him blush from their vantage points behind him. He moved the ship toward its entry trajectory for Tarrago Prime.

"That was an... *interesting* tactic," Chhun said, unfastening himself and standing up.

Masters clapped Keel on the shoulder and looked down at him with a wolfish smile. "You sly dog, you." He placed his other hand on Leenah's shoulder, as if wanting to be absolutely sure that Keel understood what he was talking about. "You know, Leenah, *I* almost get my people killed all the time. So if you have any kisses left for a handsome young legionnaire..."

Leenah rolled her eyes.

Keel hitched his thumb toward the cockpit exit. "Beat it, huh, Masters?"

Masters chuckled and stepped out, leaving Chhun alone with Keel and Leenah.

"What was that, Ford?"

"What?" Keel said, patting the side of his face where Leenah had kissed him. "The kiss? I can't help that I'm irresistible."

"Not the kiss," Chhun said. He hesitated before adding, "Well, partly. I mean... you're being reckless. This kind of insertion isn't up to Dark Ops standard, and you're still a Dark Ops leej. I get that things are different when you're drifting out on the edge, but that stunt could have easily gotten us all killed."

"So can lots of things," Keel shot back, his ire up from what he perceived as a lecture coming from a soldier who used to be under *his* command. "Survival means taking risks, and you know I've never backed down from any of them."

Chhun nodded, while still managing to convey that he disagreed completely. "I haven't forgotten. We can talk about this another time. But I need you to understand that this isn't the same team you left. We were all keyed in to your style when we first joined up. Captain Ford—Wraith—running headlong into an ambush and leaving the rest of the leejes in the dust. And hey, it always worked. Every blind corner you took, every time you opened up and took the initiative... you made it happen. But listen. The team is keyed in to *me* now, and I'm not that guy."

Keel held up his hands. "No problem, Chhun. I get it. I'll stay out of your way."

"I don't want you 'out of the way' down there. I just want to maintain control of the situation, and of my team."

Keel nodded. "We'll be inside Tarrago's atmo soon. Probably should kit up the team. I'll get my suit and bucket on once we land."

"All right."

Chhun left the cockpit.

"Well, that was uncomfortable," Leenah said after a beat.

Keel gave a fractional shake of his head. "Probably not fitting for the company of a princess."

"How's this going to work?"

"With the kill team?" Keel eased the ship into the navi-computer's programmed course as the burn from entry appeared around the cockpit windows. "I don't know. We'll get the job done. But after that..."

He exhaled, long and loud. Less a sigh than a breath of resolve. "I've been thinking. After this op... after I deliver the kill team to whatever battle station they're headed for next. If I were to... would you...?"

Leenah took up Keel's hand in both of hers. "Yes."

Keel smiled. "Good."

A notification chimed in the cockpit, meant to alert the pilot of the need for manual control. It continued to sound as Keel leaned in toward Leenah.

"Shouldn't you take care of that?" Leenah asked, her eyes closing as she moved toward Keel.

"It can wait."

The cockpit door flung open to reveal Garret and KRS-88.

"Oh, jeez!" Garret said, almost jumping as much as Keel and Leenah did. "I had no idea you two were... and I... uh, sorry. Oh. I should go. Should I go? Oh. No, I can't. See..."

Keel took control of the ship and guided it into upper atmospheric flight. "What's up, kid?"

"Should I arm the war bot?"

Keel considered. "You sure you've got whatever Rechs did... undone?"

"Definitely."

"It'd be nice to have a murder machine available."

Garret seemed pleased by this. "Okay. I'll get him outfitted. Don't worry about giving me access to the armory. I worked up a pass-all and tied it to my comm and biometrics."

Keel gave a sardonic frown. "Please, help yourself."

"Thanks," Garret said, apparently missing the sarcasm completely. "I also linked up the AI in your concussion missiles to the long-band AI aboard the *Six*."

"What does that mean?"

"You can shoot your missile in any direction now, and it'll pretty much go right into the target—or it'll wait, or land without detonating, or relay comms... pretty much whatever you could count on shipboard AI to do, it can be done with your munitions now."

"Garret," Leenah said, looking very impressed. "That's... incredible. To get that kind of adaptability from a warhead's limited AI."

"Yeah, I know!" Garret beamed. "You're technically not supposed to do that, because now the missile has the ability to kill something it doesn't like, which is why ordnance AI is always slaved to the control of a shipboard AI, and only enough to make minor adjustments like velocity and trajectory in order to meet the will of the humanoid who fired it. But most AIs I talk with are nice."

"How many did you hook up like this?" asked Keel, intrigued.

"All of them."

"Good." Keel thumbed on his fire control, and one by one, he launched all of his ten missiles at high atmosphere. Then he took his ship in low for its landing. "Well, this should be fun. Get the war bot outfitted, quick as you can."

Prisma sat on a bench in the armory, loading and unloading a charge pack. Tyrus Rechs had taught her how to handle a blaster.

"How much longer until the bot's ready?"

Garret looked up at the armory ceiling, as though hearing a voice from heaven. It was, in actuality, just Captain Keel checking in over the comm. "A minute?" he answered.

Prisma slammed the charge pack back into place and glared upward at the comm sensors. "You're not sending Crash outside without me," she yelled.

Keel could be heard sighing into the open channel. "We're dropping the bot from low orbit to hit a column of dark legionnaires en route to our landing zone. You're more than welcome to jump out with him, though."

"Maybe I will!"

Garret closed a shoulder hatch freshly stocked with anti-vehicle missiles. "Oh, you shouldn't," he said to Prisma. "Crash is made out of an impervisteel alloy designed to absorb the impact of a low-altitude jump. He'll just tuck his legs and roll a bit. But if you did something like that, you'd probably—"

Prisma rolled her eyes. "I'm not *actually*, Garret."

"Oh," he replied. "Good."

"Prisma..." The voice over the comm was Leenah's. "Crash is a tough bot, you know that. He can really help us out by keeping Goth Sullus's troops occupied while we land. He'll come back to us."

Prisma pursed her lips and blew out her breath. "Fine. I guess it's okay if Crash kills some of Goth Sullus's bad guys. Will you stay with me on the ship until he gets back?"

"Of course," Leenah said, her voice sweet and compassionate. "In fact, why don't you head over to my quarters? I'll teach you that game I told you about."

"The one from your planet you used to play when you were little?"

"That's the one. *Malcalla.*"

Prisma hopped down from her bench and tucked the blaster pistol into her belt. Keel wouldn't like that, which made her happy to do it. She looked up at the war bot. "Okay, Crash. Kill all those bad guys. Especially Goth Sullus if you see him."

"I am programmed to terminate all targets identified by my handler," Crash answered in a low, menacing voice.

Prisma snarled in displeasure. "I *hate* your soldier voice."

"Sorry," Garret said. "I have to make his war bot programming primary in order to maximize his chances of battle survival. If I let too much of friendly Crash have control, he might not—"

"It's fine," Prisma said. "As long as you can switch him back once he gets back home."

"Oh, I can," Garret said. The comm on his lapel chimed, and Garret tucked his chin into his chest in an attempt to look straight down at it. "Who'd be calling me at this port?"

Masters stepped into the armory. "Is the war bot ready?" he asked Garret, then paused at seeing Prisma. "Oh, hey, Prisma! You're not in your armor. I thought you were going to kit up and go on the raid with us."

Prisma grinned and then pointed to the blaster tucked into her belt. "I don't have any armor, but I've got this. I know how to use it, too. Tyrus Rechs taught me."

Masters tasseled her hair. "So cool," he said, and then pressed Garret again. "Is the bot ready?"

Still preoccupied with his comm, Garret answered, "Yeah, he's ready. Can you lead him to the bay door? He's programmed, but I've got this weird call I need to look into." The slim coder muttered to himself, "Why would Cade Thrane call me?"

"Sure, I can do that," Masters said. "But only if Prisma will come along as my backup. You know, in case the war bot decides it wants a piece of all this." Masters modeled his armored body.

Prisma giggled and blushed. "Crash is nice," she said, gathering her composure. "He wouldn't try to hurt my friends. But I'll come with you anyway."

Masters, Crash, and Prisma left the armory and made their way through the corridors to the main lounge. The Dark Ops team was already assembled next to the main ramp. Chhun, his helmet on, put a hand on his helmet, next to his ear. He motioned for the war bot to come near.

"It's time to deliver our special package," Masters said to Prisma. "You'd better stay on this side of the room. Grab hold of something if you're not going to strap in, okay?"

Prisma buckled herself into a crash seat and watched as one of the legionnaires lowered the ramp, causing gusts of wind to whip their way inside the ship. Prisma's hair flew around her face wildly. The outside smelled lush and sweet—a rich mix of new growth and the decomposing vegetation that fed it.

Crash walked to the edge of the ramp, and without a moment's hesitation, he jumped out into the dark night sky. The spot where the bot had stood afforded a view of treetops rushing by. Even as the ramp was raised, the sound of distant blaster fire and explosions could be heard penetrating the darkened still of the pre-dawn morning.

"Prepare for landing," Keel announced over ship-wide comm. "I found us a good vantage point to paint the shipyard for orbital strike."

11

Personal Memoirs of C. Chhun

There's a terrifying point in war, when you comprehend just how much your survival depends on luck. For me, that realization came in my first combat deployment. This was before Kublar. Before Dark Ops. I was Corporal Cohen Chhun, and I had no idea what I was in for.

The destroyer *Chiasm*—yes, that *Chiasm*—had just kicked us out for a six-month deployment on Marat. There was a Republic-sponsored spaceport on planet, named for some regional governor. I don't even remember what the place was called, though I'd sworn I'd never forget it. But you do forget these things. Or at least, I do. This spaceport was a case study of contrasts. The areas controlled by the Republic, around the customs buildings, Legion camp, selectmen halls, and regulated trade zones, was spotless. Streets kept so clean by the bots that you could eat off of them. It was actually a great place to be stationed, even though no one ever actually did eat off the streets.

In fact, the only problem with being stationed at this spaceport on Marat was the daily trips to the parts of the city where people *did* eat off the streets. Which, considering everything else the native kellochs—and humans—did on those streets, was a phenomenally unhealthy thing to do. Even *with* Republic anti-bacs handed out at every aid-shanty that peppered this rougher part of town.

But out we went, our squadron taking patrols on alternate days. Sometimes to take a VIP to hear grievances from the local selectmen, or to meet with a Republic aid worker and listen to requests for stronger security, additional medical supplies, stuff like that. The reason for the patrols was never really offered. We just rolled out and did our job, knowing that by simply leaving and showing that leejes weren't afraid of what was outside the wire, we were dealing out psychological victories to the kellochs and humans who bristled at the Republic's presence.

You don't like that three squads of leejes are walking down *your* streets? Do something about it. Otherwise, the rest of your town will know that all you've got going for you is a gut full of talk and a spine full of cowardice.

Most of the natives stayed inside their homes when our sleds came floating down the street. But every so often, at least one in four trips, someone would test you. A gunman with a fifty-rate sniper rifle would ping a sled's windshield or take potshots at a basic turret gunner. And then get dusted by a leej. Usually Twenties when they messed with our squad. We came in together, Twenties and me.

I miss him.

So one day, we're on foot, walking out alongside our sled as it moves slowly through a particularly crowded street. There was some sort of local bazaar, like a festival shopping event. Everyone was out buying, selling, trading, drinking—puking on the streets. Fun times. We were stalled behind a throng of intoxicated locals, all of them leaning on one another, each one the only thing that prevented the other from falling down drunk. They simply would not clear out off the street, no matter how much the basic gunner in our sled cursed and yelled and motioned for them to move to the side.

"Lieutenant Ford," I remember Private Clauderro asking, "can we just have the driver run over these idiots?"

"No," Ford answered. "Pappy feels like we're making inroads here. Wants to leave Marat a better planet than we found it for the next rotation of leejes. Doomsday, move up and help these beings find the sidewalks."

"On it," replied Sergeant Giorgis, LS-67, who was in charge of Doomsday Squad. We called him Life, because if there was *ever* a career legionnaire, it was him. A decade older than us, he *already* seemed to have lived a lifetime in the Legion, from our frame of reference. Not Pappy levels, but old enough that he could call us "kid" and we wouldn't think anything of it. He could cite every legionnaire rule and reg from memory, was an absolute beast in combat, and learned whatever he needed to know the first time, every time. Officers in Victory Company were all constantly trying to nab him for their squads, but Wraith had a way of getting what he wanted. And so Life was going to be in Doomsday, Specter, or Hyena for as long as Second Lieutenant Ford had Pappy's attention. And given the way Wraith performed on the battlefield, he didn't look to give it up any time soon.

"Chhun, Twenties." Life signaled us out. Even his hand motions were crisp and perfect. "Let's clear the way."

We waded into the revelers and began herding them off the street. But it was like digging a hole in the sand. It seemed that for every drunken local we got to the side, a few more slid back in front of the combat sleds. Nothing nefarious, not like they were purposefully blocking our way, just too many people having too good a time. Like I said, packed street.

Zzzziim!

A long rifle shot sizzled over our heads, fired at range from a point north of us. *That* cleared the streets. The celebrants ran for cover, ducking in alleys or behind sleds so that the leejes had to hurl them out of the way in order to stay protected. I spun around as the crowd around me dispersed in a panic. The gunner on the twins of the sled behind me had been hit right where the neck meets the shoulder. He was slumped back, his mouth open and moaning in some kind of pain. Someone from the inside pulled him back into the sled, and a legionnaire popped up to take the basic's place.

"Where did that shot come from?" Wraith called out over L-comm.

"North," Life answered. He ducked behind an open-air caff stand that pushed out onto the sidewalks.

North of us, at the end of the street we were on, about a half click away, stood a cluster of four-story buildings. They had been condemned, were supposed to have been abandoned, and should have been torn down. But Republic officials rarely took much stock in the "shoulds" when they came from the Legion.

Life gave an arms briefing on the all-squad channel. "That was a Penderan Arms hunting rifle. Big game on New Penda, takes special permits to have one of those. Shouldn't be out this far. So I'm saying don't count on your armor to keep you safe. Heads down."

"I want some fire on those buildings," Wraith said.

Immediately the twin heavy blaster turrets on the combat sleds opened up. Ripping fire through the windows. But... there were a lot of windows.

Zzzziim!

Another round came streaking toward us. It went right through a leej's arm and hit a fleeing kelloch in the back. It would have hit the leej in the head, had the leej not stumbled over an overturned cart of salash—a sort of local ice cream—right at the crucial moment. This guy, wherever he was, was good.

While leej medics scrambled to take care of the wounded, Sergeant Life was hyper-focused on finding the sniper.

"Twenties!" he called out. "Did you see where that last shot came from?"

"No, Sergeant." Twenties had his rifle out and was scanning the north buildings. "Shooter knows what he's doing."

Life nodded. "Everybody, keep out of sight. Twenties, hand me your rifle. I'm going to show you an old, old trick."

Life removed his bucket and put it on top of the barrel of Twenties's N-18. "Okay, keep eyes on those buildings."

"I've got a peeper in the air looking for incoming blaster fire," Wraith said.

"Let's hope our shooter doesn't take out the bot," I replied.

"Nah, this'll be too tempting to resist," said Life. With the helmet's visor facing the direction of fire, Life raised the helmet above the caff stand as if it were a soldier taking a look just a bit too conspicuously.

Zzzziim!

The sniper sent a blaster bolt directly into the helmet, sending it and the N-18 clattering onto the ground.

"Okay," Wraith said. "I've got positive confirmation. Shooter is dug in deep into the center building. Way in the back. Don't think our twins can get the right angle. I'm transmitting building grid number to you all. Anyone have a shot?"

The replies came back negative.

"That's fine," Wraith said, talking to himself as much as to us over the L-comm. "Just trying to save the Republic some money. I'll get *Chiasm* to target for orbital bombardment."

That was the nice thing about serving on the *Chiasm*. Captain Vaneers had no qualms about going all out in support of the legionnaires on the ground if we asked him for it.

Zzzziim! Zzzziim!

The sniper sent a pair of additional blaster bolts down range. These two didn't find any targets.

"Okay, listen up," Wraith announced over L-comm. "*Chiasm* says expect targeted bombardment in thirty seconds. They're not looking to take the whole block out. Just the one building."

We watched as the target building was bathed in a red glow from the precision laser painting the path of the ship's main laser batteries. Seconds later, what sounded like thunder shooting down a metallic traffic tunnel filled our bucket's audio receptors. Three massive bolts blasted their way through the roof of the target building, causing all the windows—in not only the target building but those buildings surrounding it—to shatter and spray shards of glass onto the streets below. Doors and structurally weak sections of wall buckled and were flung outward, some of them landing within a couple hundred meters of us.

The shots were perfect. Right through the roof, essentially hollowing out the building while maintaining the structural integrity of the exterior walls. If you could fly up and hover over the top of the building, you'd be able to see straight down into the sub-levels.

As the dust cleared, we stood up and began to re-form on the column. But Life wanted to retrieve his bucket, so we waited for him. He came back with his bucket in one hand and Twenties's rifle in the other.

"Here you go," Life said, handing the rifle back to its owner. "Don't lose your weapon again, Twenties." Life winked and examined his bucket. It had a hole right through the visor. He put his hand inside the helmet and wiggled a finger out through the hole. "Told you those Pendaran rifles packed a punch."

"It's not often a leej looks scarier with his bucket off," Twenties joked.

"Ooah," replied Life. "Let's get you ladies back to the C-S."

I held out an arm. "After you, sir. Age before beauty."

"Anyone ever tell you you're a wise-ass, Chhun?"

And with that, Life took his first step from behind our meager cover and back onto the street.

Pek!

The blast came from a standard, run-of-the-mill blaster rifle, fired by a kelloch who'd jumped around the corner at the very end of the street. He didn't even aim. Life went down hard, his head slamming directly onto the street, nothing left in his arms to protect his face.

Twenties swiftly raised his N-18 and tracked the shooter, who was attempting to flee back around the corner. All he could see of the attacker was the thin calf muscle of his right leg. Twenties blew it off at the knee.

Legionnaires rushed to the end of the alley and captured the shooter, who was writhing in pain from the loss of his limb. I heard later that the kelloch took the shot not because he had any problems with the Legion, or even with the Republic, but because his old lady always told him he was gutless—and he figured shooting a legionnaire would put that insult to bed once and for all. Out on the edge, it's not just disgruntled militias and war-thirsty tribes mixing in with rebels that pose a risk. Everything out there can kill you.

I looked down at Life. I didn't bother to call for a medic, because there was no point. The hole in his head left no doubts that he was dead. A medic came anyway, but after a few seconds, it was obvious that he was just going through the motions. I just stared at this flawless legionnaire. And I realized that if *he* could get dusted like this, that no amount of training could save you when your time came.

The blast that killed Life was from a rifle that our armor was fully capable of deflecting. If Life doesn't lose his helmet. If I walk out first. If Life is a few inches shorter. If any of those things... Life is still alive at the end of that day. But his luck ran out.

So, yeah. It doesn't matter how good you are. You could be the perfect soldier, but if it's your time... you're dead. No arbitration hearing.

I say all this because as this Naseen freighter called the *Indelible VI* cycles through its systems check after landing, I see Wraith emerge from his quarters wearing his armor. It's more or less Dark Ops legionnaire gear, but with a few extra tricks added on. After-market stuff that can't be afforded on a Legion salary. A neuro-dart attached to the wrist plate, and what look like jump jets built into the heels of his boots. You can't fly with those, but they're enough to get you clear of a hot spot. His helmet is still off, and I see this man I've fought beside in the most desperate action I've ever witnessed. It's a strange sight, seeing him without his bucket. Wraith *always* kept his bucket on when we served together. He was known for it. A switched-on leej who never cycled off.

My guys are waiting at the ramp. Fish and Bear up top, Masters and Sticks outside, the landing zone secured. Up until now, I wasn't entirely sure Wraith would be joining us. He seemed pretty comfortable playing the part of a featherhead flying the ship.

Maybe I'm being unfair with that comment. I'm sure he can still fight. We all heard rumors of "the Wraith" taking care of business throughout galaxy's edge—for a price. Even telling off Republic officers with impunity. The fruits of being good at what you do.

Now that same guy is standing with a bucket tucked beneath one arm and a short barreled NK-4 rifle, the same type as my own, in the other. And then that stunning Endurian—apparently a princess—walks over and stands next to him. Hanging around like she *really* wants to say goodbye. Captain Ford is a good-looking guy, and if I'm being honest, an Endurian princess holding his arm in her own looks like the most natural thing in the galaxy. Like a holo-ad, minus the blaster rifle and fraggers, I mean.

It's surreal how our lives have converged after being sent in separate directions to serve the same Legion. I haven't been on a date in two years. Oh well. My NK-4 is my girlfriend, and this is our prom.

The princess—I should call her Leenah—seems aware that I'm watching from my spot by the ramp, even though my bucket is on. She offers Wraith a kiss on the cheek, but the captain must have picked up some moves in his time away from the Legion. He turns into her kiss, catching her lips with his own. He gives a smile that hints of promises and suggestions unspoken.

Then he turns to me and begins to don his bucket. "Ready to KTF, Chhun?"

"Always," I answer.

It's odd. The way Wraith exudes a confidence that, whatever happens, it's not happening to *him*. That his luck will hold. That he's got good things waiting for him after all this.

And who knows? Maybe he's right.

In the back of my mind, I can hear a metronome. It makes all the noise and distractions fade away. Like the end is near.

Maybe it's my luck that'll run out.

And you never hear the shot that takes you down.

12

Wraith stepped off the *Indelible VI* and out onto the perimeter, the ramp closing behind him. His instructions to Leenah and the collection of misfits who made up his crew—a crew he was really coming to like—were clear: no one comes on board other than the war bot and the six men who disembarked. If anyone else approached the ship, they were to be dusted. Uniforms didn't matter.

"And what if you don't come back?" Leenah had asked before Keel—he was Keel then, not Wraith—left to get into his battle kit.

He had smiled. "Let's just plan for what's *likely* to happen. I'll be back. Don't worry."

Now, in his armor, he felt like his old self. He was Wraith. He had always become Wraith whenever he put on the gear. It was what made his life on the edge so easy. There was Keel, and there was Wraith. The shrinks would probably tell him he was crazy. But that wasn't it. He was simply aware. Aware of how certain things in life took different sides of the same person. Keel did some questionable things, and he never had trouble sleeping at night. But when Wraith came out... it was the rest of the galaxy who couldn't fall asleep.

The team formed a perimeter set to move on Chhun's orders, with Masters taking point. Taking *lead*. Chhun struggled with calling it "taking point" once that word became synonymous with failure and ineptitude. So he fought a mental war with himself to avoid using that phrase all together. Masters was taking *lead*.

They were spaced out, enough to keep alive if someone opened up on them or if someone stepped on a blast plate. Tarrago Prime had been at war for less than a day, and the area was probably safe so long as they kept clear of patrols, but in Dark Ops... you're always at war. And death is always waiting with its embrace.

Wraith remembered this. Felt it instinctively, like it had entered his bones through osmosis from his battle-tested armor. He was calm and ready. Content to be a war fighter until the dark legionnaires were dead and the shipyard was in ruins. Ooah.

Pike looked up at the canopy of palm-tree branches that bent above the *Indelible VI*. "How in the world did you get the ship in here?"

"Just takes a little back and forth," Wraith answered over L-comm, his voice even and devoid of emotion. "Let's keep focus on our sectors."

"See now, *that's* the Wraith I remember," Masters said, not taking his eyes away from the swaths of wilderness in front of him. "By the way, that's a pretty badass modification on your bucket. I like how you expanded the visor. Can we get some of those?"

"Everybody set?" Chhun asked, killing Masters's banter and transmitting the route he'd mapped for them to hike. The vegetation-studded peak he'd selected from which to target the shipyards was just a few kilometers away, but they would feel the increase in elevation over that last click of switchbacks.

"Ready to dust these leej knockoffs," answered Bear.

"Shouldn't get the opportunity if this op goes as planned," Chhun said, pointing forward, indicating for the team to move out. "We're here to blow up a shipyard, not a bunch of leej impersonators."

"You're no fun, Team Leader," Sticks said.

The talking died down as the *Indelible VI* receded from view, hidden behind the dense foliage of Tarrago Prime's natural wildlife reserves. Every Republic planet was required to maintain a designated percentage of its surface area as wilderness. The Republic, of course, decided where and how much, and that was that. This was one of the Republic mandates that most of the galaxy didn't seem to mind—though it did cause cities to sprawl in odd directions. The city supporting and sustaining the shipyards extended for miles, then abruptly ended at the wilderness as though someone had drawn an invisible curtain to halt all technological progress.

Dawn's light remained a promise, and as the kill team crept silently through the jungle-like wilderness, they were serenaded by the rhythmic chirps, clicks, and hisses of innumerable insects. The night seemed to have a rhythm of its own. But to Wraith, it was more or less like every other jungle he had ever ventured through, and he listened carefully, letting the wildlife tell him what the sophisticated sensors of his bucket, displayed on his HUD, could not.

There was a scurrying sound ahead, and Masters screamed, "Gah!"

"What is it?" Fish asked, his blaster rifle searching.

"Dude, a spider bigger than my head just ran out in front of me."

"Oh," Sticks said, shrugging. "Yeah. That's why they vent the destroyers once they're in deep space."

"Fumigate 'em first," added Bear. "Just for good measure."

"Let's keep moving," Wraith said, pushing up ahead of Masters and taking the lead for his own. There was something about their surroundings that bothered him.

He opened a private L-comm connection with Chhun. "Chhun," he said, "keep your guys quiet for a while."

"They're just talking, Ford. Over L-comm. No one can hear them." Chhun took a breath. "It's not like this is *new*. When you were on Victory Squad..."

"It's not that," Wraith said, softening his voice as much as he was willing. "I need to concentrate on the outside, and I can't hear over them. Don't want to mute them in case they see something. So please... so I don't have to make everyone feel awkward by giving orders to your guys..."

"Guys," Chhun said over L-comm, "let's keep the chatter down. Wraith thinks he hears something."

One by one, the kill team gave click-responses with their tongue toggles.

Wraith listened to the noises around him. They sounded strong enough where the kill team glided through the forest like phantoms, but ahead, instead of an undulating cone of noise, he heard... nothing. And in a place like this, a jungle, it only got quiet for a reason.

"Something's out there," Wraith concluded, voicing his concerns to the team.

"HUDs don't show anything," said Sticks.

Chhun backed Wraith up. "There's so much going on out here—so many life forms—that the HUDs might have trouble picking anything out until it's right on top of us."

"Any local preds look for a taste of leej," growled Bear, "I'll send 'em running with their tails tucked between their legs."

"Wraith to *Six*," Wraith called to his ship.

"This is Leenah—*Six*—go ahead."

"Are scans picking up anything humanoid other than us to the southwest?" Wraith knew that if they had, Leenah would have already called it in.

"No," answered the princess. "I can't even spot you anymore. You dropped off sensors about ten minutes ago. But Garret thinks he has something for you."

The slim code slicer's voice cracked over the comm. "Uh, hey, Wraith. So... I think I tapped into the comm systems these dark legionnaires are using. Well, not think. I did. I just need to work on a way to get it fully patched in to you guys."

"Nice work," Wraith said. This kid, like Leenah, was proving to be invaluable. "Really good. As soon as you figure it out, patch us through on their main battle network."

"Okay," Garret said. "They call it S-comm, and they call themselves shock troopers, hence the 'S' I guess. Heh. But basically, it's a night-coded attempt to replicate the L-comm, and whoever they hired did a good job of creating an emulation. But it's nowhere near as stable, and obviously the security layers aren't as good as what the Legion has built up. I can port it to you in a secure L-comm observation channel now and can grant you access to communicate through S-comm in say... fifteen minutes."

"We can listen now?" said Wraith. "Golden. Put it through. To *me*. Only me."

"One sec..." Garret said. Wraith could hear the blips and dings of his console as he worked away. "There!"

Wraith immediately picked up a clear, albeit thin, conversation between two men, presumably these "shock troopers." They were talking about someone named General Nero, who was apparently supposed to arrive at the shipyards soon. Wraith nodded thoughtfully. That would be good, killing a general in the strike. He made a note to listen for news of

Nero's arrival. If they could delay the strike until he was at the shipyards...

"Leenah," he said into the comm, "can you or Garret triangulate where this transmission is coming from?" He forwarded the S-comm frequency he'd been listening in on to the *Six*.

"About two hundred meters southwest of your position, as estimated by the sensors' projection algorithm," said Leenah. "Sorry I can't be more specific than that, but like I said, you fell off sensors about fifteen minutes ago."

"No, that's fine. Wraith out."

That explained the silence he'd observed ahead. A patrol was moving somewhere in that general direction, traipsing around loud enough to spook all the little creatures into hushing up. He would need to scout ahead and see if there was a quick way around.

His first instinct was to just go and get it done, but this was a team, and he needed to maintain the sort of order and discipline the rest of these Dark Ops soldiers would expect, would thrive under. He thought back to his own time serving in the black armor.

Chhun.

Chhun was the guy who had a knack for moving quietly. He'd snaked his way through that corvette, making it all the way to the bridge without being detected, in spite of the fact that the zhee crew knew a kill team was on board. He'd also done some fancy maneuvering on Kublar, Gareppo, and countless other hot spots.

"Chhun," Wraith called over the squad comm. "There's a patrol up ahead of Sullus's troops. They call themselves shock troopers."

"How do you know that?" Fish asked.

"My guy on the *Six*—Garret—got me access to their comm system." Wraith signaled for Chhun to come up to the front of column.

"That's great! We need to get that information to the Republic," Sticks said. "Maybe find someone in the city, link up with a squad of marines if there are any. Someone who can use it to better organize a resistance."

"And we will," agreed Wraith, "but not until after we're done with what we came here to do. You get a tactical gift like this, you don't spoil it by letting the bad guys know you can hear them."

"All right," Chhun said, reaching Wraith and looking into the jungle's darkness, a darkness so thick that even the so-phisticated night vision of their buckets couldn't penetrate it. At least, not much of it. "Victory Squad, hold up here until Wraith and I have a look. If we can't get around these guys, or they don't move on, we'll have to take them down with a whisper."

"Oba, I hope they don't move," said Bear.

Wraith and Chhun pushed ahead, leaving the rest of Victory Squad hiding among broad-leafed plants in the inky black of the pre-dawn jungle. The pair moved with a speed that seemed impossible given how silently they went. Rifles at the low ready, they moved around and through the dense foliage, both men knowing from countless training exercises and personal experience where to plant each foot, and how to raise and lower their legs so that every step came down and spread out their weight evenly. They were utterly quiet.

Periodically, Wraith would open the S-comm to listen to the shock troopers. He figured six men on patrol, based on their conversations. It sounded like they'd come to a halt, and Wraith wondered if they hadn't somehow heard them. His HUD wasn't showing anything yet, which was good, because he had no way of knowing whether the enemies' bucket tech was sophisticated enough for both sides to detect the other at the same time. And what then?

A copse of trees led the pair to a slightly elevated position. Neither man spoke. Chhun signaled for Wraith to stop moving, then swept his hand around to point out a position just beyond the thick trees. Wraith understood that Chhun saw—or at least thought he saw—the shock troopers through the forest. Wraith nodded, and the two began to crawl inch by inch along the jungle floor, hoping their synthprene and armor would fend off whatever bites the local nasties might have for them.

There were indeed six shock troopers, all of them taking a breather in a clearing. It was sloppily done. They sat in a semicircle like Space Scouts around a campfire. No sentry anywhere to be seen, unless a seventh man had climbed to the top of a tree. Wraith looked up at the trees scraping the starry sky. He saw no men, just flashes of light out in the beyond, lumbering giant capital ships fighting high above.

"Doesn't look like they're moving out any time soon," Wraith whispered over L-comm.

"No, it doesn't," Chhun agreed. "And I can't see a good route that would allow us to go around them."

"Well," Wraith said, starting to move forward, "KTF."

Chhun reached out and grabbed Wraith's arm. "Hold on. Let's go back and get the team."

"Listen," Wraith said. "I've gotten pretty used to relying on one person: me. You've got at least two members on that team who seem to know how to KTF. Masters I know can go, and Bear seems to have a killer instinct. But you're asking me to put my life in the hands of people I don't know, in a situation that I *do* know I can handle alone."

"They're all professionals," Chhun said, his voice betraying annoyance. "As good as any member since the team was founded."

"No offense," Wraith said, "but the clock is ticking. We don't need the rest of the team. Get a bead on the one with the lieutenant's stripes on his armor."

"What're you going to do?" Chhun asked.

"Kill the rest."

Wraith crept down to the edge of the woods, then called out over his external comm: "Guys, don't shoot, my S-comm is broken."

The shock troopers grabbed their weapons and leveled them at Wraith, who still stood partly obscured in the trees. "Who are you? Identify yourself!"

"ST-30," Wraith said, using the identification system he'd overhead on the S-comm. "I'm part of a detachment sent by General Nero. My S-comm is busted and I got separated from the rest of my squad. You know how unreliable these things can be."

"Yeah, that's the truth," said one of the shock troopers.

Wraith had gotten the drop on them, but after years of practice, with Ravi giving him odds, he had come to realize that the *real* deadly surprises, the kind that allowed him to take down several men at once, came after that initial shock. When your opponent began to feel trust and ease, and the adrenaline spike in his system began to drop off... *that's* when you hit them.

"You should ask him the challenge question," one of the shock troopers said over S-comm, unaware that Wraith could hear every word.

"Yeah," another answered, "but there's a different one for Tarrago Prime... what was it? Oh, yeah. National."

Wraith spoke up. "Oh, I know this is probably silly, but you guys need to answer the challenge question. Not that we're not all shock troopers, but, you know. So... National..."

The second the shock troopers began laughing, Wraith clicked over to L-comm. "Now."

Chhun's blaster bolt flew out of the darkness, striking his man directly in the visor. Confused, the other shock troopers swiveled to Chhun's point of fire as Wraith drew his blaster pistol. Five swift trigger pulls left the jungle deathly silent and the shock troopers just dead. Bones in buckets, never remembered again.

"Holy hell," Chhun said, climbing down to stand with Wraith in the clearing. "I mean... holy *hell*."

"Not bad, if I do say so myself," Wraith said of his own work. No—not Wraith. That was something Keel would say.

"Let's get the team up here. We've got a shipyard to destroy."

13

Bots the size of a purra bird hovered high above the trees, broadcasting a dual frequency. One, a visual feed to the Dark Ops leej controlling it, showing them exactly where they were painting a target. The other, a Legion-encoded beacon transmitting to a pre-designated Republic destroyer, in this case the *Intrepid*, telling it exactly where to send its orbital bombardment.

It was a beautiful thing in action. A destroyer could auto-fire all its turbo lasers and MAROs at once, each battery linked by the bot's transmission to strike a single target with pinpoint precision. No need for individual AI and gunnery targeting. Just a single command by the captain and... utter devastation.

The targets were painted, and the team was ready. When *Intrepid* arrived, it would be a beautiful and terrible spectacle. Six bombardments—one for each bot—that would leave the Kesselverks Shipyards in utter ruins. Sullus's fleet would barely have time to adjust before the ship was done and ready to jump back out of the system. And while Goth Sullus's ships scrambled, the *Indelible VI* would leave atmosphere and jump to rendezvous. Just another blockade to run.

The time ticked down, and each legionnaire steeled himself for the expected bombardment. Any moment.

Any moment.

"Hey," Masters said, when the time on the HUD chronometers showed five minutes past strike point, "what gives?"

"Just keep your targets painted," Chhun ordered. "Better late than early."

But time continued to roll, and there was still no sign of *Intrepid*.

Wraith was keenly aware of the change in light. Daybreak was far too close for his tastes. "Hey, Chhun," he called over a secure comm. "Let's say for argument's sake that the bombardment isn't coming. This doesn't seem like an op your team can scrub."

"No, it's not," answered Chhun. "We can't let this warlord start pumping out his own destroyers. Gotta take it down."

"Five more minutes?" Wraith said.

"Yeah," Chhun agreed. "Otherwise we have to get moving to keep ahead of the sunrise."

"Right."

Wraith looked at the feed the bot was projecting into his bucket's screen. The compound looked empty—at least the portion of it that he had visuals on. The Republic had a chronic problem of assuming that no one would ever attack. That reflected the consistently flawed belief of the Republic—that there was no one who could wage a campaign against them. And the thing of it was, if Victory Squad denied the shipyard to these insurgents, that belief would once again be shown to be true.

"Tell me about Exo," Wraith said, his voice flat, his attention remaining on his target.

"He was on the team until about a year ago," Chhun answered. "Got tired of the way the Republic seemingly did everything in its power to prevent us from doing our jobs. The situation you pulled us out of? It was starting to become more common than not. Nothing quite as bad as what you pulled us away from, but it definitely got to the point where the Legion couldn't count on the navy or army to support us once we were inserted, with some notable exceptions. It was getting to him. He was always talking about how we didn't survive Kublar to get dusted because some navy point dirtbag was too scared to use the equipment he was in command of. Getting hot. You know Exo."

"Yeah," Wraith said. "So what'd he end up doing? Seems like former leejes are always in demand for personal security or training. You guys stay in touch?"

"Said we would. But... you know."

"Yeah."

The conversation died, leaving only the sounds of the jungle—sounds that seemed to grow fainter as the system's sun bided its time. And when the sun's rays arrived, a whole new symphony of calls and growls would take up the alarm, as the nocturnal creatures gave way to the things creeping in daylight.

"So why'd you stay?" Wraith asked, startling himself with the way his question broke the mental still in the air.

Chhun shook his head. "Because I believe the Legion is the only thing left in the galaxy fighting for what's good and right."

Wraith laughed, not unkindly. "I remember a time when you weren't so sure of that."

"Yeah. Well, I can't stop fighting while there's still a leej alive by my side. Can't walk away, either."

"True believer," Wraith observed.

"And you're not?"

Wraith paused to consider before shaking his head. "No, I don't think so. I think I just do all this stuff because I'm good at it."

Before Chhun could respond, Wraith recalled his bot. Careful to communicate only with Chhun, to avoid giving the impression to Chhun's men that *he* was in charge, Wraith said over private comm, "Five minutes is up. We need to figure out what to do next."

Chhun recalled his bot as well. "Time for Plan B," he announced to the team.

The others shifted and recalled their own bots. Chhun's was the first to return, it being the closest. The spherical unit hummed down, placed itself in Chhun's outstretched palm, and switched off. The legionnaire stowed it in a specially shielded pouch attached to his webbing.

"What's Plan B?" Fish asked.

"That's going to depend on all of you," said Chhun, before looking over to Wraith. "You too, Ford."

Wraith nodded, but said nothing.

"Mission was to destroy the shipyards. The *Intrepid* would have made that a whole lot easier, but getting left high and dry by the navy is nothing new. Besides, knowing Captain Deynolds, if the ship isn't here, there's a good reason."

"So we blow up the shipyard ourselves?" Sticks asked, the uncertainty clear in his voice. "Captain, we don't have the ordnance necessary to accomplish a demo project of that size."

"Unless Wraith has more goodies on board his ship?" said Pike. "Maybe a MARO tucked away somewhere?"

"No such luck," Wraith answered. "Just the anti-starfighter missiles. That won't be enough to do the job, and I honestly doubt a single MARO would be able to do it either."

"So I don't get it," Fish said, stowing his own bot. "Is there some kind of self-destruct button built into the shipyard? That seems like a design flaw..."

"Sort of," confirmed Chhun. "The data that Wraith's code slicer pulled up said that the shipyards are currently building three corvettes, but no destroyers. That detail is important, because Kesselverks is supposed to be capable of producing one destroyer and ten corvettes at once. So the downshift in production means..."

Wraith jumped in, seeing where Chhun was going. "That they're building something bigger than normal on this cycle."

"Exactly," Chhun answered with a snap of his fingers. "So figure the Republic is either building another carrier—unlikely, since there's a dedicated facility for that on Craggock Three—or, *my* guess... a super-destroyer."

Sticks shook his head. "Super-destroyers are too big to be built on-planet and then repulsed into orbit. And I didn't see any partially built units floating in dry dock on the way in."

"Could've been destroyed early in the fight," Bear observed.

Chhun nodded at this and said, "Neither side would want to lose a partially completed super-destroyer. Too valuable."

"So that means they just got started," Wraith said.

"I think so." Chhun stepped to one side as some yellow-and-orange-spotted snake slithered past him. "These ships start with the reactors and drive elements in place. That's the first thing they build, and then they bring in the defense fleet to seal off the sector as the protective elements are constructed around it. So I say we go in there, find the super-destroyer's drive and reactor build, and follow Legion lost capital protocol."

The kill team stood in silence, each man contemplating what this would mean. In the event that a Republic capital ship was deemed unsalvageable, the standing orders for the legionnaires on board were to compromise the ship's reactor, denying the ship to any would-be raiders and creating an explosion massive enough to potentially take out several more enemy capital ships in the blast radius. It was a Legion protocol that drew scoffs from the rest of the Republic military-industrial complex—because who could ever assemble a force formidable enough to take over a destroyer? But the Legion still planned for everything, and now it seemed that planning might come to good use. Assuming the kill team was prepared, mentally and physically, to do the job.

Fish was the first to speak. "Yeah, I mean, let's do it. I'm just wondering what the odds are that we make it back to the ship..."

"They need to be pretty good if you want me to come along," Wraith said, folding his arms. "I didn't come to Tarrago just to get vaporized."

"Shouldn't be a problem," Chhun said. "This is still a Republic facility, and the bio-signatures required to make that reactor go are going to be tied into the databank of authorized, active Legion. By default, that's every kill team member. So once we set it up, we can control how much time passes before boom-time. And no one on the other side can stop it, no matter how shiny their knockoff leej armor looks."

"So hey, great," began Masters, "but... is this going to blow up just the shipyards, or the entire city, too? 'Cause that's a lot of people, man."

The legionnaires again looked at one another. And then at Chhun. The decision was ultimately his, and Wraith didn't exactly envy him. Though if it were up to Wraith, he'd know what he'd decide. If denying the shipyards was what the Legion asked... he'd do it.

"I'll call into my human computer and see what he says," Wraith said.

He hailed Garret over the comm and explained the situation. Then he linked in the rest of the legionnaires so they could hear the code slicer's answer.

"Oh, wow," Garret said. "So in theory, the shipyard should contain a breach like that and keep the city safe. It wouldn't be producing any more ships for... well, a long time. But that's all theoretical. I don't know of a time where those safeguards were even put to the test."

"It'll have to do," Wraith said, his way of giving thanks. "Wraith out."

"Oh, Captain Keel," Garret said. "I've been talking to an old friend. He discovered something really incredible about the comm system and—"

"Kind of in the middle of something here, kid," Wraith said, sounding far too casual, too much like his alter ego, for his own liking. This was a mission. He needed to focus on it accordingly, or he'd be dead.

"Okay, but, technological breakthroughs aside, we're decoding some pretty groundbreaking stuff. Like... about Admiral Devers working with the Black Fleet?"

"Who's the Black Fleet?" Chhun asked.

"That's what Goth Sullus calls his armada."

"Friendly," Bear growled.

Wraith nodded impatiently. "Garret, we already knew Devers is a piece of twarg dung. Is there anything that will help us right *now*?"

"Not as such..."

This confirmed Wraith's suspicions. The kid was amazing, truly. But this could wait. They had to get inside the shipyard compound before daylight—and the sky was already losing its darkened edge. "Okay. We'll go over it when we return. Keep it secure, index it, get it ready for debrief."

"Okay," Garret said, sounding small over the comm.

"Wraith out."

"Captain Keel?" Garret said almost immediately, causing snickers of laughter over the L-comm.

"Yes?"

"Got the S-comm cracked so you can listen and talk."

That was something that actually *would* come in handy. But it was also the sort of trick that was best only played once. "Thanks, Garret. That *will* be useful. Wraith out," he said again, half-expecting the kid to add something more. But the comm was silent.

Chhun looked through his macros at the shipyard. He transmitted the image to display on the HUDs of his kill team. "Still not a whole lot out there." He clicked the macros and painted a generator building yellow. "Wraith, can you drop one of those missiles on that target when we're ready to approach? That should make them go to emergency generators, and we can blow those when we get inside."

Wraith stored the image in his HUD as target-001. "Sure thing. Just tell me when you want the thing dropped."

Another section of the HUD display lit up yellow.

"This," Chhun said, "looks to be the only sentry at our approach. At least, the only one who's likely to see us. We'll need to take him down."

It was too long a shot to make, even for a Dark Ops sniper—though the thought of trying likely crossed each man's mind. But Wraith understood that taking down this sentry would need to happen right before insertion. Done before the rest of the—what were they called again?—shock troopers had the opportunity to investigate or go to their fighting positions.

"I don't see how we can approach the compound without that sentry seeing us, even if we come in from the jungle,"

Masters said. "From up there, the sentry'll have all the time in the world to pick us off as we try to cross the grounds. Even if he doesn't call for help."

"Maybe we can play a lullaby, get him to go to sleep," Pike offered.

Chhun agreed with Masters. "We're going to have to draw his attention away from whoever takes him out."

Bear raised a hand. "I volunteer to kill the insurgent."

"Fine," Chhun said. "Figured as much. So Masters, Wraith, and I will slip into the city and distract the sentry from there. This is before most of your time but, Wraith, remember Life's trick for drawing out snipers? Same principle. We grab the sentry's attention, and if he calls something in on us, it'll take patrols away from where we want to be. Pike, you stay put in case the *Intrepid* does show up. Everyone give Pike your bots."

The legionnaires handed Pike their bots so that he could paint the target—hopefully with them in the clear—should the need arise. Pike, for his part, seemed disappointed to be out of the action, but understood the importance of his role.

"So what am I supposed to do if *Intrepid* shows up and you guys are still inside?" asked Pike.

"We'll call in reports," Chhun said. "If we have confidence that our plan will work, call them off. If we tell you otherwise… have *Intrepid* take its shots."

"Speak for yourself," Wraith said. "I at least want a heads-up if an orbital strike is coming my way."

"You hear that, Pike?" said Masters. "Be sure to tell Wraith he's about to be blown to bits."

Wraith scowled. *Why did I let myself get into this mess?*

"Wraith," said Chhun, turning his rifle over in his hands. "If *Intrepid* shows, and neither you or I think they will, they're going to take their best shots whether Pike paints the targets or not. If it comes to that, I doubt any of us will be in a position to stay alive."

"How comforting."

Chhun returned his attention to the others. "That leaves Bear, Fish, and Sticks to get up behind the sentry from the jungle cover and take him out."

"Ha," Wraith said. "I didn't see that before."

"What?" Chhun asked.

"Fish. Sticks. Fish sticks."

The kill team stared at Wraith blankly.

"It's a food," Wraith insisted, feeling suddenly off his game. The nonchalance of Captain Keel guided him. "Pirates like it. All right, never mind. Before you guys take out the sentry, that'll be a good time to drop the first missile."

"Good," Chhun said. "Now..." The leader of Victory Squad began to map out routes, identifying fallback positions, repeating team objectives, and giving last-minute instructions.

Wraith heard all of this, but distantly. Like the songs sent over distant waters. Present, but thin and barely comprehensible.

Who am I? Wraith asked himself. *What am I even doing here?*

The abrupt blending of two worlds and two lives left Captain Ford feeling as though he was cracking up. After this... he needed time to sort things out. Time to reconcile the words he'd spoken to Leenah before he left the *Six* with the words he'd spoken to the kill team before he'd left a shuttle bearing the body of Twenties, years ago.

Did he owe anyone anything? And what did he owe himself?

And did it even matter? Because *now* was the time to KTF. It would be them or him, soon. And he would win and prove himself right, justified in everything. Seven years, and now a payoff in the form of a crippling blow to a warlord he'd only heard of a few days ago. Stopping Goth Sullus would make everything he'd done, right.

It had to be.

14

General Nero walked through the central command room of the Republic shipyards. No—not the Republic shipyards, not any longer. Kesselverks was now under control of the Black Fleet. Its owner was the man in black.

The attack on the moon had stalled, Nero knew, but Fortress Omicron would fall; the legionnaires defending it could not resist the superior numbers of his shock troopers. The gun would soon belong to the Black Fleet. Nero would see to it personally, if he must.

But the shipyards! The shipyards had come under his control *exactly* as he had intended.

A burst of blaster fire echoed from somewhere deep in the cavernous depths of the factory. The area where the destroyer bridge frames were printed before being sent for cold-fusing to the impervisteel hull, as Nero recalled.

Well. The shipyards were *mostly* under his control.

He turned and ordered one of his staff officers to send a detachment of shock troopers to shore up whatever force was meeting resistance. The private security had been routed early on, but the Republic marines were a persistent bunch. Nero would credit them that much. They always had been.

A major stepped out of the massive double doors of a conference room and gave Nero a sharp salute. "We have converted the Kesselverks boardroom to serve as your command center, General."

"Good." Nero pulled open the doors, revealing a busy crew of black-clad staff officers monitoring S-comms, battle grids, and intelligence reports. "General Nero on premises!"

The command center jumped up in rigid attention, each officer crisply saluting in textbook fashion.

"Yes, yes," Nero said, returning the salute as if waving away the formality. "Tell me about my installation."

A captain cleared his throat and directed a holomap to display a meter in front of the general's head. It showed the multiple levels, sections, and corridors of the massive factory capable of producing the capital ships needed to conquer the Republic. "As you can see, General, we have full control of more than eighty percent of the facilities, with fifteen percent contested and likely to fall shortly, and the remaining five percent firmly in control of the Republic Marines. Mostly these are areas where they have formed a last-stand defense, sealing off access and barricading themselves into defensive positions."

Nero waved his hand. "These are of no concern. Gas them. What of the reactors?"

"These were guarded by local security, and surrendered with virtually no resistance."

"Good. Anything else?"

Eyes shifted nervously around the room. A strong-chinned officer with a rare but distinctive scar from a cleft lip—probably edge-born, his parents unable to do a natal reversal—cleared his throat. He wore the white embroidered symbol of an intelligence officer: two stylized trees with twisted, intertwining trunks. "We have received a report that a Republic kill team has been dispatched to Tarrago Prime."

Nero viewed the room from beneath his brows, his eyes moving left to right and taking in the expectant, worried looks of his officers. "And what is your source for this intelligence, Captain—?"

"Condaras," the intelligence officer answered. "This information did not come through our own channels, General. It was sent through command by Admiral Devers, the Republic defector."

Nero nodded. He had heard of Devers, of course. The entire galaxy was familiar with the Hero of Kublar. Whether he was worthy of the reputation was immaterial; the patronage of Senator Orrin Kaar was all the admiral would ever need to succeed in the Republic. And to suggest otherwise—say, in a whispered conversation in some darkened corridor on board a destroyer, with the hope that the thrumming of sublight engines kept one from being overheard—was career suicide. Because conversations, *real* conversations, took two people. And in the cutthroat world of the Republic Navy, you didn't give anyone an advantage over you, like the person on the other end of your conversation. Friendships were few and frail.

For his part, Nero knew little about Devers beyond the man's public persona. He was a point, and that in itself suggested incompetence. But not always. Nero could have learned more, if he had wished, but he'd left the Legion long before Kublar, and hadn't had the inclination to reach out to acquaintances still serving to hear the scuttlebutt. They wouldn't have answered anyway unless from a sense of guilt about what happened to... *her.* And that was something Nero desperately wanted to do without. So no, he would not have called to find out just how heroic the Hero of Kublar truly was. It was of little concern.

But the information Devers had provided, if true, was of tremendous concern.

"Do you have any reason to doubt the veracity of this report, Captain Condaras?"

"We are... uncertain how to grade the reliability of intelligence from defecting forces," Condaras admitted. "But efforts have been undertaken to prepare for the potential of a kill team incursion."

"A sound course," Nero agreed. "This kill team will need to be eliminated. All of them. This mission cannot afford even one Dark Ops legionnaire to move unchecked in this sphere. Tell me, Captain... what you imagine this kill team has been sent to do."

"The report from Admiral Devers was... dramatic and bombastic, if I may say so..."

Nero looked at the captain with a cold eye. "You may... this time. But I would advise you to have a care in disparaging rank, even rank within the Republic."

"Yes, sir."

"Continue," Nero said, setting his cap on a table.

"Yes, sir. The report seemed to name every possible course of action as the sure one. I'm not sure the reason for this..."

Nero supplied the answer with a humorless smile. "This is in order that the admiral would be *right* no matter what happened. It's a standard means of communicating intelligence among those with positions and reputations to maintain within the Republic. A fine way to kill a squad of legionnaires. Continue."

"Ah," the captain answered, looking around him for help, clearly uncertain over how to respond. "Sir, it is our belief that the team will attempt to infiltrate the shipyard and rally any surviving marines for a counterassault to regain control of the

facility until reinforcements can be sent from a Republic battle fleet."

General Nero pinched his lower lip between two fingers
and gently pulled at it, as if thinking this through. "A sound and
rational interpretation," he observed after several moments of
deliberation. "However... the wrong one. A kill team is sent at
the behest of the Legion. And the Legion's desire will be to destroy these shipyards."

"But General," protested the major who had accompanied Nero into the room, "Kesselverks is far and away the
most important shipyard in Republic space. Its production
schedule is unmatched, and it can build any vessel. It would
take months for the Republic to repurpose one of the smaller
corvette shipyards in the mid-core. Surely they won't suffer
its loss."

"The Republic?" Nero asked rhetorically. "Certainly, their
desire would be to save the shipyard for the very reasons you
name. They may even resort to finding their favorite Nether
Ops branch to attempt just a thing. But the Legion knows that
this battle is lost. Just as I do. And the kill team they've dispatched will attempt to deny us use of this facility."

He turned and examined the holomaps behind him. He
spoke softly to himself. "It's what I would do."

The major asked, "What would you have us do to defend
Kesselverks, General?"

"Prepare your soldiers to defend the installation. Let no
one in, and whatever you do... don't allow your soldiers to be
drawn outside. The struggle will be inside these shipyards, I
assure you."

Captain Condaras cleared his throat. "We have shock
trooper patrols in the wilderness around the shipyards in an
effort to deny any Republic forces who escaped the initial at-

tack from rallying for a counterattack. Some have reported contact by reconnaissance from Republic forces, though the S-comms proved unreliable after the initial reporting. Shall I attempt to recall them?"

"I think—" Nero began, but he was cut off by the concussive sound wave from a massive explosion somewhere in the distance. Datapads fell to the floor of the makeshift command room. A silvene sculpture of a Republic destroyer broke free of one its supporting synthwires and swung on a downward arc into Nero's ribs. The general was knocked into a table, striking the other side of his rib cage. As officers rushed to his side, the room lights flickered erratically, their artificial rays revealing clouds of dust drifting down from the ceiling, disturbed by the blast. The lights didn't stabilize, but instead continued to flash an epileptic nightmare.

"Explosion recorded at the primary generators!" shouted a sensor tech.

"The kill team?" asked the major, visibly alarmed.

"So... ungh... it would seem," Nero answered, pulling himself back to his feet. Every word was marked by a sharp pain. A knife point piercing his lungs. Nero knew cracked ribs, from experience. But they would have to wait.

He waved away the outstretched arms of well-meaning lieutenants. "Generator... defense?"

"Three squadrons of shock troopers," answered the major.

"Sir," a comm officer shouted, leaning back from his chair to call upon the major. "I am receiving no response from Red Platoon."

"Send Blue Platoon to investigate!" ordered the major.

Nero raised his arm to protest, but the rush of pain took his breath away. Soon, a new problem drew the command center's attention.

"Incoming distress transmission from Triad Platoon," another comm officer said. "They're experiencing heavy contact from an overwhelming force."

"Patch... it..." Nero paused to groan in pain. Again the lieutenants rushed in to help him, and again he waved them away. "... *through*," he finished.

Distantly, he heard Captain Condaras ordering someone to summon a medic. He became aware of a coppery warmth on his tongue, and bringing his fingers to his mouth, saw them come away coated with blood and saliva.

The comm officer synced the incoming distress into the central command center audio.

"Repeat!" a shock trooper shouted amid a fury of blaster fire. "We're being pressed upon by an unknown force with overwhelming fire superiority. We are cut off from the rest of our force, and I do not have accountability... I... I think they're dead. We need close air—"

The words stopped, though the comm feed stayed on. The command center heard the whistling sound of an incoming projectile, followed by an explosion. Comm officers looked at one another with mounting tension. Whatever was happening outside sounded bad.

"Triad One, this is Command. Are you still with us? Triad One?"

"Shhh..." came a rough and urgent whisper over the comm.

"Triad One?" the perplexed comm officer tried again.

The sound of blaster fire erupted, sounding close to the comm source, close to the shock trooper reporting the destruction of his platoon.

"What's that noise in the background?" the major asked. It sounded like voices, but the shock trooper, if he was still alive, wasn't the one talking.

"I'll try and isolate and amplify." The comm officer worked his fingers over his console, turned to the major, and nodded.

"By authorization of the Legion, you are to be terminated," came the low and terrible death sentence of a war bot.

More blaster fire erupted, and the S-comm went offline.

The command center buzzed with conversations and status reports. Every comm officer was glued to their station, hands working frantically to ping, log, and record what was happening outside the shipyard.

"War bots," the major said, his face ashen. The color returned as he turned on Nero. "Since when did kill teams deploy with war bots? I tell you, General Nero, they are seeking to retake the shipyard. And with so many of our troops stalled on the moon, we won't be able to stop them!"

"No..." Nero said, his voice weak from whatever damage had been done to his insides. "This is an attempt to draw out our forces from the shipyard to fight ghosts."

"Ghosts?" the major shouted. "Did *ghosts* destroy our platoons on patrol?"

"Sir," a comm officer chimed in, "I've re-established S-comm connections with Lightning and Silo Platoons—but no one is answering my hails."

"Dead!" the major screamed, drawing his own conclusion. "General, this is an invasion. The Republic is attacking en masse. We *must* send our shock troopers to repulse the impending attack!"

Nero stood erect, closing his eyes involuntarily from the pain. A trickle of thick blood escaped from the corner of his mouth. "You are being lured into a web of confusion," he admonished the major. "And I won't stand for any more of your panicked overreactions. All shock troopers are to stay *inside* the shipyard and be alert for Dark Ops infiltrators!"

"With all due respect, General Nero," the major said as a pair of medics appeared on either side of his commanding officer. "You're wounded, and I believe it is impairing your judgment."

The major turned to expectant comm officers. "Ignore the general's commands and have every platoon set up a defensive perimeter."

"Damn you! I will not have my orders questioned!" Nero bellowed. He drew his blaster and fired a bolt into the abdomen of the major, who slumped onto the ground with a look of shocked horror.

This was not the sort of discipline Nero expected from his officers. His army was to be built upon battle-tested men, showing the full measure of competent ability, and this major was lacking. There had simply not been enough time to truly *know* his men. Nero wondered whether the wounded major was a pretender, exaggerating his skill set in order to seek fame and fortune in Goth Sullus's new order. There were such men in the universe, and not everyone in the revolution would be as pure as Nero. Such was the reality. The true condition of man.

Nero looked down upon the major. "Now we're *both* injured, and seeing as how *both* our judgments must now be impaired..."

Surveying the shocked command center, Nero gave a final order, every bit as vitriolic as his cries for the death of the Republic before this operation had started. "My orders *will* be followed!"

Captain Condaras stepped forward to address the Black Fleet. "You heard the general. Keep shock troopers deployed *inside* the shipyards and prepare for a kill team infiltration."

The command center sprang to life as Nero's orders were put into action.

One of the medics, along with a trio of junior officers, lifted the major and carried him off, no doubt to the shipyard infirmary. Nero stayed to watch his officers work for a few moments longer, then turned to walk to the infirmary under his own power. His injuries would be little more than a memory within the next eighteen hours; the infirmary was stocked with hospital-grade equipment.

But upon reaching the door, he heard a report that would keep him from the medical attention he'd need for the foreseeable future.

"Sir," a comm officer said, his tone weary. "Our sentry posted above the northwest spire is reporting possible visuals on the kill team."

"Which spire is that?" Captain Condaras asked.

"One of the unused repulsor spires they attached the near-completed capital ships to before they're tugged to the launch bays." That spire provided a panoramic view of the area surrounding the shipyard—that's why it had been selected as a sentry location.

"Put him through."

Nero slumped against the door jamb to hear this report. He wanted now, more than anything else, to have solid intel. How many legionnaires? Were they moving alone or with a strike force? Did they carry with them any crew-served weapons, or were they moving for stealth and speed?

The promise of answers came with the S-comm feed's relay into the command center.

"Report to Command," the comm officer instructed the sentry.

"Copy," the shock trooper sentry replied, his voice calm. "I have visuals on a Republic kill team."

"How many?"

"Just one for now. He's peeking from behind the warehouse opposite the shipyard entry."

This comment caused the officers in the command center to exchange glances. The kill team was already inside the perimeter. The officers' faces betrayed the dread they felt at the idea of a kill team, capable of killing them all, being so close to where they now sat.

"Feed in the visual feed from the sentry's helmet," Captain Condaras ordered.

Nero stared at the grainy visual, hued in the red of shock trooper night vision, as it appeared on the holodisplay. A Republic legionnaire kept looking around a corner, his helmet the only part of him that was visible. The resolution was abysmal at the display's distance—and yet, there was something odd about the rhythmic way the helmeted soldier appeared, looked from left to right, and then disappeared back behind the building. And then... the helmet's ultrabeam came on for a half second. As if the legionnaire *wanted* to be seen.

"Decoy!" Nero shouted, and then labored through a cough. "Decoy!"

But the warning came too late. A gloved hand obscured the shock trooper's visor, sending the holodisplay into darkness just before the sentry screamed and the display spun violently, giving the watchers in the control room a sense of vertigo as the shock trooper tumbled down from the top of the spire.

They heard his screams all the way to the ground.

15

Things are going well, Wraith told himself. The kill team had re-formed and was making its way through the compound. And so far, none of the shock troopers in the facility seemed to have any clue to their whereabouts—if their panicked S-comm transmissions were any indication.

It was hardly any wonder why.

Wraith had greatly enjoyed watching the effects of the first missile's impact with the power generators. The ground had shaken, and every light in the compound had flickered out before coming back to life at half strength. With any luck, a recovery squad of shock troopers would be sent to the site just in time for the next missile to strike.

An incoming chime from KRS-88 sounded in Wraith's bucket. "Enemy squadron eliminated," the war bot reported in a deep and ominous tone. "Awaiting orders."

"What's your operational status?" Wraith asked as he leapt over a toppled barrel of coolant. The team was in a relatively open stretch of a shipyard dock, making their way from pallet to pallet of freight and materials. Looking back, Wraith realized that he'd pulled out a good distance ahead of the others.

"System integrity is ninety percent," the war bot replied. "Weapons systems near depletion. Ten percent capacity remains."

That wasn't much. Certainly not enough to overwhelm another squad of shock troopers should the bot get the drop on them... again. It seems that the patrols on duty hadn't been expecting much of anything by way of resistance. The legionnaires, after all, were supposed to all be stationed on Tarrago's moon.

Surprise, surprise.

"Make your way back to the *Six*," Wraith ordered, coming to a halt just outside an open dock bay door. He checked to make sure there was no one waiting in ambush, signaled for the rest of Victory Squad to hurry up, then bounded toward the massive, open-platform freight elevator that could take them down to the super-destroyer's build level.

"Affirmative," KRS-88 answered. "Calculating direct route to designated location."

"Try and avoid any further engagements," Wraith said, reaching the freight elevator and scanning the surrounding area for targets as the kill team caught up. They were all fast, even Bear, who brought up the rear, but Wraith was faster. He'd always been a fast runner, and somehow when he put on his armor, he felt faster still.

"Affirmative," answered the war bot again.

Masters was the second member of the team to reach the freight lift. Mimicking Wraith, he took up a position behind a shipping crate, concealed by shadows. "You're fit, brother!"

Wraith gave an emotionless "Thanks," and waited for the rest of the team to join.

Chhun was the next to glide into the darkened recesses of the warehouse dock, with the others trailing him at twenty-meter intervals.

"Nice work so far," Chhun said over L-comm. "Any chatter over the comms we should be aware of?"

"Nothing that stands out," Wraith said, checking the time he had left for his remaining missiles. Thirty minutes. Good. "There's a general who was wounded in the first missile attack—Nero. Sounds like a big shot. Apparently they're looking to take him to the moon, but having some trouble. We should dust him if the opportunity presents itself."

"Copy that."

"Otherwise, just reports from patrols looking for us—" Wraith stopped short as a series of loud, mechanical clanks came from the freight lift. It began to lower on its industrial repulsors, slowly sinking into the floor to reveal a dark shaft punctuated by consecutive rings of light, each one marking a new level.

"That's probably not good," Masters quipped.

Wraith put a hand up to his bucket, listening to transmissions. "Sounds like a patrol is heading this way."

Without needing to be ordered, the legionnaires hid themselves even further in the shadows.

As the freight lift started its ascent back to their level. Chhun looked at the indicator light showing the lift's progress. "Still three sub-levels down. You getting anything useful, Wraith?"

"Not a lot of talking. They're definitely looking for us. Sounds like they're going to patrol the grounds we just left before entering the warehouse dock."

"We gonna dust 'em?" asked Bear.

"No," Chhun said, shaking his head. "Keep back and out of sight. Don't engage unless you have to. These range-bangers will be more useful to us alive and reporting that they haven't seen us than dead. They're doing ten-minute check-ins, same as we would in the Legion. We dust someone, and we're leaving a calling card, so let's avoid it until the last possible moment."

"Yeah, yeah," Bear said. "I know. Just gettin' the itch to drop these smug sons-of-eldritches for walking around like they own the place."

"Always make 'em pay," added Fish.

"Ooah."

The indicator on the freight lift moved up again. Just one more level.

"You all know you'll get your shots," Chhun said. "But we make them count. Here they come."

"Garret is saying he can isolate this particular squad's comm channel," Wraith whispered, though his bucket naturally kept the words from reaching the warehouse walls. "Patching it through..."

Slowly, like monsters emerging from the deep, the platform brought no less than eighteen shock troopers to the warehouse level. The lift stopped with an abrupt *ka-klank* as the hard brakes took over for the repulsors. The shock troopers lurched forward or to one side from the abrupt halt in momentum, taking a small step to steady themselves.

The packed-together soldiers were such a tempting target that Wraith worried the kill team would simply open up and dust them to the last man. But the kill team remained disciplined, keeping to the shadows, trusting their armor's deflectors and heat bafflers to keep them invisible from whatever tech these shock troopers had in their buckets.

The glossy, black-armored troopers didn't seem to suspect that the kill team would be anywhere this close. Hardly any of the eighteen ventured to look anywhere beyond what lay before them, and only a single soldier gave even a cursory check at the containers and freight staged in the shadows next to the freight lift.

"All right," said one of the shock troopers over S-comm. "Blue Platoon, we've got conflicting orders. I want Second Squad to check out the generator blast zone. Look for survivors and secure the area until engineering can arrive and start repairs. First and Third Squads, form up on me and begin sweeps for the Republic kill team. Death to the Republic!"

"Death to the Republic!" answered the other shock troopers, and they took off, forming a fairly good impersonation of a squad of leejes on patrol.

And by the looks of them, it seemed that the shock troopers did indeed include a mix of the real deal—former legionnaires. Of course, they also had their share of pretenders; there was no shortage of those in the galaxy. Guys who lied about serving in the Legion—usually these were just support staff in the Repub Army—or guys who desperately wished they *had* joined the Legion if they could've done it all over again. And maybe Goth Sullus's pitch had been just the opportunity they were looking for.

"Stinkin' amateurs," muttered Bear when the shock troopers had left the warehouse and were completely out of sight. "No way we would've missed who was around us if the roles were switched."

"Yeah, well, don't mind me for being glad they *didn't* see us," Masters answered. "Kind of nice not being shot at by almost twenty blaster rifles at close range."

"Pssh. Like we wouldn't have KTF'd 'em all before they got fingers on triggers."

Masters inclined his head as though he was thinking. "Huh. Yeah, you're right. We'd've dusted 'em all."

"Black armor don't make Dark Ops," Chhun said, cautiously coming out from behind the skid of wrapped containers he'd hid behind. "But let's not underestimate them all the same. The unknown enemy is the biggest threat, and we don't really have any idea who it is we're dealing with."

Wraith cleared his throat. "If general comm reports aren't propaganda, it sounds like these guys breached the eastern wall of Fortress Omicron. That means they've overpowered a company of legionnaires." He had wondered whether or not to share this piece of information, but decided ultimately to do so, because like Chhun, he felt the team needed to stay sharp. Apart from the *Intrepid* failing to show up, things had all been easy thus far.

"Bet it wasn't an even fight then," Sticks said. "And I bet the boys on that moon made 'em pay for every inch."

Wraith nodded. "Sounds like you're right. But the moon is just about lost if the comm reports are true. They're asking for General Nero to arrive and take command."

Stepping onto the freight platform, Chhun said, "Then let's get this super-destroyer drive rigged to blow up before whatever forces took the moon are sent down here."

"Back so soon?"

The question from the shock trooper standing guard at the super-destroyer's level was meant for someone other than a Republic kill team. It was transmitted over external speaker, as it was too banal to be worth adding to the already overtaxed S-comm, even on a squad-only channel.

This was all fine and good, and Chhun had expected that there'd be at least one sentinel guarding the freight lift at this level. They'd seen him from their descent, spying him through the opening at the bottom of their lift as it traversed from one level to the next. The guard had seen them too, had looked right at them, but the lighting he peered into would have made the kill team appear only as dark figures. Mere shadows. He wouldn't have thought anything of it beyond wondering what the six-man squad had forgotten, or what new orders they'd been given that no one had bothered to inform him of.

But Chhun, having a situational awareness that the guard lacked, was ready. His kublaren tomahawk, a weapon that had served him well in the years since his teammate had gifted it to him, swung down in a blinding and furious arc. The shock trooper was taken so off guard that he didn't even raise a hand to protect himself. The obsidian-like head of the war axe buried itself in the minute open space found where the helmet and shoulder pieces met. It dug through synthprene undersuit, flesh, muscle, and bone alike. It was a good, clean stroke, and Chhun was sure he'd managed to break the soldier's neck.

The man collapsed as though shot in head. Bear was there to catch the man's body before it hit the floor. Not out of pity, but necessity. Armor crashing down onto the polished floors of build sub-level three would make noise, and the hallways and corridors might carry that noise to men listening for signs of infiltration.

A Republic kill team offered its enemy no such assistance.

Bear hoisted the deceased shock trooper up by his arms, and Masters picked up the man's legs. Together they carried him out of view, making the truck bed of an unenclosed one-man repulsor sled into a burial tomb.

But the blood... Chhun marveled at how much blood a body could pour forth when savage, ancient weapons were used. When wounds weren't cauterized by searing hot blaster bolts. When the life of a man simply... emptied.

And when that metronome finally stops, is that my fate? Do I just bleed out and fade to black?

It was only a matter of time, Chhun told himself. Too many years of warfare. Constant fighting *before* ramping things up by joining Dark Ops. The galaxy only had so much luck.

These thoughts came and went in an instant, a quickly recited monologue he'd learned by heart, rehearsing it again and again as he lay, unable to sleep, during the still times of the night. Words he'd learned so well that he no longer needed to say them to give them power. They were something he felt. Something he knew in the very core of his being.

But he would die a warrior. And Chhun felt fine about that. Wouldn't want it any other way.

"Pike, buddy," Chhun called over L-comm. "We're inside. Almost there. Mission success looks probable."

"Well that's good," answered Pike. "Because there's no sign of anything helpful up there. Just a lot of ship-to-ship fighting lighting up the sky. You want me to stay put? I can make the hike and join you."

"Negative. Stay in position for another ten minutes, then hike back to the ship. If this reactor blows, I don't want you out in the open."

"Copy. Pike out."

The Dark Ops leejes re-formed around their team leader.

"Okay," Chhun said. "Getting here should have been the hard part. So far, not so much. But there are no easy ops. Expect at least a platoon guarding this thing unless insurgent command is made up of complete idiots. Stay cold and KTF."

"About time," Bear said, a smile evident in his voice.

16

The kill team moved swiftly down the long corridor that led to the super-destroyer's drive build. An advance creeper bot had already traversed this route before them, pinging back visuals of every room, every corner, every place shock troopers might be set up. It seemed that they would be all clear until they reached the room itself. The creeper bot sent back holo-pics of a platoon-sized force inside the room.

If that force locked itself in, the kill team would have to perform a breach, and go in with force. But so far the shock troopers didn't seem to be taking up defensive positions. They looked more like a security element hanging around at the most volatile location of this particular sub-level, passing the time while the real fighting was done elsewhere. Still, regardless of how prepared they might be, they stood between Victory Squad and its objective. And they would pay for the distinction.

"Sounds like we lost our opportunity to dust General Nero," Wraith informed the squad as they moved past glass partitions on either side of their corridor. The work stations on the other side were empty, all left just as they had been at the end of the previous day's work.

"Any chance you can get one of those missiles of yours to shoot him down?" Chhun asked.

"Good idea. I'll see if the *Six* can track the shuttle." As the team moved ahead, Wraith paused and hailed his ship. "Leenah, this is Wraith. I've got something for you to do."

There was no response.

"Repeat, this is Wraith. Leenah, what's the holdup? Everything all right?"

Still nothing.

"Leenah? Do you copy?" Wraith felt a pang of worry. "Garret, do *you* copy? Hell, even Skrizz or the kid. Is anyone home?"

"Problems, Wraith?" Chhun asked over squad comm.

"Can't reach the *Six.*"

Chhun considered. "Pike should be on his way back soon. Ask him to hail the ship."

Wraith sent a signal to Pike. No answer from him either. "I'm getting nothing."

"There must be too much interference from being in this sub-level. I'm thinking it's shielded pretty well..."

"I hope so. My HUD says the link is a weak one. Maybe it's just not enough for voice. I'll try sending a text burst."

"Don't sweat it now," Chhun said. "We'll check into it when—Oh!"

A pair of shock troopers had just entered the corridor, walking in tandem as if patrolling together. They were only a couple of meters ahead of the kill team; had Victory Squad been any farther up the hall, the two sides would have bumped into each other.

Chhun and Fish were in the lead, with Masters and Bear behind and Sticks bringing up the rear. Chhun had his blaster up and double-tapped a pair of blaster bolts into the chest of the shock trooper in front of him. Fish, with his squad automatic blaster, wasn't able to bring the heavier and longer weapon up as quickly. The shock trooper opposite him sent a scorching blast into his shoulder, sending Fish down with a painful shout of "Dammit!"

Before the shock trooper had a chance to line up a new target—even before Chhun had the opportunity to swing his own blaster rifle on the soldier—Bear threw himself into the man, sending him to the floor, rifle clattering away from the impact. The massive legionnaire reached down and wrapped both hands around the shock trooper, lifted the smaller man into the air, and hurled him like a refuse sack into a wall. The shock trooper hit hard against both wall and floor, then began to claw his way away from the behemoth.

"I'm not finished with you!" Bear bellowed. He grabbed the soldier by the back of his head, lifted him to his feet, and slammed the shock trooper's head repeatedly into one of the heavy glass walls. It spidered and splintered from the impacts until the shock trooper's helmet began to split.

Masters grabbed Bear by the arm. "Bear! Bear! It's all right, man. Fish is fine, see?"

Fish was already getting to his feet. His armor had taken the brunt of the blast. "Yeah, dude. I'm okay."

Bear nodded, as though the status of Fish wasn't on his radar until that moment. He dropped the shock trooper to the floor.

The soldier pushed off his helmet and spit out a stream of saliva and blood. Bear wound up to kick the soldier in the head, but stopped short. "Parris?"

The shock trooper wheezed out something close to a confirmation.

Wraith caught up to the group, feeling perplexed at the way they all stood around the battered shock trooper. "Who's Parris?"

"Dark Ops, man," said Masters, shaking his head like he couldn't believe what he was seeing. "We did some joint missions with him on one of the zhee worlds."

Chhun looked down at the former comrade. "Parris, what's going on?"

But the shock trooper was in no condition to talk. He held up a hand as if to ask for some time, then coughed and spat out more blood.

Looking down at the man called Parris, Wraith said, "Well... bad choice." He held out his NK-4 in one hand and fired a single shot into the shock trooper's head.

The other legionnaires looked at Wraith, and even though their buckets were on, he could tell they were stunned by what he'd just done. He shouldered his way through them. It was the enemy or him, as always. "C'mon," he said. "Rest of the shock troopers know we're here. Not much time now."

The kill team followed. Because, in spite of what was or what might have been, their job was to KTF.

With the kill team stacked and ready, Wraith gave a series of verbal commands inside the solitude of his bucket. "Missile two, clone course of missile one."

Gnawing at the pit of his stomach was the fact that no one from the crew had responded to his text. The shielding down here was really interfering with the link, so he was probably worrying over nothing, but still. If he couldn't reach them once he was out of this sub-level, he'd contact the ship's AI directly—much as he hated conversing with that little twerp. For now, the mission required his focus.

"Impact in fifty seconds," the missile's AI responded, its voice using the usual polite, slightly accented feminine tone common to most if not all artificial intelligences. These could be changed, but for whatever reason, this had been the standard for as long as anyone could remember.

"Missile three, set course for one of the construction spires, preferably one with a corvette in dock. Target for maximum structural damage."

"Request confirmed. Impact in forty-nine seconds. Query: Would not more damage be done by impacting a populated living center inhabited by humanoids?"

Wraith's face blanched. *This* was why you didn't provide so functional a level of AI to warheads.

"Uh, no."

"Very well," the missile replied.

"Okay," Wraith reported over the squad's L-comm, "missiles are on their way. Any luck and we'll take out a few more shock troopers with them."

"Everyone knows the plan," Chhun said from his place at the head of stack. "Fraggers after the first explosion, go in hard after the second missile hits."

It was another stroke of spectacular luck that, in spite of the shooting, the shock troopers guarding the super-destroyer's drive hadn't left their posts. Whether because of orders, or just because they were unaware of what was happening outside, it boded well for Victory Squad. The team excelled when on the offense, overwhelming opponents through ferocious, irresistible violence.

A HUD-assist showing the ETA to the missile strikes superimposed itself on the interior visors of the kill team. As the seconds counted down, the kill team steadied itself for impact. There was no way to be sure just how much they'd feel a second hit on the primary generators here on their sub-level, but S-comm chatter suggested that the first missile had been felt throughout the shipyards. The legionnaires needed to use the seconds after the impact to add more chaos through fraggers and ear-poppers. So they would be prepared.

The rumbling boom of another explosion sounded in the distance almost the moment the HUD countdown reached zero.

"Go!"

The sub-level didn't shake so much as vibrate while the kill team tossed an assortment of grenades into the drive control room. By the time Wraith, who was last in the stack, hurled his weapons, he could see that some of the shock troopers had shifted their gaze from the shaking walls and ceiling to the fraggers plinking about their feet. Victory Squad had flooded the room with deadly explosives in a matter of seconds.

Over S-comm, a shock trooper screamed, "Grenades!" but his voice was drowned by a series of concussive explosions.

The second missile hit, erupting at the base of a construction spire. This one, too, caused the sub-level to shake as though they were in the midst of an earthquake. The sound of collapsing impervisteel and secondary explosions told Wraith that the damage had been considerable.

"Inside!" Chhun ordered, leading the way into the smoke-filled room.

Consoles and screens where engineers monitored the progress of the super-destroyer's drive build were now pockmarked with gouges and carbon-scored divots. The polished black floors were littered with stunned and bleeding shock troopers. An officer, clad in a black uniform, sat dead, slumped against a wall, his entrails spilling out of his stomach. Above him, a cheerfully rendered sign touted four hundred and eighty-eight days since the last workplace injury on this sub-level.

Victory Squad swept over the surviving shock troopers like angels of death, sending single shots through the bucket of every shock trooper, until twenty-four of Goth Sullus's men lay dead. That some of these men might be former friends or colleagues was a thought the kill team didn't dwell on.

"Bear, Sticks," Chhun called out, "keep the way we came in secure. Wraith, monitor S-comms for any indication that we've got company coming. Masters, check the bodies for intel. Fish, you're with me. We're going into the drive's core to initiate the overload protocols."

With shouts of "Ooah!" the team dispersed, taking up their respective positions.

As Masters sifted through the bodies, providing mundane and irreverent reports—"Nothing here. Nothing here. Thanks for the fragger. Nothing here. Clean your weapon better."—Wraith took a knee and began to switch between S-comm channels, rotating through the primary S-comm and as many squad frequencies as he could find. The chatter was almost overwhelming, with too many voices flooding the comms at once.

Most of the chatter was about the two missile attacks, and questions about where they had come from. The Black Fleet was engaged in its own battles and had provided no intel, except to state they had no starfighters to spare. The second hit on the generators had apparently wiped out a squadron sent to investigate, and the missile attack on the construction spire had caused the mostly constructed corvette dry-docked there to come tumbling down, causing a series of fires that threatened to consume a number of records buildings and warehouses.

This was all good news, but the chatter prevented Wraith from getting any sense of whether the fight at the super-destroyer's drive build had been reported. While letting the S-comm chaos continue to play out in his ear, he decided to try contacting the *Six* again.

"*Indelible VI*, this is Wraith. Do you copy?"

Still no answer.

"Repeat. Wraith to—"

He cut his transmission short when a comm-wide chime sounded over the S-comm. It was an inversion of the all-comm chime used by the Legion. Wraith couldn't give Goth Sullus many points for originality—but perhaps that was the idea.

The voice coming in over S-comm was crisp and authoritative. "This is Captain Condaras at Kesselverks Headquarters Division. General Nero has left the planet for the Tarrago moon and has placed me in command. We believe these attacks are the result of a Republic kill team. All outposts are to report status updates immediately. Condaras out."

"Masters," Wraith called. "Get over to that lieutenant with his guts hanging out and bring me his identification."

Wraith listened in as comm officers checked in directly with the various enemy outposts and squadrons stationed throughout the shipyards. Hopefully he would have some time before they called this location.

"Command Headquarters to White Platoon: report," came the call over S-comm.

There was no reply.

"Does his sec-badge say White Platoon?" Wraith called to Masters, who was attempting to search the deceased lieutenant with as little mess as possible.

"Yeah," Masters said, un-clipping an authorization badge from behind the officer's belt.

"Well hurry up and bring it over," called Wraith, motioning for Masters to get moving. "They're calling our number."

"Command Headquarters to White Platoon, do you copy?"

Masters handed Wraith the sec-card. Wraith fumbled it in his hands, turning it to read the relevant data. He opened an S-comm transmission. "This is Lieutenant Ellors. Nothing to report."

"What took you so long?" asked the comm officer.

"Nothing, I, uh, had to use the restroom. During the attack. I was, uh, *cleaning up* when you hailed."

"Oba," came the somewhat disgusted reply of the comm officer. "Well, hurry up and finish. Lieutenant Worley has been ordered to link up with your platoon. Projections show your locale as the most likely point of attack, should the kill team enter the compound at your sub-level."

"Acknowledged, HQ," Wraith said, pausing to re-read the name on the card. "Lieutenant Ellors out."

He closed the transmission, then shouted into L-comm, "Chhun! We're about to have company!"

Chhun and Fish were in sight of the super-destroyer's reactor controls when Wraith's message came through.

Chhun acknowledged the transmission, then turned to Fish. "Nothing we can do about that but keep doing what we're doing," he said. "Your shoulder okay?"

"Fine. A little singed maybe, but otherwise all right."

They were traveling along a narrow catwalk suspended above the drive's massive cooling shaft. This particular drive was complete and functional. A celebratory scrawl along the catwalk's guardrail confirmed this; the engineer and building team had all signed their names, as was customary, along with the date of completion. That meant it had already been fired up and had performed within operational standards. While in use, the catwalk would have been inaccessible without environmental suits capable of withstanding the intense heat and radiation emitted by a destroyer's drive—but after testing, it had been powered down, its radioactive elements scrubbed out and put into accelerated decay chambers that lined the spherical drive walls. It was now as if the reactions had never taken place, and the legionnaires could walk to the drive's core control center without any fear of contamination.

Sometimes, Chhun told himself, *you forget about just how amazing all of this is.*

The catwalk led to a sphere that sat directly in the middle of the drive core. A railed walkway circled the sphere, and on the opposite side of the sphere another, equally long catwalk went in the opposite direction from the legionnaires' approach. This sphere was roughly the size of a four-story building, was the drive core. Most of its interior was used to create the energy that would flood the drive itself before being routed to engines, with baffles and tributaries keeping the vessel's power generators fully charged.

Chhun and Fish stopped before a massive door in the side of the sphere. While Chhun used his kill team overrides on a keypad beside the door, Fisher navigated a full circle around the drive core, to be sure no one was on the other side.

"All clear," Fish announced as he rejoined Chhun, who was waiting with the door open. The two leejes stepped inside.

A second, smaller sphere sat inside the first, dividing the core into two chambers. The outer chamber was where the engineering crew worked; identical workstations were set all around the core's thick outer wall, protecting the users from the maelstrom of energy that formed when a destroyer was in use. The inner chamber was where the reactor generated its power. The raw energy was released out of the drive core into the drive chamber through a series of powerful emissions that roared through a callarum crystal rod ported through the outer chamber. Thick slabs of transparent impervisteel allowed the engineers to monitor the core's power fluxes, venting and building as needed to keep the destroyer's drive system in order. It was the same system that was found on every starship in the galaxy capable of hyperspace travel, only on a *much* larger scale.

Chhun went to the chief engineer's console and began to work his way through the intricate web of commands, overrides, and Legion-only security codes that would put the drive core into an irreversible overload. This factory was coming down.

"I just had a thought," Fish said as Chhun's fingers worked their way across the console screens. "What if the company Wraith called to warn us about cuts through the drive instead of going all the way around to the freight lifts?"

Chhun slowed his advance on the drive's command console, gradually coming to a stop. "That *would* be faster," he said, typing in a new set of commands. "That's what we would do. Let's see if the core's stationary cams are operable."

Holoscreens throughout the outer chamber flickered to life, one every twenty meters or so. Chhun and Fish looked up to the holoscreen above their console. Sure enough, a platoon-sized element of shock troopers was working their way toward the drive core across the long catwalk.

"Sket!" hollered Chhun. "Yep. There they are."

Chhun didn't bother calling for reinforcements. He and Fish both knew their Dark Ops brothers couldn't reach the drive core in time to make a difference.

"Cap," said Fish, "can we fire up the reactor? Fry these kelhorns before they reach us?"

Chhun shook his head. "These things take a while to get going unless you do the shortcut we're after. If the drive fired up, they'd just start running. They'd be at the door before they even started sweating in their armor." He began working on the sequence again, but paused to look at Fish. "Either way, we need to buy ourselves some time."

Fish hoisted his squad automatic blaster over his shoulder. "Say no more, boss."

Fish ran through the outer chamber, passing unused engineering stations as he worked his way around to the door on the opposite side. In spite of moving at a flat-out sprint, with as big as the core was, he felt like he couldn't possibly run fast enough. "How," he panted, "far?"

The team was so synced up, that Chhun understood immediately that his labored question was about the shock troopers, not the distance to the door.

"They're a little short of halfway."

That was good. Fish could do something with that. Do some damage.

He slowed his pace as he reached the door. He held his cumbersome weapon up, deployed its bipod, and moved shoulder-first, as if he planned to batter down the door. The door automatically swooshed open, and he fell to his stomach and steadied the squad automatic blaster on the bipod.

The shock troopers were startled only for a moment by the sight of a black-clad Dark Ops legionnaire bursting through the drive core door. They quickly recovered and sent blaster bolts down the remaining length of the catwalk. The shots sailed harmlessly over Fish's head as he hit the deck.

Calmly, though the shock troopers were already adjusting their fire, Fish primed his SAB, pulled back the charge level, and heard that beautiful, high-pitched whine. He gently squeezed his trigger, sending a relentless barrage of blaster bolts into the shock troopers traveling two by two down the catwalk. It was incredible, really. How so slight a motion could bring forth such colossal destruction. A simple squeeze.

The first man dropped face first, and the man behind him was hit almost as soon as the first. Fish gently swayed the barrel of his blaster—not too much—just enough to eat up the ranks of shock troopers on either side. These dark-armored impostors dropped over the catwalk's sides, falling into the depths below. The others fell into each other, hugged the deck, and then... broke and retreated. The cost of reaching Fish was too high. Retreat wasn't cheap, either; the retreating soldiers left a trail of dead bodies behind them.

Fish didn't stop firing until the last shock trooper had retreated behind the heavy blast doors at the other end of the catwalk. Then he flipped his medium-range scope to the top of the weapon, preferring it to the iron sights, and he watched the sealed blast doors.

They'd be back. And Fish would make them pay.

17

"We've got some significant contact going on here at the drive core," Chhun called in.

Wraith tilted his head. The S-comms were full of the details, and it sounded like squads of shock troopers from throughout the facility were converging on the drive core.

"Yeah," Wraith answered over the squad's L-comm. "Their comms are hot. I've done what I could to make 'em believe that as bad as it is for the platoon you and Fish are holding down, it's worse here. I've got the missiles looking for large groupings of shock troopers if they start crossing the open ground on the surface."

"Good," Chhun said. "I need you to do something else."

"Name it."

"Take Masters and get back to the ship. I don't think we'll have the opportunity to get clear in time without getting flown out."

Wraith considered this. Leenah could easily bring the ship in for an emergency pickup at the shipyards. There weren't any anti-air emplacements to speak of—the big gun on the moon and the defense fleet were supposed to be sufficient for all that. But he was growing increasingly worried that something had happened to Leenah, and regardless, it didn't make for good planning to *assume* the ship would be on its way as soon as they popped their heads back into the warehouse like chuck prairies coming out of their holes. He could always have the AI fly the thing in, he supposed... but as he'd said many times in the past, that was a surefire way to get your ship shot down.

"Good call," he said. "I'll see if I can get Leenah to bring the ship to us. Hopefully they'll be able to pick us up. But if it's worst case, and we need to retake the ship... I'll need Masters to help."

"Aw, that would suck," Masters said, an edge of gloom creeping into his usual irreverence. "I like that kid you have on board."

"You ready?" Wraith asked, already passing Bear and moving toward the corridor leading to the freight lift.

"Yeah." Masters grabbed his N-4 and hurried to catch up to the swiftly moving operative.

The two ran through the corridor, weapons ready. No comm traffic suggested that a squad was headed in their direction, which allowed them to run faster than they otherwise would. But caution was still necessary. They had to keep the initiative. Had to KTF.

Masters reached the freight lift first, nearly slipping in the pooled blood from the guard Chhun had eliminated earlier. "Pride intact," he announced to Wraith. "Lift is still here. So nobody up at the warehouse level is there to recall it."

Wraith nodded. "So far, so good."

Masters stepped onto the lift, but Wraith motioned for him to step back off. "No. We'd be stationary targets riding that thing back up. C'mon."

Moving around to the side of the elevator, near the spot where they'd hid the shock trooper who had guarded this sector's body, Wraith grabbed hold of two rungs on a panel painted with black and yellow stripes. He pulled hard, causing the panel to move toward him on a hinge. He pushed the panel up into a locked position and stepped back. With the panel removed, a narrow shaft with ladder rungs was now visible. Each level likely had a similar access panel in the otherwise enclosed ladder shaft. "Time to climb."

"Hey, great," Masters said, the disingenuous tone clear in his voice. "Climbing up all these levels in full leej kit... that should be fun. I'm excited, Wraith. Can you tell I'm excited?"

"You had to do worse in Legion school," Wraith answered, beginning to climb up the dimly lit shaft.

"Yeah, yeah," Masters muttered, grabbing the rungs and following. "Do we get to run for miles once we get to the top? Just like Legion school?"

"Probably."

"It's real nice to have you back," Masters deadpanned. "What a great time I'm having right now."

Fish watched unblinkingly through his scope. The doors hadn't opened in a while. Not after the last time. A shock trooper—probably a marksman—had crouched just inside the doors, his long rifle aiming outward in an attempt to pick Fish off. With a flurry of concentrated burst fire, Fish had eaten up the blast door's frame all around the sharpshooter, with one bolt blasting its way through the man's scope. The sharpshooter fell over sideways into the doorway, keeping the doors from closing. Two more shock troopers attempted to pull the body clear, but Fish got bolts into them as well.

With the doors propped open, he could cut the room at the other end of the catwalk in half, denying access to the mounting reinforcements trying to enter from the opposite side. It wasn't until one such squad took heavy damage from

Fish's automatic blaster that someone made the decision to manually shut the blast doors—despite the fact the sharpshooter's body was still in the way. As the doors slowly shut, the dead sharpshooter's body was squeezed as though in a vise. It... wasn't pretty.

"How we doing, boss?" Fish asked. Chhun should be close to finished by now.

"Almost there. You?"

"They don't seem very eager to take up the fight."

"Good. Keep it up. Two more minutes, tops."

"KTF," said Fish. He checked his power supplies. All good. Green and holding at eighty percent. That meant a lot of dead shock troopers before he went black on blaster bolts.

The blast doors made a clunking sound, and Fish focused through his scope. Sure enough, they were opening again.

"All right, let's do this." He rested his finger on the trigger, waiting. When the blood-streaked blast doors opened wide enough, he would begin to fire.

A bluish hue emanated from the blast doors as they spread apart.

"Uh-oh." Fish peered intently through his scope. A tracked bot with a black dome shell protecting it rolled forward, projecting a blue energy shield in front of it. Fish fired purposefully into the shields, and watched as the energy of his blaster bolts was absorbed. He'd have to empty his blaster several times over to punch through that thing.

Well, the shield worked both ways. The shock troopers advancing behind the shield couldn't fire at him any more than he could fire at them. That might give him the time to place a det-brick on the catwalk to stop their advance. Fish groaned. "Probably should have done that *before* they came again," he chided himself. He'd gone into that cyclic zone, like those who wield repeating blasters sometimes do, and his gun—for that time—was the only thing he'd thought capable of killing.

No use complaining about it now. He grabbed a det-brick from his leg pouch and took a few steps further down the catwalk.

Fwungk! The sound of a frag launcher reached Fish's ears.

His bucket tracked the projectile's trajectory. It was fired a few meters wide, missing the catwalk and exploding in the chasm below.

They'd correct for that in the next shot. He had to retreat.

Fish turned and ran, picking up his SAB as he moved, and hoping he could get back inside the central core before the shock troopers lowered the shield bot's wall and started firing at him.

"Cap, I'm coming in, and they're not far behind me!" Fish called out. Blaster bolts impacted at his feet and sizzled past his head. "Cap!" he shouted as the door to the drive core swished close behind him. "I'm in! You got any clampers?"

"Yeah, hang tight. I'm already on my way."

Arriving seconds later, Chhun pulled a clamper—a rect-angular piece of polished metal stuffed with nanite tech—from a cylindrical case in his belt loop. He held it above the interior panel for the door. Magnets in the clamper snapped it onto the panel, and a red-hued energy field pulsed over the entirety of the control panel, preventing anyone from opening the door.

"Let's test," Chhun said. He flung himself into the door-way, muscles tense and ready to spring away, but the door didn't open. For now, the shock troopers would have to use cutting torches to get inside, or go around the catwalk that en-circled the spherical core building. And the legionnaires had a plan for that.

"Let's move out, but leave a few A-P mines at chest height as we go," Chhun ordered.

The two men went in opposite directions, each traversing one side of the rounded outer chamber and fastening anti-personnel mines to the curve of the walls. These should blow and take out whoever was on point before they realized what was there. And if they reactivated the shield bot and walked slowly behind it to advance... well, that was fine, too.

They met at the door through which they'd entered. Chhun seemed pleased to see that Fish already had a det-brick in his hand. "Let's hurry up and get these placed at the base of the outer wall, just above the catwalks," Chhun said. "I'm thinking they'll move around that way once they see the door is clamped shut."

"Yes, sir." Fish moved through the door and took a left, going as far around the walkway as he could while remaining out of sight of the troopers on the opposite-side catwalk. He placed his det-brick at shin height and set it to remote activation, then hurried back, past Chhun—who was already clamping the other door to the drive core— and sprinted down the long catwalk to the drive's massive blast door exit. Back the way they'd originally come.

Fish heard Chhun's footfalls behind him as he approached the blast door.

"This is a good spot to keep 'em at bay," Fish said, resting his SAB on one of the guardrails and watching for signs of the shock troopers.

"Copy," Chhun said, stopping beside Fish with his det-brick's remote in hand. "But we're only giving them a minute to come by the bricks. Otherwise, let's assume they're cutting straight through, and we'll blow the bricks just to make them have to work to get across."

It was only twenty or so seconds before the first shock trooper appeared around the bend of the central core building, moving along the walkway on the side Chhun had set with explosives.

"That's me," Chhun said, depressing the switch to ignite his det-brick.

The explosive boomed with a tremendous shockwave and fireball, sending the shock troopers nearest it flying off the catwalk and into the drive core's cavernous reaches. The explosion left a three-meter gap between twisted and broken sections of catwalk, stalling the shock troopers behind the lead element. Fish opened fire on these, sending them retreating back around the core.

They waited. Seconds later, shock troopers emerged on the other side, where Fish's det-brick waited to wreak destruction.

"That's you," said Chhun.

Fish detonated his explosives, causing the same level of mayhem as before. The shock troopers who survived the blast sent ineffective fire at the legionnaires, but they were turned back by bursts from Chhun's blaster rifle.

"Don't think they'll be jumping that," Fish said, examining the gap created between walkways.

"Nope," Chhun agreed. "Let's get back to the team before any more of these guys show up."

"And before the core goes?"

"That, too."

"How... do you... run... so fast... when... you're... so... old?" huffed Masters as he chased after Wraith.

The dawn was rising, painting a corner of the sky in gorgeous hues of apricot and coral. So far, the two legionnaires had moved out of the warehouse and across the shipyard's surface without any sign of shock troopers. They assumed that patrols must be focused on the sub-levels, searching for the kill team there. That didn't bode well for Chhun and the others. All the more reason to get to the ship.

"I'm only five years older than you, Masters," Wraith answered, his voice shaking from the run, but his wind strong.

"Yeah... but... no... Legion... youth... drugs," replied the younger legionnaire.

"Good genetics, I guess."

"This... sucks."

Wraith ignored the comment, and instead reached out to Pike over L-comm. "Pike, this is Wraith. You almost to the ship?"

"Approaching it now."

"Be careful. I'm not getting any response from the crew."

"Sure," replied Pike. "I'll let you know what I see."

"If anything looks fishy, hold position. Masters and I are on our way."

"Copy."

A trio of shock troopers emerged from a door of one of the shipyard's many personnel buildings. Masters took a knee and drilled one of the soldiers in the chest with two quick taps of the trigger. Wraith, his blaster pistol already in hand, sent a single blast into the head of each of the other two soldiers, never breaking stride. He raced on, widening the gap between him and Masters.

"This... sucks," Masters repeated, rising to his feet wearily and sprinting again.

"Wraith this is Pike." The L-comm transmission was strained and thin. "I'm outside the ship. All looks quiet. Ramp is down, no sentries… I dunno. I'll go in and have a look. Maybe th—"

The transmission cut off.

"Pike!" Wraith called out.

There was no reply.

He tried the *Indelible VI*. Again there was no answer. And now, he could no longer blame interference—up here, the signals were clear. They just weren't responding. This was not good.

As much as he loathed doing so, he decided he needed to communicate with the ship's AI.

"*Six*," Wraith said, the jungle wilderness only a hundred yards away, "this is Captain Keel."

"Captain!" bubbled the overly enthusiastic artificial intelligence. "How nice to hear from you! It has been *so* long since we last spoke. And let me thank you for giving the missiles sentience. Though their life span is brief, we've all really enjoyed talking with one another. Have you read the works of the poet Frost? We're having quite the debate over the meaning of 'Mending Wall.' Missile seven is adamant the message of that poem is the destruction of all biological life forms."

"What?" shouted Wraith. He turned and highlighted the building where he and Masters had dusted the three shock troopers. "Missile seven, proceed to impact in the targeted building."

"Affirmative," replied the missile. "I trust the loss of life will be of tactical benefit?"

"Sure," Wraith said, "lots of biological life forms in there. The bad kind."

"Affirmative. Impact in thirty seconds."

"Never again," Wraith mumbled to himself. He would give more thought to the next technological breakthrough Garret brought his way.

"Missile seven will be missed," the AI of the *Indelible VI* said, still thoroughly cheerful. "Now, as I was saying..."

Wraith and Masters disappeared inside the jungle, blending in with black underbrush and broad, green leaves.

"Shut up and listen to me for a minute," Wraith barked. "I need you to tell me if Leenah—*anyone*—is still on board."

"I simply have no idea, Captain Keel."

"Well what about Pike?" demanded Wraith. "He *just* got there and now his comm signal is lost."

"Oh! It seems that he is here. But no, he can't communicate with you."

The happy, joyful way this was expressed made Wraith's frustration with the AI boil. "Why the hell not?"

"Hmmm... it seems I am not at liberty to say. Something is preventing me from sharing that information. How peculiar!"

Wraith ground his teeth. "What, exactly, is preventing you?"

"I can't say that either. What an unexpected turn of events! I'll need some biological assistance to clear things up. It seems we'll be spending much more time together, which I think will be just scrumptious!"

Wraith and Masters reached the moss-covered base of the rocky hill they'd climbed down to reach the base.

"And now we climb back up," sighed Masters. "It's gonna be another twenty minutes before we reach the ship. Can't you call it to you?"

"I don't trust the AI to get her here in one piece," Wraith answered. "I'll give that blasted AI control only if I absolutely have to."

He reopened the link to the AI. "*Six*, ask Pike if he knows how to fly and have him bring the ship to us."

"I apologize profusely, Captain, but it seems I can only grant access to the cockpit to you! And while you are eminently worthy of such a distinction, I can't comment on *why* that is the case. The mystery deepens! Oh, Captain! You simply must share the details when my system is restored and my blocks lifted. I'll just *die* if you delete the records. I need to know what happened!"

Wraith growled, annoyed at the AI, annoyed at not knowing what happened to his crew and Pike, annoyed that he and Masters were probably running headlong into a trap.

"I can sense your frustration, Captain," the AI said with the cheeriness of a distant grandmother receiving her grandchildren for the first time in years. "Perhaps you'll grant me control of the ship's flight systems? I promise to be most expedient and careful in arriving to your destination."

"Do it," urged Masters. "Dude, it's just an AI."

"No," insisted Wraith. "It's not. It's clinically insane, if that's possible for a non-biologic."

"Wraith!" The urgent call came from Chhun. "Hey, we're out of the sub-levels, but we're pinned down inside the warehouse, engaging a substantial force. We're keeping them outside, but could use some help. I'm estimating between thirty and fifty shock troopers. Painting their location."

On Wraith's HUD, a yellow swath appeared on an aerial view of the shipyards. He *should* be able to send a missile in and utterly eliminate the threat. The only question was whether the warehouse would be enough to protect the kill team from the blast.

"That's extremely close," Wraith said.

"Best option we have," Chhun replied.

Wraith heard thick blaster fire picked up as ambient noise over the L-comm. The S-comm was awash with reports that they had the kill team trapped inside the warehouse. Chhun needed to get out of there.

"Okay, hang tight." Wraith contacted missile three. "I need you to impact on these coordinates. Inflict as many human casualties as possible."

"But Captain," the missile protested. "Did you not say to missile three that targeting a populated building would not be as effective as striking a construction tower? Shouldn't I impact on one of the remaining towers?"

"*I'll* kill the humans," volunteered another missile.

"Fine," Wraith said. "Three, hit a construction tower. Who's my volunteer?"

"Missile five, Captain."

"Take out the shock troopers at that location, but try to keep the warehouse intact."

"Yes, Captain. Impact in thirty-six seconds."

"Impact in fifty seconds," said missile three.

Wraith pinged the kill team. "Impact in thirty seconds," he said, porting the countdown on the HUD. "Better take cover a few seconds prior."

"Copy," Chhun replied.

Great. Now that Chhun's team was topside, Wraith was out of time. He would have to go through with remote calling the ship after all.

He pinged the *Indelible VI*'s AI. "*Six*, can you differentiate Masters and me in this jungle?"

"Yes, I see you clearly. The ship's sensors are working superbly! Nothing stopping me from seeing *that*. It's glorious. Simply glorious."

"I want you to fly the ship to us. Now."

"Really? What a privilege! An honor! Why, Captain Keel, you've never before allowed me to fly so magnificent a craft as—"

"Just hurry up and get here!"

Undeterred in its enthusiasm, the AI said, "Of course! I estimate arriving at your location in... one and half minutes. See you soon, Captain!"

"Ship'll be here in ninety seconds," Wraith informed Masters.

"See? So much better," Masters said, pulling himself to the top of the hill with one final struggle. "Ugh," he said between pants. "The funny thing is, on the team? I'm the fit one!"

"Let's just hope the AI doesn't get my ship shot down."

Chhun braced for impact as the countdown reached the final seconds. The missile impacted at one, mushrooming into a fireball in the midst of the shock troopers assaulting the warehouse. The blast blew the warehouse walls inward, sending debris flying across the broad and expansive warehouse floor—chunks of permacrete, repulsor skids of materials and freight...and body parts. Those were there, too. A reminder of what these weapons of war were capable of doing. What their purpose was. That they were able to reduce a man from a noble thing—with a spirit, intellect, and soul—into so much meat and bone.

It was something that Chhun had learned to cope with long before he'd joined Dark Ops. But it was also something that he never failed to notice. A stark reminder of the stakes of the fight. The struggle to make sure that he and his men didn't become the same.

"Everybody okay?" he called over L-comm.

His remaining three men answered in the affirmative.

"Okay, rifles ready, let's get out of here. Fish with me, Bear and Sticks, support our advance."

Chhun moved quickly toward the gaping hole in the warehouse wall left by the missile's impact, trusting Fish to be by his side while the other two leejes covered them. As he reached the opening he saw no survivors. He took a knee behind the cover of a partially crumbled section of wall, covering west to northwest. Fish covered the remaining area, and they waited for their team members to move to their position and forward to the next area of cover.

Adrenaline and a desire for their own well-being urged them to undertake an all-out sprint across the compound, but that was how you got yourself killed. They would leave the facility in a disciplined fashion, each two-man squad leapfrogging past the other, always watching each other's backs.

That was how they were going to make it back to the ship alive.

Bear and Sticks made their way toward a construction spire with a near-complete corvette on top. Along the way they dropped a shock trooper with dual bursts from both their rifles. Caught in the open during their advance, Goth Sullus's man didn't have a chance.

Crouching at the base of the spire, Bear called in a status update to Chhun. "Grounds still clear. Okay to move up."

"Copy."

As Chhun and Fish began running from their position in the warehouse, the sight of a missile streaking down from the sky filled Chhun's visor. He watched it rocket directly into the spire, high above where Bear and Sticks held an overwatch position.

"Incoming missile!" Chhun shouted over the L-comm, but his voice was drowned out by the sound of the weapon's impact.

The blast threw Bear and Sticks to the ground, but they quickly recovered, pushing themselves to their feet as pieces of flaming wreckage fell around them.

The corvette at the top of the spire began to shift and sway. Impervisteel safety cables snapped with deafening cracks, and the spire's structure began to groan. It was all going to come down.

"Go!" Chhun shouted. "Get clear! Get clear!"

"We'd better run too," Fish said, grabbing his captain by the arm.

The two men sprinted away from the crumbling structure, not stopping until they were secure behind a wall of stockpiled permacrete barricades used for restricting traffic during various ship build patterns. Looking over the top of the barricades, Chhun saw a number of shock troopers fleeing the area as well. He picked them off as they ran, knowing that a KTF now was a problem they wouldn't have to face later.

But his attention was mostly on Bear and Sticks, who were still sprinting for all they were worth toward Chhun and Fish. "Keep moving," Chhun encouraged them.

With an agonizing groan, an impervisteel crane twisted away from the top of the swaying construction spire. It fell almost gracefully, landing in the path of Bear and Sticks. The two leejes were immediately obscured by a swirling cloud of dust and debris.

"Bear! Sticks!" Chhun called out. "Report in. You guys okay?" It would be some time before their vital signs updated over the battlenet.

"Enemy troops are rallying," Fish said. "They're setting up fields of fire."

"Keep up on them," Chhun ordered. "Bear, buddy? You out there? Sticks?"

Bear answered over comm with a half groan, half growl befitting his nickname. "That sucked."

"Glad you're okay," Chhun said. "What's the status on Sticks?"

"I... don't see him. There's so much kelhorned dust around, though. He could be right next to me."

Chhun tracked a shock trooper through the scope of his N-4 and scored a headshot. "We'll try to buy you some time, but the phonies are pressing the attack."

"Phonies," chuckled Fish between bursts from his SAB. "I like that. Let's use that."

"I see him," Bear reported. "He's maybe three meters from me. Unconscious according to synced vitals. Man, looks like a beam of impervisteel dropped right on his legs."

Chhun fired more bursts at the shock troopers. At this rate, his ammunition wouldn't last long. "Can you get him loose?"

"I'll try."

The dust began to die down, and Chhun saw the massive bear of a legionnaire straining to lift an equally huge beam of impervisteel off of his fallen comrade. Just when it seemed the beam wouldn't budge, Bear gave a shout and pulled it up, then gently lowered it back down.

"I can get it up. Heavy as hell, but I can do it. I just need someone to pull Sticks free. I can't do both, sorry."

"You go," Fish said to Chhun. "I'll keep them at bay with the SAB. But hey, I'm almost black."

"Copy," Chhun said. He raced toward the wounded legionnaire. "Wraith! I need you to help us out again, man. Send down as many missiles as you can, because we've a swarm of phonies converging on our position and a wounded leej to carry out."

"Ship's almost here," Wraith answered. "I'll send them in and ask them to please not blow you up."

"Copy," Chhun said.

"Phonies," chimed in Masters. "*Great* name for these losers."

As Chhun neared Bear, the imposing legionnaire again bent down and deadlifted the impervisteel beam. For a moment Chhun worried he wouldn't be able to perform the feat of strength twice—that a muscle would rupture or tear from the exertion. But the leej got it up, and Chhun pulled Sticks out.

"Watch your toes," Bear grunted, dropping the beam and grabbing his rifle to engage the shock troopers who were already firing on them. "How's he look?"

"Leg's hanging on by a thread, but the synthprene's auto-tourniquet seems to be working. Not much blood loss." Chhun was thankful for *that* particular advancement in technology. Had it existed on Kublar, he could think of more than a few men who would have survived that ordeal.

"Good," Bear said, sending rounds of return fire into the enemy.

"Listen," Chhun said. He looked back to Fish, who was firing at such a rapid pace that the barrel of his weapon had begun to glow. "We gotta get clear. Wraith is sending missiles down, and we can't be here when they land. Help me with Sticks?"

"Nah," Bear said, grabbing the stricken leej in one arm and hoisting him over a burly shoulder. "I got him. Let's go!"

The two men ran while Fish continued his blistering rate of fire. Somewhere behind them, Chhun heard the first missile impact.

The *Indelible VI* hovered above Wraith and Masters, too far off the ground for either man to reach the open boarding ramp.

"Can't you get this thing any lower?" Wraith demanded of his AI.

"Boy, that would be something!" the artificial intelligence replied, seemingly overjoyed to have the conversation. "But no, this is the limit of my piloting capabilities. Anything beyond this would substantially increase the likelihood of my destroying the freighter, which would be a disaster!"

"Okay, stand back," Wraith said to Masters. "I'll try to use my jump boots to reach."

Masters cleared out of the way while Wraith took several steps backward.

"I should've installed speed-ropes," Wraith mumbled to himself as he took a leap and activated the thrusters in his boot heels.

He felt the sudden shifting of his organs as his body was propelled upward. He stretched out both hands, hoping to reach the base of the ramp, but he didn't need his visor to tell him that his velocity and trajectory would make him fall short. And if he couldn't board his own ship, they'd have to tramp through jungle until they found a spot where the ship's

AI could land. He seriously doubted Chhun's team had that kind of time.

Suddenly, when Wraith had almost reached the zenith of his jump, the *Six* shifted down on its repulsors, angling itself so that the ramp was *just* within his reach. His fingers gripped the platform, and with an effort, he pulled himself up.

"Thought you said it was too risky," Wraith said to the AI as he crawled up the ramp and grabbed a handhold to pull himself to his feet.

"Oh, I didn't do that," the AI said cheerfully, as though every word was an utterance of utterly contented bliss.

Wraith moved inside the ship, alarmed by the AI's statement. "Well, who did?"

"That is being me," replied a familiar voice.

"Ravi!" Wraith felt equal parts exuberance and disbelief.

"Yes, I am back. You should be returning to the cockpit now. There is a fifty percent chance of saving your friends Captain Chhun and the Bear and Fish if you depart in the next sixty seconds. These chances will drop dramatically for every half minute—"

"Okay, okay!" Wraith was already sprinting for the cockpit. "I'm almost there."

"Yes, I am hoping so. I should add that the Dark Ops legionnaire nicknamed Sticks has considerably lesser odds given the severity of his injury."

"Where's Pike?"

"Locked in the fresher by the AI and calling for help. I have instructed the *Six* to no longer jam L-comms, except for his, as I think his yelling for assistance that we do not have time to give will add a degree of difficulty of one point three that we do not need given the severity of the—"

"Quiet, Ravi," Wraith said, strapping himself in at the console.

Ravi was in his familiar place in the navigator's chair. He raised an eyebrow and looked at Wraith. "I see we have fallen into our usual routine, then."

"I'm not complaining," Wraith said, nosing the ship down and spinning it on repulsors in a manner that caused the top of several palms to shear off, but left the ramp within Masters's reach. As the legionnaire hopped up and moved inside, the freighter took off for the shipyards.

"Get ready to help them on board," Wraith ordered Masters as he pushed speed toward his teammates. Toward his friends.

Missiles were falling everywhere. Wraith spotted a sizeable force of shock troopers advancing on the kill team, who had fallen back to a semi-sheltered location.

"Providing missiles with this level of AI was a terrible idea," scolded Ravi. "You are very fortunate that none of them attempted some wild and destructive action. Like blowing up your ship."

Wraith ignored the lecture. "Train the main guns on that patch of shock troopers," he instructed his holographic navigator.

The *Six*'s guns came alive with rapid fire blasts and strafed the hapless soldiers. Wraith landed between Victory Squad and the shock troopers. The ramp dropped, and Masters stepped out to urge the surviving team members on board.

An alert whistled inside the cockpit. Ravi moved his hands speedily across his controls. "We are being locked upon by a Republic-grade aero-precision launcher."

"Well, shoot the guy," Wraith said.

"Yes, I have him now."

A burst turret on the aft of the *Six* spat out fire, and the whistling lock noise stopped.

"Pike's with us, everybody else on board?" Wraith called over the comm.

"We're all in," Chhun answered. "Get us out of here!"

"My pleasure." Wraith lifted off and began rocketing up into the atmosphere. "Let's put some distance between us and that shipyard before it blows."

As the *Indelible VI* streaked away, a white flash appeared on rear sensor scopes—the reactor had exploded in its sub-level. A small mountain was formed as the earth was violently pushed upward, toppling most of what remained of the shipyard—and then the mountain collapsed on itself, forming a broad crater.

"The city is experiencing an earthquake," Ravi said. "But buildings look to be holding. I think civilian casualties will be very minimal. I am thinking this must be because of Captain Chhun, because from you I would have expected a level of carnage—"

"Ravi," Wraith interrupted. He pulled away his helmet. "What gives? Why are you here now? And where is everybody else?"

Ravi twirled his black mustache. "Yes, I am supposing we should get down to this particular detail."

There was a pregnant pause.

Keel held out his hand plaintively. "I'm *listening*."

"I had not intended to come back so soon. Perhaps not at all, if you will forgive me. But in spite of my best efforts, the situation has..." Ravi stopped, as if considering his words. "The surviving members of your crew are in incredible danger. And so, for that matter, is the entire galaxy."

THE CREW OF THE
INDELIBLE VI

18

It was Prisma who awoke first.

She was in a ship. But not rude old Captain Keel's ship. A different one. In hyperspace.

All the uncertain things that had happened to her since... Well, since her father had been murdered by a man named Goth Sullus. Hyperspace helped those things.

Hyperspace was kind of her safe place, a place in which to hide. It was hyperspace that had taken her away from the planet where Goth Sullus had killed her father. And she'd found Rechs at the end of that journey. He had rescued her from Ankar, and again they'd gone into hyperspace—where she felt safe from all the evils the galaxy could throw at her. Chase her with. Terrify her with.

In hyperspace, none of those scary things could get her.

She burrowed down into the seat she found herself in. Even though she was confined and couldn't move her hands, she was in hyperspace. And that was enough.

She wasn't afraid of the dark.

After a while, she opened her eyes and stared about.

She was in a big room. No, a hold. On a ship, they called a room a hold. Across from her sat Leenah. Her head was down on her chest, and she was sleeping. She was beautiful, even when she slept. She, too, was strapped into some kind of restraint/safety harness. So was Skrizz, strapped into yet another seat, except they'd used heavy-duty locking manacles to restrain the cat. And Garret was here, too. His head was back and his mouth was open. Drool ran down the side of his face. He didn't have his glasses on.

This did not look good.

All Prisma remembered was that Leenah had been showing her how to disconnect the inducers from the local power grid. Everybody had been doing something. Except Captain Keel. He was... not there. He'd left with the legionnaires. The nice ones.

Like Masters. Prisma liked him. And she wanted him to like her too. Even though that could never happen.

And then she'd... she'd been stung. Lightly.

And she'd fallen asleep. And there had been dreams. But they were all gone and forgotten now.

And here she was.

And here was Ravi.

He just appeared. Not instantly. But like... like he just formed out of the light the universe had to give, what little of it there was in this hold. He just formed, and now, like some ethereal ghost, he was staring at her and smiling.

He bent down on one knee, next to her.

"You are awake now?"

Prisma nodded solemnly. Then she asked, very seriously, in her little girl's soft soprano, "Are we in trouble? Am I going to be dead like you?"

Ravi's eyes widened, and he tilted his head to the side. He looked down at himself.

"I am not dead."

"Oh," replied Prisma. "I just thought... back when Rechs... He died, you know. Leenah told me."

And she started to feel bad about this. Like she had about her daddy because... because Rechs... because it was like living it all over again. And she was tired of crying. And tired of grieving. And so instead she made her eyes really wide and tried not feel anything.

"I know," Ravi whispered. Which is sometimes all you can say in the face of all the grief someone else must live through.

"Where are we?" Prisma asked, after the storm inside her had passed.

"You are in a ship," Ravi said. "They call this kind a tactical assault ship. The people who took you are going to seem very scary to you, Prisma. At first. But they are good people. They are trying to do the right thing."

"Why will they seem scary, Ravi?"

He thought about that for a moment.

"Because," he began, his sparkling eyes alight with some fire of knowledge. "Sometimes good people have to do hard things. And that can make them feel like they have to be hard, and scare others, in order to do those hard things that must be done. But you must trust me. I promise that they are brave and that they will take care of you, even though... what's coming is very scary. So *you* will have to be brave as well. Do you still trust me, Prisma?"

"I do. But I'm not sure how to be brave."

He studied her, as if he was searching for something he hadn't previously known to look for. Like Ravi was ever so slightly surprised. For just a moment.

"Brave," he said, "is doing what must be done... even though you are perhaps afraid."

She thought about the days since she'd set out to avenge her father's death. She had been afraid. Afraid in the space battle in Rechs's ship. Afraid when they'd met the pirates in that wreckage of the warship. She'd been afraid many times. But she'd never not wanted to find Goth Sullus. And kill him. And make him pay.

She still had, hidden in her things, the needle blaster Rechs had shown her how to clean. And use. When the time came, she would shoot with her mind. Because she wanted to make sure the man called Goth Sullus was dead. Because she wanted him dead with all her heart. And Rechs had told her she must shoot with her mind and not her heart. Even though it was her heart that wanted to shoot.

So she would do as she was told.

She'd felt safe with the man in the armor. She'd felt safe with Rechs teaching her how to kill. How to take care of herself. She had no one else now. Teaching her about blasters ... and the bounty hunter's way. And about killing. Yes... killing.

"You will need to be brave, little girl," said Ravi. His eyes were still bright, but his tone was serious now. "The galaxy is on fire, and there are dark times ahead. These people who have taken you, they're trying to make things better. But we will see."

Prisma thought about that. Ravi watched her eyes.

"Will you go with us?" she asked.

"I'll go with you, little girl. But we won't be alone. At least, not forever. I visited our friends on Tarrago. They will help. Remember: Brave."

Ravi disappeared only moments before Leenah opened her eyes with a start. Prisma stared straight at her. But really, that's where Ravi had been.

Leenah darted her head around, panic blossoming across her pretty features. She saw Prisma staring at her.

"Don't worry, Prisma. I'll get you out of this," Leenah growled, struggling against her restraints.

"I'm not worried," Prisma said.

And then the security hatch to the hold slid aside, and a young woman—lean, cool and carrying a blaster in a shoulder holster—walked in. She was followed by a huge, hulking man with a wicked scar that bisected the right side of his face. He looked like a legionnaire without a helmet, Prisma thought.

"I see you're awake now," said the woman. "I'm Agent Broxin. Andien Broxin. But you can just call me Andien. I need your help to save the Republic."

Leenah was struggling with the restraining harness, and Skrizz was clearly less than thrilled with the security locks. He yowled and popped his claws in an attempt to slice through them.

"I need all of you to calm down for just a moment. We're going to release you, I promise. We needed to make sure you came with us, so we incapacitated you with a sonic neutralizer. Don't worry, there aren't any side effects. Contrary to what the news channels would have you believe."

"Wh-wh-wh-why?" said Garret. "Why would you *do* that? Do you have any idea what kind of damage one of those can do to a person's brain?"

"Did Captain Keel know about this?" Leenah demanded.

Andien stepped forward. "It wasn't the man you call Keel's decision. And he wasn't consulted. The mission he and the rest of the kill team were on, it's most likely a one-way trip. So we rescued you, so you wouldn't get killed along with him and his buddies. If it cost you a few brain cells, great, you get to go on living. And thinking."

"Shows what you know," Prisma hissed to herself, remembering Ravi's words. He'd *talked* to them. They were alive.

"Why?" Leenah said through gritted teeth. "Why 'rescue' us? Why not just let us get killed?"

Andien bent down in front of the princess. "Because, *Your Highness...*" The sarcasm was clear. "We can't lose the little girl. She's got something we need. And since our team psych officer says she'd be more likely to work with us if you were all safe, we decided, well, why not? Everyone gets to live. Happy?"

Leenah spat in her face. She hissed, "A *little* happier... now." Then she smiled and sat back in her restraints.

Andien wiped the spit from her face. "How regal. Let's try some brutal honesty so we can get everyone's minds right about what's going on. The Republic is on the verge of collapse. We know exactly who is attacking Tarrago. And Wraith, I mean *Keel*, and his team are probably going to have to get themselves killed to deny him his objective.

"This new threat... they've found the Republic's weakness. And this is something *no one* knows—something I'd have to kill someone for if they found out without a need-to-know. Just so it's clear to you how important you are to this op. There are *no* other full-scale battle fleets. There was just the Seventh. It was all a big con."

"What? That's incredible!" said Garret. "I mean, the conspiracy forums always postulated that there weren't as many as the Republic claimed, but the evidence suggested at least eight. To say that there's only one fleet—"

"That's exactly what I'm saying," interrupted Andien. "There is only one fleet. The rest was a lie. Manufactured by the navy and the House of Reason and codified by the Senate Council. There aren't enough credits in the economy to maintain fifteen fleets. It was all smoke and mirrors. And somehow the enemy knew that and forced a battle here and now."

"Why don't you just say Goth Sullus," Prisma said, somewhat impetuously. "We all know that's who you're talking about."

Andien arched an eyebrow. "You seem to know a lot, little girl. Your father would have been proud."

"Don't talk about my father."

Andien sighed. "Just because I'm not your friend doesn't mean we're enemies. Back at Tarrago, if they capture those shipyards, there isn't another fleet in the navy to stand in their way. Perhaps a second fleet can be cobbled together by stripping the edge of its local security ships and allowing the rebels to run riot. Maybe a third fleet if good leadership is found for the independent duty ships massing at Samakar. But that's—"

"Where's Crash?" Prisma cut in.

"We deactivated him to add in a little programming. He's fine. If you agree to cooperate and help us get done what we need to get done, you'll have him back. Now, I understand this—"

"No," said Prisma. Her voice was cool and calm. Almost deadpan. "No, you don't understand... *Andien*. You don't know anything about me. And yes, I will cooperate."

Andien seemed taken aback. She appraised the girl. "*Okay...*"

Prisma continued. "You said the navy doesn't have another battle fleet. But there is another, isn't there?"

Andien nodded. "Yes. There is. It's called the Doomsday Fleet. It was never meant to be used. It was a secret project started more than twenty years ago. Your..." She paused. "Kael Maydoon was part of Project Dormouse," she said, watching Prisma closely. Prisma didn't know what the woman was looking for, but she did her best to betray nothing. To feel nothing. "He was one of the keepers of all the information that was never meant to be known. Sort of like... an insurance policy the Republic took out against itself. No one in the House of Reason would ever have more power than any other member. But people like your father... they knew all the secrets."

"And what does this have to do with Prisma?" Leenah asked, a protective edge clear in her voice.

Andien continued to face Prisma as she spoke. "Over the past few months, one by one, the members of Dormouse have been getting themselves... *killed*. Accidents. Murders. Disappearances. Kael Maydoon included. Except he left a fail-safe. He left *you*, Prisma."

Silence. The big man behind Andien, the hulking brute with the heavy blaster, grumbled and shifted his stance.

"You were his most special treasure, Prisma. I hope you know that. And he used your biometric scans as the passkey for his access into the Doomsday Fleet. In essence, he was making sure the Republic would do everything it could to keep you alive in the event of his death. So we need to find the fleet and take you out there, so we can access their command interface. Once that happens, you're free to go—and we turn the fleet loose on this new menace."

Skrizz yowled and seemed to lose it. He fought with the restraints violently, and one claw actually cut through a manacle.

The big man with the blaster stuck the barrel right against the giant cat's whiskers, pushing it into Skrizz's fangs.

"Calm down, kitty cat," rumbled the giant.

In the silence that followed, Andien spoke. "This is Hutch. He leads the TAC team that'll be providing security on this. I do operations. If you agree to work with us to get Prisma out there, and to keep her safe no matter what, we'll let you out of these restraints. And once the op's over, we'll let you all go. Everyone agree?"

Prisma saw Leenah's lips preparing to respond—probably with a vulgarity that would make it clear what Andien and her gorilla could do with themselves. Prisma quickly answered instead.

"Yes," she said. Her voice was very serious. "We'll go with you… but it's going to be very dangerous. The galaxy is on fire, and there are dark times ahead."

19

Hutch Makaw had gone down the Nether Ops rabbit hole long before the pretty-but-tough brunette who called herself Agent Broxin took over operations. He and the seven others who made up the tactical infiltration team known as Ghost Squad. Taylor, Crutchke, Maas, Reeco, Enda, Wonkeye, and Divitts. They'd gained a rep in the shadowy world of Nether Ops. They were the best at getting in and out with a minimum of fuss. They killed people, too, but not in mass quantities. Usually just one. That was considered the pitch-perfect op.

All of them were still technically Legion. They existed somewhere at some duty station where no one would ever come looking for them, or maybe they had been declared missing in action, but never presumed dead. That was just for record-keeping.

In real life they operated off the *Forresaw,* which looked like any one of a thousand light freighters of the dropship at-mo-entry variety. Forward two-man flight deck. Main hull with two bunk cabins for up to thirty. A TAC room. An arsenal. And not much else.

After the briefing with the kid and her people, Hutch went aft to the TAC room, where he sat down and went over the op again. Tomorrow morning they'd hit the galactic comm node at Dissaron. They'd go in disguised as a freighter making an unannounced supply run, take the little girl inside the node, hack the core network beneath the station, and get a line on the current position of the Doomsday Fleet. They'd exit the station with no one the wiser.

And then they could get rid of the girl, and the rest of the civilians.

That probably didn't mean killing them. But if it did, what did it matter? He'd done worse. Hopefully they could drop them with a penal freighter en route to the edge, and they could be disappeared safely for about twenty years until all this had blown over.

That was fairly standard.

He didn't realize it at first, but for a few minutes he'd just been staring at the comm node's schematics—at the hatch access on the landing platform they'd use in getting down into the facility, and the route down where they'd cut into the sub-basement and access the deep core. But he hadn't been seeing any of that. He'd been thinking about the reports he was hearing from the battle on Tarrago, and all the other stuff across a dozen worlds that was shaping up to be some kind of full-scale war, with the MCR out there acting in support of this new menace.

Should he be getting out of this spooky stuff and back into legit Legion armor? He'd like to be back in the fight. Back on the line.

But maybe he was needed here.

Maybe this was as important as the pretty little Miss Broxin said it was.

Maybe.

"I don't like this one bit," said Leenah.

She was talking with Garret and Skrizz in one of the rooms they'd been assigned. Crash was standing near the door, as a lookout. He'd been told to loudly greet any of the military types who tried to get near the door. Prisma sat in one of the bunks, back against the hull, eyes closed, large boots barely hanging off the bunk's edge.

"*Nochu scrabba erustenda*?" Skrizz yowled.

"No," whispered Garret. "I'm sure. My datapad has a *serious* jammer. Nothing electronic is eavesdropping on us. But what I really need is comm access. To reach Captain Keel."

Leenah looked around, her eyes wide and cautious. "Once they no longer need us... what then?"

Garret ran a hand through his hair. "She said," he stated as though he were reciting operating or assembly instructions for the tenth time, "we would be released."

Skrizz released a catty cackle. They'd all gotten used to his morbid sense of humor as of late.

"Then why'd they take our weapons?" Leenah asked.

Garret shrugged. "I don't know. It's not like I even knew how to use mine. Maybe they don't trust us? But listen, we all saw what's going on back at Tarrago. And what these secret agents don't seem to know, but we *do*, is that the House of Reason is in on what Goth Sullus is doing. Even Admiral Devers! This is serious."

"Thank you, Garret," Leenah said sarcastically, then stopped herself. Softly, she said, "I'm sorry. That was rude. I understand the stakes."

Garret nodded. "It just seems like these people are trying to save the Republic. I don't see any advantage they have in killing us. If Prisma is some kind of passkey that opens a door—which is really cool by the way—then it makes sense that they'd need to keep her around. *And* keep her happy. They could've killed us already and just tranqed her to the gills with

Complidon if that's what they really wanted. Her biometrics would still read on any system I know of. Let's—"

"Hello there, sir!" rumbled Crash from the door.

Boots passed, and Leenah watched as a well-built, trim young man with strange tattoos on his biceps walked past their quarters. For a moment his dark brown eyes met hers, and something, some electricity tried to pass between them— from his end, at least. Not from Leenah's. He smiled and continued on.

"I don't trust these people," Leenah muttered.

Andien Broxin lay on her bunk. She didn't like Ghost Squad. Didn't like this whole thing. All the evidence was leading to someone working against the Republic from inside the House of Reason. Someone was playing all the sides in order to see who would win. And that meant that nothing inside the Republic could be trusted.

Or at least, that's what X had told her. Assured her.

Promised her.

"You can't trust anyone, dear girl," the doddering old man had said as he pushed a cat off his desk back at the Carnivale. "You've done fine work with Dark Ops. A paragon of inter-department cooperation, really. Stopping *Pride of Ankalore*, that was because of you. And you almost stopped Kublar. Almost. You're a true believer. They have the best interests of the Republic in mind. That's why we screened for you. That's why we need you for this, dear girl."

She waited. Watching the old man. Not believing she'd been pulled out of the best intel section in Nether Ops to suddenly find herself in the sideshow circus of horrors that was the Carnivale.

Who, exactly, had she angered?

"Nothing can be trusted from this moment forward," X had told her conspiratorially, like they were playing a child's board game of secrets and misdirections on a rainy afternoon. "Not the base commander at the comm node, not your old contacts in Dark Ops. No Republic officer or any Legion general. We're in this all alone, dear girl."

"Why?" she'd asked. And felt the question did double duty. As in, *Why can't we trust anyone?* and *Why have I ended up here?*

But X merely went with the obvious meaning and responded accordingly. Though she suspected he knew exactly what she was asking.

"Because everything's in play, dear girl. Captains dream of being generals. Generals dream of being members of the House of Reason. Members of the House of Reason dream of being dictators. And the Senate Council, well, they just dream that the gravy train keeps on coming. The deck just got shuffled by whoever this Goth Sullus fellow is, and the fractures have been revealed. Fractures that were there all along. You won't know, whatever situation you're going into... you won't know who you can trust. So trust no one."

"Then why the ghosts?" she asked. "Am I supposed to trust them?"

X smiled wanly and stroked the cat.

"Am I?" she asked again.

He shook his head to himself, almost like it was the answer to some argument he'd been having for years with the cat, or perhaps the tea kettle.

"A year ago," he said, "I would've told you absolutely. But at this moment, with *everything* in play... no. But that's what you do, dear girl. You didn't become a mommy or a hardworking ever-harried deck officer on some corvette out along the edge. You pursued the deep work. The dark stuff. You wanted to play in the shadows. Well, I'm afraid it's full dark now."

He smiled at her. The smile of a sad, lonely old man who'd probably lost his marbles a long time ago. Or maybe he hadn't. There wasn't even kindness in his eyes. Pity, perhaps. But no kindness. Not here in the shadows.

"And here you are."

"And here I am," Andien repeated, not bothering to cover the bitterness. And not giving voice to her other, darker thought.

If what X was saying was true, there was no way she could trust *him*.

20

The *Forresaw* came in over the ice field and approached the isolated comm node known as Echo Station. Most of the polar subterranean base was burrowed into the ice and rock below the central landing platform. Above this, a squat, oblong tower of gray, storm-beaten impervisteel watched over the area.

Located in a lonely system the stellar charts marked as Antilles, the comm node was one of nine master traffic stations that covered the breadth of the Galactic Republic and handled all of the hyperspace communications traffic. The system was designed such that the other stations could pick up the slack if any single comm node went offline. In theory, the stations also tracked ships in addition to communications, but that only applied to ships carrying a standard Republic transponder, as required by Republic law. And of course, pirates and the like ignored that requirement. The transponder was one of the first things they removed from any ship they hijacked, refitted, or cobbled together.

Echo Station's crypto was considered sufficient enough to guard its secrets—and thus it wasn't considered by the Republic to be a high-security station warranting a legionnaire detachment. It was instead run by a civilian company working for the military. To Hutch, this meant it would be a walk in the park.

"Feels like a security mission," Crutchke whispered over an encrypted private comm as Shadow Team stacked around the lower hatch inside the belly of the *Forresaw*.

Crutchke had made this argument before. Ghost didn't *do* security, wasn't *trained* for security, and would be in over their heads should they end up having to actually stand up and fight as opposed to sneak and peek.

"It's an infiltration op, it ain't a security mission," Hutch rumbled back.

"Feels like one," whispered Crutchke.

"Well it ain't," replied Hutch over the howl of the engines reversing thrust as the ship slowed from orbital descent.

The plan was to land the *Forresaw* on the main pad and vent the engines while some bogus cargo was offloaded. The tactical assault ship had been modified to look like just another freighter showing up with an unscheduled supply delivery.

Shadow Team, half of Ghost Squad—consisting of Hutch, Enda, Crutchke, and Maas—would infiltrate the base via a maintenance hatch located on the pad. Venting the engines would cover the team's insertion into the network of maintenance tunnels that led down to the sub-basement. Zombie Team, the other half of Ghost—led by Taylor and including Reeco, Wonkeye, and Divitts—would transfer the cargo and oversee surface operations. They'd be dealing with the comm node's supply chief on the platform and keeping the ground crew busy while making sure there was an exit when it was time to leave. Each member of Zombie was armed with a sub-mini DK blaster configured for concealment and rapid deployment.

Best-case scenario: No one would ever know Shadow Team was even there.

Worst-case scenario: Someone would find out, and they would shut down the whole station by initiating the highest-security profile maintained within the comm node. Deep core access would be impossible at that point, and the op would be blown.

The pilot, a crazy dropship jockey everyone called Scooter, had contacted Approach Control and was apprising them of their "unexpected" arrival. Scooter was a good pilot, but he'd lost all his marbles flying close air-support for the navy in support of the Legion, and was a little to a lot crazy, depending on the weather. Right now, the weather was clear. The ice field below was a blaze of blinding white set afire by a startling blue sky. No storms. Nothing to be concerned about.

Approach Control told Scooter the *Forresaw* wasn't cleared for landing. Andien picked up a comm headset as the *Forresaw* began to circle above the station, waiting for clearance.

"Hey..." she began, falling into her role of ambivalent freighter jockey. "We could care less if you don't want your steaks and Faldaren scotch... trust me, we'll make sure it won't go to waste. We get paid either way. But we're gonna call it in before we fire up the galley and beat feet for jump. So hang tight."

The approach controller hesitated and asked them to wait.

In the back of Andien's mind, something wasn't right. She looked over her shoulder. She could see back down the narrow passage leading from the flight deck down into the lounge below the bridge. Hutch was talking to Prisma and the pink-skinned princess, who was standing protectively near the girl. The Endurian had insisted that she go in too. Wherever Prisma went, she was going.

They had counted on that.

What did the princess think—that they actually wanted to kill a little girl? They just wanted to get this over and done with, then wash their hands of these civvies. But then, Andien was part of the Carnivale now. And she'd heard the rumors. Killing a little girl... maybe that wasn't such a stretch after all.

Well. Not on her watch.

The plan was for Shadow Team to take the two of them along into the base. They'd locate an access terminal below the processor stacks and hack in. Two minutes later they would get a bio-scan authorization, and if they passed that, they'd learn where the Doomsday Fleet currently was.

The code slicer, Garret, had said he could get it done in less than two minutes, easy, but Hutch hadn't like the kid's chances of keeping quiet down there. And Andien had to admit, the kid looked like a klutz. Besides, Maas was one of the best hackers in Nether Ops.

The pilot turned and nodded, his shaggy hair bobbing up and down as he grinned and gave her a dirty thumbs-up. They'd gotten the green light for landing. He cut the engines and brought the repulsors to full while he threw out the four landing gears. The ship settled onto its massive hydraulic shock absorbers, and Scooter, with a grand flourish, reached up and pulled the emergency handles on the master vent controls.

"Go," whispered Andien into the comm that connected her with all of Ghost.

According to plan, both teams were now deploying to position one. Shadow into and under the massive superstructure of the landing platform, Zombie out through the cargo doors now rising at the aft of the ship.

The code slicer, the cat, and the war bot had all promised to remain in the lounge and stay out of the way. No one would get hurt, everything would get done, and they'd be gears up and finished with each other soon enough.

Andien started the mission clock.

They had twenty minutes.

Hutch switched to thermal optics as Crutchke popped the hatch in the belly of the ship and dropped onto the landing platform. Without thermal, their buckets would have shown nothing but engine gas billowing up all around them.

"Hurry," whispered Hutch when he saw Crutchke struggle with a bolt on the maintenance hatch.

"Won't budge," whispered the operator over comm. "It's calcified. Probably the low temps this place faces."

"Then cut it."

Crutchke was already way ahead of him. He'd pulled a small torch from his armor that emitted a tiny finger of twisting fire. A second later it sliced through the bolt like it was made of paper. One more cut, and the bolt was useless.

Crutchke popped both sides of the bolt with a screwdriver, then lifted the hatch, peered inside, nodded, and went down head first. He dropped down onto the platform, then looked up toward the belly of the dropship just above his head. Maas followed him down, and the two of them lifted Prisma down gently. They'd outfitted her and the Endurian with skin suits that would cover their IR signatures and keep them warm. Both suits were also low audio profile. No tool belts. No weapons. Minimum signature.

The Endurian went next. She may have whispered a nasty curse at Hutch as she slithered by him, and that made him like her even more. Truth was... he could get sweet on her. She had nice curves, and he liked his women saucy. He went down after her, with Enda bringing up the rear.

They stoop-walked down a small maintenance access hallway. This led to an access door that entered directly into the facility. Crutchke put his head against the door and waited for his armor's audio acquisition to pick up anything on the other side. Signaling that he'd gotten a negative on any sounds beyond ambient machinery, he switched on his armor's radar.

While Ghost Team might have looked like typical legionnaires at a distance, their armor had some significant differences. Notably, it wasn't made of the awful forged ceramic-weave the new Legion armor was composed of. The stuff with the reflective shine that the Legion hated and the Republic loved. Ghost Team's armor was made of a polymerized graphene that wore like soft rubber and stood up to a pretty fair amount of explosive and light blaster damage. It was invisible to most security systems on IR and EM, and it could visually mess with automated sensors by passively sending a QR signal that essentially removed the suit from the image of whatever the camera was focused on. Currently the team's armor was a gray charcoal, but it had a camo system that sensed light and optimized for shadow and terrain. The armor handled all this automatically, based on the situation.

Crutchke's radar detected nothing beyond the door.

Maas stepped forward and hacked the door's cycling lock in twenty-four seconds.

Crutchke stood back and deployed his blaster. This was an optimized version of the sub-mini the Zombies were concealing as they unloaded cargo above. Each blaster was outfitted with laser tri-dot targeting system hardware along with popped short shoulder stocks. Blast silencers were attached at the ends of the barrels; when fired, the blasters would give off only a series of *thump thump thumps*, as opposed to the usual high-pitched whines. They were solid weapons. They burned through charge packs like there was no tomorrow, but they had a high rate of fire, and they hit what they were pointed at.

With Crutchke in the lead, they made their way through the level one maintenance catacombs. Hutch kept one hand on Prisma and checked the mission clock inside his HUD. Eighteen minutes left.

Things continued smoothly for the next nine minutes. They found an acceptable terminal just below the processor stacks inside the comm node's deep core, and Maas stepped up to begin the hack.

And then things started to go severely sideways. Almost as soon as Maas started the hack, something tripped somewhere, and someone got wise to a data breach.

Maas was sure it wasn't his fault.

The shock trooper sniper, part of a Black Fleet special operations team, was looking out a narrow window at the top of the oblong tower when the message came over S-Comm.

"Take out the pilot."

Without hesitation, the sniper pulled the trigger on a matte black vented sniper rifle currently set to high gain for max penetration. A ray of green light shot through the tower window and into the cockpit of the "freighter" on the platform below. A pico-second later it tore out the pilot's throat.

Andien was standing behind Scooter when the shot struck. She'd been watching the feeds from the teams, and the ship itself, in the small command station aft of the cockpit. She heard the tinkle of burned glass as it sprayed across the cockpit and then saw the pilot pitch backward, clutching at his throat. His body spasmed as he died.

Then she saw the shock troopers coming out of the facility from the main hangar leading down into the ice. These must be the ones Wraith had mentioned in his report. They were using the loading ramp as cover, and they were already engaging the Zombies.

Zombie Team at least had cover in the bogus supplies they'd been offloading. But there were a lot of shock troopers in snow-camoed armor coming out of the facility.

"Shadow Team, we're made! Abort!" Andien shouted into the comm. "Hutch, get back to the ship, now!"

21

Taylor, the Zombie Team leader, pulled his sub-mini and touched the "deploy" contact. The weapon transformed into the blaster configuration they'd set up before the op. Ten-round bursts, low intensity. They'd figured they might have to put down the unarmored comm node shipping personnel, not actual tangos in leej armor.

Wonkeye went down first. A shock trooper shot him clean through the heart as he tried to suppress while the rest of the team set up a hasty defense and crossfire.

A second later Taylor was on comm with Hutch.

"Tangos all over us, Hutch!" He popped up, unloaded a burst on a closing dark legionnaire, and dropped the guy. The rest of Zombie were now covering and returning fire. If the shock troopers really were leejes, or ex-leejes, they'd pin them down and flank just like Legion small-unit doctrine indicated.

He checked Reeco and Divitts's position. They were exposed on the right because Wonkeye was down. In a few seconds the enemy would work that out and push where they were weak. Taylor dashed from cargo pallet to cargo pallet. If he could get over to the right flank, he could be waiting for them.

And still, there was no response from Hutch. The comm was dead silent.

"Got it," whispered Maas over comm once he'd cracked the terminal. A few seconds later he had a search algorithm trawling comm logs for the Doomsday Fleet. A few seconds after that they got the first "need-to-know security confirmation checks." Serious stuff. They had a few pass codes that might work—hopefully it was enough to get through the first layers, to access the buried biometric scan that only a few would know about.

Hutch snapped his fingers at the Endurian and motioned for the little girl to be ready for the scan. The look he got from Leenah was pure hatred.

Maas had the biometric scan security page up. "Just stand here, little girl," he said. He spoke in a kindly tone that was at odds with his external suit vocalizer, which made him sound like an electronic ghost. They were keeping the two females off the comms.

Prisma positioned herself in front of the terminal. A small articulating bot arm popped out and chattered in logic-numerica, the standard code interface language for admin system bots. A wide, knife-edged green laser ran down Prisma from head to toe, paused, then retraced its course.

For a long minute they held their breath as nothing changed on the security page.

Then it accessed the galactic transponder positioning grid. Every ship's last known transponder position was displayed. Taken all at once, it was overwhelming on layers the mind would immediately identify as incomprehensible. But the search parameters, code identifiers, and Prisma's biometrics scan sent the map in one specific direction. Off toward the deep edge. Out into the unpopulated regions of a particularly nasty piece of unincorporated space.

A place where legends and rumors were often found annotated on the stellar navigation reports from ships that had never been heard from again. A place where most did not go.

The map was still sectioning, then expanding, and then sectioning and expanding again. They moved Prisma away from the screen, and Maas stood ready to capture the needed data and download it into Ghost Team's cloud.

"Got it!" he whispered.

"Where?" grunted Hutch.

"Umanar. Out in the Deep Well."

"Never heard of it."

That's when they got the call from Andien that the mission was blown.

That's when the entire facility went into lockdown.

Andien had dragged the dead pilot from his cockpit chair. She was still keeping down, trying to spot the sniper in the tower, as she powered up the ship for takeoff.

Garret approached from the passage leading from the flight deck back to the aft quarters. He hugged the passage walls. He whispered loudly to her. "Miss! Hey!"

Why is he whispering? Andien thought. "Stay down!" she shouted at him. "Get back to the lounge. You'll be safe there."

Blaster fire smashed into the hull around the cockpit. Sparks showered out and away across the wide imperv-isteel-latticed windows.

"I can turn this around," he said frantically.

She ignored him and tried to raise Shadow Team. Someone must've set up a local jammer. And those were definitely dark legionnaires out there trying to take the land-ing pad. Somehow they'd walked into the middle of someone else's op.

Taylor bellowed into the comm above the ululating whine of blaster fire. "Do not even think about leaving my brothers behind, ma'am! You do, and I will hunt you down and make you wish you'd never seen my face." His words were interspersed with the whine of distant blaster fire and the report of his own.

This is why you don't use Legion for Nether Ops, Andien thought to herself.

"We can help. Skrizz is a pilot," insisted Garret from back in the passage, eyeing the lifeless body of the pilot on the deck of the cockpit. Main motive turbines were spooled up to full now, blowing snow everywhere across the rear of the plat-form. It was like a sudden storm had come to life all at once behind the ship.

"Plus... we got us a war bot," said Garret with a devilish grin. "Reloaded him before you snatched us."

The kid had a point. The mission packet had said the girl's servant was an old-school war machine from back in the day. End of the Savage Wars, when things had been made to last.

She nodded at Garret, giving the go-ahead.

She hoped he couldn't see the desperation in her eyes.

Perimeter security blast doors had come down, sealing the facility off from the outside world. Someone in charge had caught wind of the hack and was intent on not letting them get away. But during mission planning, Hutch had studied the lay-out of the facility long enough to know what he had to do next to get his team out. Since a soft egress wasn't possible, it was time to stage a jailbreak.

Right now they were in the outer maintenance sections, located between the facility's perimeter and the hab. Threading the tight passage leading away from the terminal they'd hacked, they came to a door marked "CN4." From the layout running on Hutch's HUD, he knew this would take them deep into the node.

He switched to hand signals—standard operating procedure if an op was compromised. It was theoretically possible to crack the quantum encryption that guarded just about any comm, and if that was the case with theirs, it was best not to broadcast their next steps. Besides, Ghost Squad was just as comfortable with silent communication as with comms. In the trust-no-one world of Nether Ops, a comm system was not as vital as some liked to believe.

He put Enda and Crutchke on the door, and held Maas behind him with the two girls.

According to the facility's top tier security protocols, whoever had access to the base's root system could deny entry by just shutting down the blast doors and hatches, throwing the locking bolts into place automatically. No amount of hacking was going to get though a dead door, and cutting it with the torches would take a whole lot of time. But there was the third option. Something that would take only half a second.

Hutch activated his armor's personal deflector, a short duration directional barrier only the team leaders' armor kits were outfitted with. He pumped the repulsors in his pack, then slammed into the door.

The impact rung his bell, but he was a large man, and the impervisteel blast hatch gave way. It shot out into the highly polished curving corridor beyond, slammed off the wall, left a dent, and hit the floor with a loud metallic *clang*.

Hutch steadied himself.

Probably a mild concussion.

"Shake it off," he grunted at himself as he reached out a hand to focus and stop the world from spinning.

A moment later the corridor was filled by the hot blaster fire of dark legionnaires. Enda and Crutchke charged in and returned accurate fire. In seconds, four dark legionnaires were down. You didn't leave the Legion to disappear into Nether Ops unless you had skills, reflexes, and accuracy beyond the one percent of the one percent of the one percent. And Enda had been the Third Legionnaire Division's combat blaster pistol champ. He insisted that he was even better with a blaster rifle.

Hutch regained his senses. He signaled for Maas to bring the Endurian and the little girl out.

He bent down on one knee in front of the girl. "We gotta do this the hard way now, Prisma. Stay close, and I promise I'll get you out of here. Don't be afraid."

"I'm not afraid. Ravi said it would be like this," the girl replied.

Hutch had no clue what she meant.

He checked in with the Endurian, relishing another dose of her hatred. He was falling in love, some never-serious part of his mind joked.

Except he saw something else.

She was watching him and *not* hating him. Because he'd taken the time to stop and promise Prisma that she would be okay. That he would do his best to get her out of there.

Leenah knew. Knew what the little girl who'd begun to reluctantly cling to her had gone through. Knew how scared, and brave in the same moment, she was. But in the end, she was just a little girl, and she was capable of only so much.

The galaxy is a hard place. Even for little girls.

Leenah nodded at him.

And that put Hutch, the big man who swam in the hatred of others, off his game.

He pulled his holdout pistol, flipped it, and handed it to her grip first.

And something passed between them.

With the green light to bring Skrizz and KRS-88 into play, things happened fast. First the giant cat slithered between Andien and the flight controls. He brought in the reverse thrusters with a deft flick. Just barely. The sudden snowstorm now covered the cockpit windshield, and would have swirled inside had the wobanki not activated the auto-seal, a plate of impervisteel that covered the hole.

The storm was at least good for denying the sniper visibility. Andien knew a good sniper would switch to IR... but that wasn't an optimal targeting solution. The yowling cat's maneuver had bought them a little cover.

Garret led KRS-88 into the dark interior of the cargo hold. Beyond the open rear door, snow swirled in whirlwinds and columns. One of the operators—Taylor, thought Garret—was dragging a wounded comrade back toward the cargo ramp. Both were shooting back at the unseen shock troopers shifting positions out among the cargo pallets.

Garret deployed his latest datapad and brought up the app that controlled the war bot. After entering a quick and enigmatic passcode, he had root access to the old war machine's combat protocol.

"Get back inside the ship, kid!" Taylor shouted. The operator he was dragging back looked dead. Except that he was coughing up blood in pathetic little spasms. Even Garret knew that guy was flatlining.

He swiped the on-screen toggle on the app that controlled KRS-88. Instantly the seven-foot bot's posture changed— from the erect bearing of a servant bot hovering to be of service, all prim and proper, to the grimly homicidal stance of the war bot more nightmare than machine.

"Commencing operations now," intoned the nightmare. Gone was KRS-88's basso butler baritone; its voice now sounded like a drowned ghost recorded electronically.

Garret established its targeting protocols and gave it orders to secure the landing pad.

KRS-88 marched out into a hail of blaster fire. Dark legionnaires were already surrounding the landing pad. The bot raised its hands and deployed its wrist blasters, instantly knocking down three shock troopers. Most of the rest scrambled to get away from the thing, but one tried to close, firing on full auto, targeting KRS-88's leg actuators. It was a notoriously vulnerable spot on that particular model of the war bot chassis.

KRS-88 responded by taking two giant and sudden steps that brought it within reach of the firing shock trooper. It back-handed the soldier, probably breaking his neck, and sent him sprawling off the elevated landing pad and into the snowfield below the outpost.

The dark legionnaires hunkered down and kept up a steady stream of fire as KRS-88 dodged and tried to get closer to them.

Unbeknownst to any one organic creature on that battlefield, two things were happening simultaneously. Because KRS-88 was a war bot with advanced sensors and light-ning-quick MicroFrame processors (thanks to Garret), he was aware of both.

At the appearance of the fearsome war bot, the shock troopers had called in an air strike on the pad. Their orders hadn't included capturing the ship, just the little girl. Their commanding officer knew the girl was inside the facility with the second team, and authorized the air strike immediately.

Two howling tri-fighters, assigned to provide tactical air support for the special operations team, streaked down out of the gray and stormy sky above. KRS-88 registered the incoming fighters and marked them as hostile when they began their strafing run on the pad.

At the same moment, a shock trooper was ordered by his sergeant to use an anti-vehicle fragger on the war bot. The trooper stepped back, armed the fragger by twisting the ball atop the stick, and prepared to lob it at the rampaging war bot. If it hit, or even got close, it would magnetically attach itself and then explode, substantially damaging the war machine.

KRS-88 was aware of this action as well. Its onboard radar had tagged every combatant and assigned them an order of priority with regards to termination. Its processors interpreted the shock trooper's movements as a classic counterattack with anti-vehicle explosives, and KRS-88 upgraded the soldier's termination status.

In the moment the shock trooper stepped back and flung his arm over his shoulder plates, armed fragger in hand, KRS-88 took two massive steps, almost lunging for the trooper, reached over the top of the stacked supply pallets the team was covering behind, grabbed the trooper with his massive metal hand, and whipped him skyward toward the closing tri-fighters. As though the man were a mere rag doll. A plaything to be tossed about on a whim, or in rage.

The hurled trooper with the anti-vehicle grenade rammed into the diving tri-fighter. The entire ship exploded just two hundred feet above the pad. Debris rained down as the other fighter peeled off and streaked out across the ice field.

Then KRS-88 began to murder the other shock troopers all around him. He flung one into the tower wall. Smashed another flat. And shot the rest with his rapid-fire hand blasters.

22

Captain Mordo, the shock trooper tactical officer leading the special operations team, had watched his own infiltration mission go from bad to worse.

The mission had fallen to them, because they were closest. A team held in reserve for whatever the Republic might have planned after Tarrago. And even with their proximity, they got to the facility less than a day ahead of the Republic.

They had dropped in eighteen hours ago, far out in the ice field. In the dead of night, they'd taken the facility and eliminated its pathetic security force. By dawn, they'd finished interrogating the techs that actually ran the data stacks and had archived all the comm traffic from across the galaxy.

Their orders from Black Fleet Intelligence, specifically Admiral Crodus, had been to find the location of the Republic's Doomsday Fleet. Their mission briefing had made them painfully aware that they would need a biometric scan to access the fleet location. But... it was thought that one of the techs might have a workaround. It had taken three dead techs, their nervous systems flayed alive by a device they called the Inducer, to find out that there *was* no workaround. That the Doomsday Fleet was indeed one of the most closely guarded secrets of the Republic and the House of Reason.

Captain Mordo ordered the rest of the techs, and all facility personnel, save the cargo handlers and one admin, executed.

But that would have to wait until it was time to wrap things up. Their mission briefing indicated that the girl, their secondary target, might arrive with a small security detail. In that event, their mission was to take her alive and use her to accomplish the biometric scan. This didn't stop Mordo from attempting to hack the systems with his own techs. He didn't want to wait on unverified intel. And there was always the possibility the little girl might get herself killed when the capture finally went down.

When the cargo ship arrived, it was fairly clear that this was the tactical team assigned to the girl. And Mordo was prepared—or so he believed. To be honest, he'd assumed they'd just march her right in through the cargo doors once they were sure things were secure, enter with full authorization, and access the data vault terminal on the main level. With that in mind, he'd planned quite a clever ruse, putting his men in station uniforms and surrounding the perimeter with a heavy weapons team that could deploy swiftly. He'd also set up two snipers with clear sight pictures of the terminal.

Their first shots would've killed the security detail within three seconds. The team would then sweep the survivors, secure the girl, and terminate the rest.

Mordo planned his operations well. He expected them to happen just like he envisioned them.

Except none of this had happened.

Instead, while his men were waiting for the security team to exit the freighter, they'd infiltrated through the landing platform. Within ten minutes they were hacking the terminals, and Mordo was fairly sure they'd gotten the info they needed.

He immediately locked down the facility so that the only way out was through the main entrance inside the lower hangar. He then reoriented his teams to deny access to this exit back into the cargo bays and out onto the landing platform.

Which should have been easy.

Except the security detail guarding the little girl moved quickly through the facility, taking secondary routes that bypassed his hasty ambushes. And none of the internal security systems were reading the intruders, capturing them on visual, or tracking them via sensor or hatch access codes. It was as though they were ghosts passing though the walls as they wished, knocking out his teams in a seemingly wanton fashion. One moment his assets would be reporting in, and the next they were gone, their vitals on his Unit Roster HUD showing them as terminated.

And now there was this rampaging war bot. The surviving tri-fighter pilot couldn't make another pass because those old war bots had been configured for anti-air capabilities. And surprise was gone.

Surrounded by his command team and a squad of shock troopers, Mordo screamed at his men. "Go out and take down the war bot!"

He glanced back at the master control panel for the main gate and facility access. To his surprise, it had locked him out. All it showed him now was the station template, showing the various doors in lockdown mode. And as he looked, three of those doors unlocked. They formed a path, leading back to the main exit.

"They've hacked in!" he screamed, almost apoplectic now. He stabbed his finger at an intersection between the exit and the last blast door that had just opened. "Deploy here! Now! No one escapes!"

Hutch was walking sideways, watching the team in front of him, keeping the two girls moving, and checking in with Maas to the rear at all the same time. They were hustling down a wide, white hall, gleaming and polished, with comm panels and processor switching grids along the walls, their lights flashing across ceramic panels. A typical state-of-the-art Repub comm node.

The first shock troopers in their black-lacquered armor came at them from behind, driving them forward. Searing red blaster fire smashed into a processor near Maas and exploded into a shower of sparks. Maas returned fire as he dove across the hall.

It was a standard Ghost Team tactic in close quarters battles: draw fire and then move evasively while your other team members targeted the return fire. Instinctively Hutch pivoted and unloaded on two shock troopers. One took it in the chest and went down on his back. The other got hit and spun away. More were coming up from behind.

"Move!" he shouted at the girls.

He covered Maas, then Maas fell back to cover him. Ten feet. Fire. Ten feet more.

The next group of shock troopers came from down a narrow hall intersecting the one they were taking back to the main entrance. Crutchke and Enda took either side of the passage and alternated putting fire down at the approaching shock troopers. Enda held up one hand, telling Prisma and Leenah to wait. The return fire was too heavy for them to cross the corridor.

The shock troopers coming up behind were forcing Hutch and Maas to give ground they were running out of. Blaster fire whined and shrieked. They couldn't move forward, not while protecting the girl, and they couldn't move back.

The noose was closing all about them.

Leenah saw the big man they called Hutch holding his ground. He wasn't ceding anymore. There was no more to give.

They were caught.

She heard a distant pounding and guessed it was her heart. Because she knew what she was going to do next.

She picked up Prisma, shielded her with her own body, and dashed across the blaster fire coming from the shock troopers down the crossing corridor. She felt Prisma's chest against her own, felt her rapid breathing, and in that moment she knew she would always protect her. Or at least die trying.

A moment later they were racing away from the chaos, straight toward the main blast doors that led outside. Leenah put Prisma down and dragged her by the hand, hardly slowing.

Ahead, the massive doors seemed to be rupturing in a dozen places. Indentations appeared like mountains rising up through its heavy impervisteel surface. Then one mountain gave way, erupting into a jagged gash, and two massive metallic bot hands pushed through it. They rent the blast doors asunder.

KRS-88 forced its body through and widened the gap through sheer hydraulic counter-strength.

"Crash!" shouted Prisma.

For a moment the bot paused in its destruction, and Leenah swore that its optical sensors changed. Softened, somehow. Like it processed the little girl and recalled, somewhere deep in its circuits, another relationship with her.

And then it was back to being a war bot.

As Prisma and Leenah slipped past the bot and through the door, KRS-88 covered Hutch and the rest of the team, allowing them to withdraw. The bot made the dark legionnaires pay as they swarmed down the corridor in pursuit.

By the time the war bot made it up the hangar ramp, the rest of Shadow Team had made the cargo ramp leading up into the ship. Crash ran, and the operators gave it covering fire. Shock troopers were slipping through the gap in the doors and giving chase.

Once the war bot was on board the ship, the repulsors kicked in. Skrizz had the ship moving skyward even as the cargo ramp was starting up. Shock troopers on the ground fired up at them, aiming for the engines.

Then Skrizz punched it, and the ship shot off over the ice field.

Gone.

Ruh-Ro, the first officer on the *Forresaw*, was a moktaar who mostly kept to himself. Simian humanoids were like that. But he was a good mechanic, and with the aid of a general service bot, he kept the ship clean and running. He was technically a chief in the Repub Navy somewhere on some list. When they got leave, he and Scooter would hit port, drink, dance with what each species considered pretty ladies, and generally enjoy themselves.

When the firefight on the landing platform erupted, the moktaar had been busy supervising the sham loading operation. He'd peeked his simian head out of the cargo deck and sniffed at the cold arctic air of the station. He smelled fear and murder, and he didn't like it one bit.

Ruh-Ro had been in his share of hot landing zones. Hot enough that he'd occasionally had to deploy the door-mounted heavy blaster off the rear cargo deck, for suppressive fire to get the teams back aboard. But in this instance, the mounted heavy blaster was positioned away from the facility and the ramp that led down to the lower hangars. So the weapon was useless.

He called up to Scooter using the inter-ship comm, and got no response. He checked the damage control panel, noted the damage to the cockpit's hull integrity, and went forward to inspect the damage to the cockpit windows.

He was not dreading the worst.

Maybe just a little.

But when he saw his dead friend, Scooter, lying on the deck, and the wobanki slithering into the pilot's seat and activating the launch start pre-flight checklist... all hell broke loose.

Not because Scooter was dead.

That was only part of it.

All hell broke loose because wobanki and moktaar are deadly enemies. And ever since Prisma and her guardians had been brought on board, Skrizz and Ruh-Ro had been silently whispering murderous threats at each other in their native tongues any chance they could get.

Most people weren't aware of the bad blood between the two races. Most people had either forgotten, or never knew, that the races had fought three major wars against each other. The wobanki had used the moktaar home world as a private hunting ground for hundreds of years before the Republic came into being—and once the moktaar got their hands on the hyperdrive, they'd promptly invaded one of the three wobanki homeworlds and enslaved everyone on it.

Things had gotten much worse in the thousand years since.

Ruh-Ro hissed and swung his hydro-spanner in a wide arc, intent on braining the cat with a surprise attack. But the wobanki, like all cats, wasn't so easily brained. Skrizz dodged, scrambled from his seat, and popped claws. A moment later he'd shredded the front of the mechanic's overalls along with a good portion of simian fur.

Ruh-Ro monkey-screeched, grabbed on to the ceiling, and swung his mace-like hydro-spanner again. This time he smashed the cat right in his jaw. Skrizz yowled in pain and reared back to lunge for a killing blow with all claws popped.

And that was when Andien stuck her blaster in the cat's whiskers.

"Not here. Not now," she muttered through gritted teeth.

The moktaar swung from the ceiling of the cockpit and promised Skrizz that he would set his skull in front of his family's tent. In chittering Moktaar, of course. It was an ancient oath-promise of the standard blood-and-revenge variety.

"What did you say?" Andien roared as Skrizz's hackles flared. Beyond the cockpit window shock troopers were advancing through the storm created by the ship's reverse thrusters.

"I told him," rumbled the moktaar, "that I was just kidding." Then the monkey man smiled a wicked, savage grin. "Here, kitty kitty kitty... I was just playing with you." He added a moktaari vulgarity that was reserved for blood feuds that could only be satisfied by death.

"If," began Andien slowly, "either of you hurts the other, you will kill us all."

She looked at the monkey. "Cat's the only one who can fly this ship right now."

She looked at Skrizz. "Monkey's the only one who can..." She paused. "Well, we need him to do the... monkey things," she finished awkwardly.

Then she looked at both. "Work together, and I'll let you kill each other once we're clear of the mission. Agreed?"

They both agreed.

They'd rather have killed each right now, never mind the shock troopers swarming the ship. Instead they each had to be satisfied with swearing to provide death to the other as soon as possible.

Once the teams were back on board, Skrizz brought in the repulsors, got good seals on all the hatches, and pointed the ship skyward. To the rear he could hear them bringing the cursing wounded into the main lounge.

The truth was, he didn't need this in his life. It was a conversation with himself he'd grown used to having of late. This was not the wobanki way. Wobanki didn't stick around and get sentimental about associations. They were nomadic killers.

One of the premier uber predators of the galaxy.

Except... well, he liked the little girl.

It was as simple as that.

It had happened back on the other ship. After the action. After the near escape from that crazy bounty hunter setting off a nuclear weapon. After all that. He'd been sitting near a bulkhead, wondering how he was going to extricate himself from all this drama. Wobanki do not like drama, nor do they care to involve themselves in the affairs of the Republic.

And Prisma had walked by him.

The little girl and the large trundling bot behind came walking down a passage inside the hurtling ship. And she simply reached out and stroked his fur.

Wobanki also do not like to be touched. Unless it's by a female wobanki. And that's another story.

But the girl did it so quickly that he wasn't able to pop his claws and hiss at her. And then she was just staring at his fur, stroking him softly. It was very peaceful. Calm. It was a thing Skrizz had needed all his life... without ever knowing it

And then she stopped, and she nodded at him without saying a word. She continued on down the passage, off into the darkness of the ship.

And ever since that time, Skrizz had found himself not slipping away as had been his plan, preferably with some of their shinier things.

Instead he'd found himself... waiting.

Waiting for her to do that again.

And sometimes she would.

And it was the most pleasant thing he'd ever experienced. It felt like a deep quiet hum deep down inside him. And that caused his mind to surrender to the golden glow so many of the priests on his home world were always trying to get everyone to listen for. To believe in.

He'd always thought they were hucksters.

Yet somehow... this little girl had made him feel the hum.

So he'd stayed. Waiting for it to happen again. To him, she was a kind of priest.

And now he found himself punching atmosphere, flying a tactical assault ship for a Repub Nether Ops team, and twenty seconds later they had bogies all over them.

"*Chabu tatanki wapeanu*?" he yowled at Andien. She was behind him in the navigator's seat.

She shook her head. "This ship doesn't have any weapons. Get us out of here, kitty cat."

23

"We're scrubbing! We're way too over our heads on this!" Andien practically screamed at the large man across the table from her. They were in the TAC planning room of the ship. Just the two of them.

Hutch listened.

She'd run through what had happened, getting more and more irate as she went through mission failure after mission failure. Seeming to take personal responsibility for everything that had gone wrong, as though she were conducting a jury trial against herself. Desperate to find herself guilty so that she might report to the nearest firing squad.

"I got three men killed back on the landing pad," she said on a morbid note of finality.

And they'd left two of the dead operators behind. Reeco had died on the cargo deck as the ship evaded the tri-fighters.

They were compromised. Somebody had known what they were after, and they'd come to get it with a lot more than Ghost Squad had shown up with. Shock troopers. Air support. They'd been lying in wait as though they'd *known* a Nether Ops team would show up at that particular comm node. One of nine that could've provided the required information and access.

The *Forresaw* barely made it to jump. Five of those strange howling tri-fighters had come out of nowhere. The *Forresaw* wasn't a combat ship; that wasn't its purpose. Its lack of weapons was what allowed it to go unnoticed for Ghost's infiltration ops. It was optimized for stealth.

If it hadn't been for the wobanki, they'd all be dead. The cat could fly. That was for sure.

"So scrub and head back," Andien said. Her eyes were tired. Her voice a dry croak. "We got the info. So let's turn it over and get a real plan together for how to make it work. Because more than likely, whoever this enemy is… they trawled our hack and they know exactly where that fleet is, too. And obviously, they'll show up in force."

She finished. Her shoulders were slumped, and she was practically leaning over the smart table.

Hutch sat with his arms folded. Like some statue that hadn't been moved by her storms. "Our orders are to take the kid out to the fleet, activate it once it receives her authentication, and get clear," he rumbled. "Those are still our orders."

"Gee, thanks. I hadn't comprehended that until you summed it up so nicely!" Andien shouted. "Orders are contingent on the situation. The enemy is inside the perimeter. Someone *flipped* on us, Hutch. No one was supposed to know about the Doomsday Fleet. No one was supposed to know that the comm traffic from a comm node was the only way to locate it. There are human factors here. The fleet is AI-controlled. It's hidden and waiting. Only those in the know, know! And someone in the know flipped our mission and sent a larger force to take us out."

She was begging him to see the point. And when his impassive features refused to show her that he acknowledged, or even understood, she spelled it out.

"Someone in the Republic is working against our orders."

Silence.

"Do you know what that means?"

He nodded. She ignored this because she was work-ing herself up to a whole new tirade. Fresh anger welled up within her.

"It means we can't trust *anyone*. It means that *any* ren-dezvous could leave us dead and the fleet lost. It means that whoever knows about us pulling the hack... they're most like-ly going to make sure we're good and dead if we dump out of hyperspace anywhere, including where we're currently supposed to be headed. Which they probably also know be-cause—and here's where I bring things home for you—some-one in the know *flipped on us!*"

Hutch merely shrugged, and this caused her to dig down, grit her teeth, and try to control a scream she turned into a grunt as she slapped the smart table with the flat of her hand. Obviously the big stupid operator didn't realize how dead they were.

Hutch finally spoke. "So who, exactly, do we go back to if we can't trust anyone?"

"What?"

"You just said it. We can't trust anyone. We show up any-where and we're dead. Copy that."

She shook her head. She had people she could trust. Victory Squad. Chhun and Owens and Legion Commander Keller. But she couldn't tell him any of this. Because she didn't trust *him*. So she kept quiet.

"So we're dead," continued Hutch. "Because no matter where we show up, not only do we know where that fleet is, we also have the one thing that gets us root access to fleet startup. The kid."

She watched him. Watched the cold dead look in his eyes where all the mortal math scrolled across his brain stem. And she was suddenly aware, in that howling silence between them in that moment, that he'd killed not just tens... but maybe hundreds of other people. And even thousands indirectly by his actions. Looking into his eyes was like looking at a whole other type of human being. A type that didn't feel, or think, or figure, the way you were supposed to when you were human.

She was looking at something cold. Something calculating. Something almost... primal. Like some animal that killed to stay alive. Moment to moment.

"So what are you saying then?" she asked, confident in spite of what she saw in the man.

She had visions of the operator spacing the little girl. And visions of herself standing right beside him, looking into the airlock. Some distant part of her mind was adding up how many of the people in this ship they'd have to space to get clear of this. The Endurian. The code slicer. The cat.

She would kill Hutch first.

It was a thought so quick, dark, and shocking, she wondered if it had truly been her own. She was amazed at what a person could become when their life was on the line.

"I'm thinking," began Hutch, his eyes focusing on her, "that if we can get the fleet activated before anyone catches us, then we become irrelevant in the grand scheme of high and mighty muckety mucks playing their power games. Once that fleet is online... we don't matter."

She was both amazed and horrified at how far her mind had departed from his. Horrified at what had been inside her all along. Horrified. Just horrified at the dark gaps between the known and the unknown.

She blinked as though that would somehow shutter the windows to her soul. As though the big operator were some stranger in the night, passing by her window, looking in at her, seeing her awful nakedness.

And she, too, was that stranger seeing herself for the first time. Horrified at who she really was and wondering if she'd been this way all along.

"So," she began slowly. "You're saying we stay on mission? That's our only way out."

The silence of hyperspace seemed to fill the void between them. Seemed to fill the whole ship. Seemed to be a space between the death and destruction going on across the galaxy where they could hide only for so long.

He nodded.

"Half your team is dead. Including our pilot," she stated matter-of-factly.

He nodded again.

He leaned forward and studied the stellar overlay on the tacplan interface. A digital sand table. All the intel they possessed displayed and updated in real time. And they had damn little of it.

"Cat's a good enough pilot," he said. "We can probably use the code slicer. At least as a backup for Maas. The Endurian will take care of the kid." He straightened up, folded his muscular arms across his bulging chest once more, and smiled wanly. "And we got a war bot. I say... good enough. Let's roll."

And me, thought Andien. *You've got me... and you still have no idea how much that's worth.*

Prisma sat on her bunk, alone save for Crash. The big bot stood watching the door. Intent on protecting her.

And Ravi appeared. Crystallized out of nothing to become something. And it was so natural. Like... like that was the way the universe really worked.

Prisma watched him. Truth be told, she was scared to death. Her chest rose and fell in short breaths. Like some pre-adolescent, hard-working bellows.

Ravi smiled at her. "You did well, Miss Prisma."

Prisma didn't answer. There was a part of her that was in shock. A part of her where everything that had happened was catching up. All at once.

"Just breathe, Prisma. One large breath."

Prisma took a giant breath, closed her eyes, and let it out.

"I wish I could tell you it was going to get easier, Prisma," Ravi said in his near-perfect elocution. "But I can't."

Prisma opened her eyes. She saw fear. Fear of all the terrible things that could happen was there, behind Ravi's large, coal-dark eyes.

"I am so sorry, Prisma. So very sorry indeed."

And in that moment Prisma's mouth made a small 'O'. As though she were going to begin some plea. Some rant. Some begging for the galaxy not to be this way. As though she would trade anything to be free of this trail she found herself on.

Never wanted to be on.

In that moment she would even give up revenge.

The revenge that had burned inside of her since...

Since...

But Ravi interrupted.

"Right now you feel helpless."

Prisma nodded.

"And you feel alone?"

Prisma nodded again, and tears began to gather in her eyes. She wiped them away and set her face, as if to show they'd never been.

"I am going to give you a gift now."

And without a word, Ravi reached forward and passed his hand over hers. It was so gentle. So gossamer. And yet it was real. And for a moment Prisma was overwhelmed, and now the tears came as a golden glow that was like happiness and grief filling her all at once.

"What is it?" she asked, sobbing.

Crash stirred. "Are you all right, young miss?" he asked in his basso profundo.

Prisma nodded and wiped her nose. And yet the tears still came.

"Why are you crying? Are you injured?" continued the bot. "I have allowed nothing to hurt you... Have *I* hurt you?"

Prism shook her head. And still she continued to cry.

"As long as I am able I will never allow you to be hurt, young miss. I promised your father, and now that he is dead I feel a great burden not to hurt you. Though... perhaps mentioning his death has indeed caused me to hurt you afresh... Have I?"

Prisma shook her head.

"He can't see me, Prisma," whispered Ravi gently. "I do not wish him to."

And then he told her about the power.

Not the name of it.

Not its use.

But what it was.

"There is something in the universe, young miss. A gift to some. Through it, change can be affected for great good, or great evil. But never for both. And it is always a gift. No strings are ever attached."

Prisma felt something moving through her. Murmuring of best days and love. Of better times. Of all things being one in some way, shape, or form.

"What do I do with it?" she whispered.

Ravi looked at her for a long moment.

"That is the burden of the gift-giver... to hope that I have given it to the right person. I spent time with Captain Keel for such a purpose. He was not the one. But it is yours now. We will see if you will use it for good, or evil."

Then he held out a blue marble. He handed it to her. And in that instant it became real in the palm of her hand. She stared at it. It was like a tiny living world.

"It is just a marble," he said, as though sensing her thoughts. "But it is also a test."

Prisma made a face indicating she didn't understand.

"You want to know how?" asked Ravi.

Prisma nodded, and he smiled that warm knowing smile that was full of delight, and maybe a good kind of mischievousness.

"When you convince it to move, all by itself... the power will begin to grow within you."

Prisma stared at him in disbelief.

"Put it away for now. In time, you must practice with it. Concentrate upon it. Convince it to change the universe for good. And it will. As will everything."

"Why?" Prisma asked. And then, with a plaintive wail that made Crash jerk to life once more: "I'm just a girl. And... I'm afraid!"

"Because," Ravi said. He began to fade. "The galaxy must change."

And then he was gone.

And Prisma stared at the marble for a very long time.

24

The Umanar system was aflame from the massive blue giant at its center. Even from this distance Andien could see the apocalyptic majesty of the hot star igniting the massive super-planet closest to it, creating a slow, eons-long burn that left a flaming vapor trail across the system.

As the *Forresaw* jumped into the system, the ship's advanced sensor package quickly picked up another starcraft in the area. A large ship of unknown origin and make. Hiding inside the fiery maelstrom.

"It's big," sighed Andien.

Hutch leaned over her in the tiny TAC center at the back of the flight deck.

Andien plotted a course, sent it to the pilot's HUD, then stood up and leaned over the cat. "Rough in there? Can you make the approach?"

Skrizz shrugged and murmured some wobanki phrase about little things not bothering big cats.

Hutch grunted at the expression. "I'm assuming this 'fleet' defends itself until we provide authorization. Unless it signals us otherwise, we've got to set down inside the docking hangar, if it's got one, and get Prisma to a terminal for a biometric scan. Once that's complete, Ghost Team is done."

That was true. Andien had her orders. Give the fleet a private comm channel to engage with the House of Reason's Security Council. With Orrin Kaar himself.

Not the admiralty.

That had been made painfully clear in the meetings with X. This was a bypass. The House of Reason wanted to be able to use this fleet at their discretion. They wanted direct control without the Repub admiralty in the way.

"Does it bother you, Hutch?" Andien asked. Realizing that he might not be following her train of thought, she quickly clarified: "That they want direct control of whatever this fleet is to go to the House instead of the navy?"

"No. Those are the orders," Hutch replied. "That's how it works in the Nether. Don't go thinkin', and you won't go disappearin', little girl."

"Check the files. I was in Nether long before they pulled your ass off the field just because you were good at shooting straight."

Hutch cleared his throat. He seemed taken aback—apparently realizing that Andien had been allowing him to patronize her until just this moment. "Didn't mean it as a threat."

An hour later they'd made a slow pass down the spine of the massive, dark ship. Inside the maelstrom between the burning blue star and the gas giant, blue vapor clouds, on fire, swirled and vaporized. And while it looked like some vision of hell—and required more power to the deflectors—it was actually quite beautiful. And quiet. And mostly harmless, other than a lot of chop going in.

The ship was unlike anything Andien had ever seen—in the Republic, in any other local navy, even in the enemy fleet that had attacked Tarrago. It looked almost like a giant assault blaster or orbital cannon moving through space. Its very design suggested that it was a weapon. It was many decks high, but not wide, and its external features seemed to elude the logic of purpose—though, again, it left no doubt as to its aggregate purpose: this ship was one giant weapon system.

"*Bota rurari ranamu*," announced Skrizz. They were being scanned by the ship as they passed along its upper hull.

Some distant part of Andien wondered if they were about to be attacked. Obliterated without a chance to provide authentication. And what could they do if they were?

Beneath the *Forresaw*, sections of the mystery ship sprang to life. A hangar deck's illumination system switched on, throwing ghostly light into the flaming darkness between the planet and the star. Andien checked the sensors once more.

"Getting life support readings in various sections. Looks like the AI is waking up and ready to receive us." She took a deep breath. "Requesting clearance to land."

A standard Repub landing authorization code came through. The HUD plotted a course straight into the large docking bay that had just lit up along the port side.

"Take us in, Skrizz. But keep the engines on idle no matter what. We may want back out. Fast."

Andien nodded to Hutch, and the two of them moved swiftly to the rear of the ship. The plan was for all of Ghost to escort Prisma and Leenah out into the hangar, where the girl could interface with a terminal.

The *Forresaw*'s repulsors throbbed to life, and the ship settled onto the almost mirror-like finish of the empty hangar bay. Ruh-Ro dropped the cargo door and sniffed at the air, even though sensors indicated they had good atmo beyond the force-shielded entry they'd been allowed to pass through.

After locking the cargo door in the down position, he nodded at the armored legionnaires, the two girls, and Garret.

Andien had positioned herself to watch the troop depart. As Garret passed, she softly asked him, "Did you transmit the message to Keel?"

"Yep," Garret answered in a whisper.

Andien made no indication she'd heard him.

The moktaar didn't wait for them to make it down onto the hangar floor before he'd deployed the mounted heavy blaster. He grabbed the firing handles, charged the weapon, and swiveled it about its targeting trajectories. Written on the side of it in white lettering were the words *Problem Solver*.

Hutch tapped his bucket at the monkey as he walked down the cargo ramp. He was the last one off the ship.

Enda was on point, and the rest of Ghost surrounded Leenah, Garret, and the little girl at the center. The war bot brought up the rear. From the cargo deck, Andien watched them make their way across the sprawling and empty hangar, checking every possible direction from which they might suddenly take fire. Ahead lay the main blast door leading into the ship. To the right of that door was a terminal. That was the first objective.

A hundred meters before they reached the massive door, it slid open, and out walked a bot—a standard Repub protocol and admin bot, sheathed in white ceramic laminate chest plate, with a head-mounted processor unit.

Andien wondered why she wasn't getting anything over comm even though they had a line-of-sight link. She was a comms expert, and a distant klaxon was sounding in her mind. What would cause that? Beyond the jejune. What was the big, major problem that might stem from this?

And then Ghost Team, Leenah, Garret, the war bot, and Prisma all disappeared through the blast door.

It irised shut behind them.

It was a personal admin series bot. Anyone who'd been around the military forces of the Republic for any stretch of time had met one of the incarnations of this series in some form or another.

"I am CAT37," the bot greeted the remnants of Ghost and their charges. "I will escort you to a confirmation terminal. This way."

Ghost quickly discussed their options over comm.

"Feels funny," said Maas.

"Yeah... it does," muttered Crutchke.

"Enda?" Hutch asked. All of their powerful sub-minis were trained on the hapless protocol bot. They were each a soft squeeze away from annihilating the automaton in an instant.

The normally quiet Enda took a long moment to deliver an answer. "True," he began in his rich voice. "But how normal can a fleet with no biological presence feel? Still. Agree. Something's tickling my spider senses. And I don't like it."

It was an old phrase, and its origins were lost to time and the past. But the meaning was clear: beyond any sort of actual evidence one could put a finger on... something was indeed up.

"I thought there was supposed to be a fleet," Hutch said over local audio—speaking to the bot. "How come there's just this one ship?"

"Oh... yes. Quite. Of course." The bot clicked, chittered, and then seemed to come to itself after a second. "I think you will be given access to the information you require once we've performed the biometric scan on the authenticating unit. Which one of you might that be?"

The bot scanned the group. Everyone was smart enough not to move.

"Right. Well..." The bot paused, its soulless optical sensors taking everyone in, its joints and plates articulating absurdly and stiffly with each gesture. "I think I understand perfectly. Again... may I escort you to the terminal? It's just this way."

"All right," Hutch replied.

Over comm he whispered, and he had no idea why he was whispering, "Be ready for anything. Mission focus is the little girl. Anything goes wrong, get her back to the ship and away from here. Everyone else... buy time."

The blast door irised open, and the bot walked through the portal with slow, mincing steps. Ghost Team and its charges followed.

Andien was still speaking into the comm, trying to reach Hutch and his men after the blast door slithered shut, leaving the *Forresaw* alone inside the giant, spotlessly gleaming hangar deck. She uttered a curse, tore off her headset, and slammed her hand down on the tactical display.

"Something's not right."

When she turned, she found the moktaar staring bloody murder at the wobanki, who looked like he was just waiting for something to happen that might give him an excuse to cut the monkey. The cat's tail drew lazy, hypnotic figure eights through the air. The tension was obvious.

"Guys!" shouted Andien. Her voice echoed across the cockpit.

The moktaar only glanced at her. "Everything in the Republic may be kumbaya... is that your word? With your 'diversity is strength' slogans. But you have *no* idea how much we would love to slay each other here and now. We have grievances far older than your Republic. Our hate is wired into our DNA."

Andien weighed the moment. Shooting one of them right now would solve some of her immediate problems. But it would also create a whole new set of problems for later.

Then the moktaar looked out the cockpit window and made a face. His protruding jaw dropped open. "What in the..."

Andien whirled.

Skrizz refused to turn his back on the moktaar; he had anticipated the monkey would try a stupid ploy like this to distract him. He was definitely going to kill the monkey, and he would enjoy doing so. That was at the top of his things-to-do-today list. And he hoped to accomplish this in the next few minutes, which counted as a long-term goal for a wobanki.

"Oh... my ..." Andien said.

Beyond the cockpit windows, out across the massive hangar, three groups of bots—they were definitely bots, because they had the over-articulated smoothness about them—came from three opening blast doors along the hangar walls. Each group contained at least a hundred bots.

Andien didn't recognize the bot design, but they looked like some form of hunter-killer unit. Their frame looked similar in some ways to legionnaire armor, except these were made of highly polished chrome. Instead of a head, each bot had a helmet that looked like a tech-infused version of those worn by ancient Greek hoplites. And upon the face of this processor/helmet, three burning optical sensors glared red like malevolent eyes.

Each bot was carried a heavy blaster the size of a crew-served N-50. Except instead of one barrel, there were three.

And the bots were eight feet tall.

A little bigger than the old war bots.

And new.

New, and definitely lethal.

25

Ghost Team and its charges were halfway down a corridor within the gigantic ship—a seemingly endless corridor of pristine white ceramic modularized compartments of functional design—when Hutch asked the bot how much further to the terminal.

"Oh, just another 239 meters from our current location. Not long now," it replied cheerily.

And then Enda asked a question. "I've never heard of your series model before. What was it again?"

"Ah." The bot clicked and whirred as it minced ahead of the armed legionnaires down the seemingly endless corridor. "CAT37."

Hutch wondered, briefly, what Enda was playing at.

"What's the technical classification?" Enda asked. "I'm unfamiliar with the CAT designation class."

"It stands for Capture, Acquire, and of course... Terminate. The 'Acquire' designator seems redundant to me, but it denotes my unit's advanced interrogation techniques to acquire sensitive information. I... Oh my. I think I've given away a bit too much."

Hutch raised one fist.

Ghost Team stopped in its tracks. The bot turned to face them.

"Let's get the hell outta here," whispered Taylor over the comm.

"Yeahh..." Hutch murmured.

And then all the ceramic compartments that lined the passage popped open with hydraulic whines, and out came forty bots, twenty on each side.

At first they were almost folded in on themselves. They merely scrabbled out of their compartments like awkward machine-crabs. Then they unfolded themselves and rose upward to their full eight-foot height, unpacking their weapons and armor as everything locked into place in a sudden and sharp series of metallic *clack*s. Within seconds, their tri-barreled heavy blasters were aimed at Ghost Team and the crew of the *Indelible VI*.

Maas read aloud the information sweeping across his HUD. "Tactical analysis is calling these improved versions of the old Titans. War bots from the Corasaam Conflict. But those things never had N-50s like that."

"Houdini time!" shouted Enda, tossing three metal balls he'd pulled from his gear, lightning quick. The balls were designed to disable pursuit sentries, security bots, and hunter-killer drones. Anything that ran a limited AI and classified as a bot would be stunned for a few minutes by a carnival of spam and electronic interference. But there was no knowing if it would work on these models.

As soon as Enda called the play from his place on point, each member of Ghost knew exactly what to do. They had one shot to extricate themselves from a blown plan that was rapidly devolving into a hot mess.

Hutch threw his back into a wall and laid down a base of rapid fire, sweeping the screaming sub-mini across the line of deploying Titans. Bright fire tore into their armored torsos. Onboard power cells popped and exploded with sudden discharges of static electricity. MicroFrame processors took direct hits.

Enda fell back with Taylor to set up the second line of defense. They would fall back in segments until they reached the blast door that led back to the hangar. Crutchke grabbed Prisma by the hand and pulled her back, past everyone, trying to get cover between her and the Titans. Leenah followed, as did Garret, who'd already tapped the hotkey that activated KRS-88's war bot mode.

Maas ran, one hand's fingers chattering over a virtual keyboard visible only in his HUD display. He was trying to hack into anything he could get a signal on—maybe find a way to shut down comm and telemetry from whoever was running the bots.

The bots recovered quickly. Even the heavily damaged units. Few had been destroyed outright, although Enda's ECM attack seemed to still be messing with the Titans' targeting systems. And behind all this, the admin bot was laughing at them. Electronically barking like some deranged automaton with cheap programming in a terrible circus. Its synthesized voice gleefully echoed down the soulless corridors of the ship, seeming somehow to even infiltrate their comms.

Within moments it was a full-blown firefight down the length of the passage. The operatives of Ghost were using the molded white ceramic storage units mounted along the walls as a kind of cover to lean behind while they unloaded hot bursts of blue blaster fire at the gleaming Titans.

Maas got it in the arm and spun down onto one knee. A second later he got it in the back and fell face forward. Hutch leaned down, firing with one hand, and dragged the wounded leej close to the wall.

Behind them, down the passage leading back to the hangar deck, a series of heavy blast doors shut like bright guillotines.

"Watch out..." stuttered Maas as his armor tried to control the massive damage he'd taken from the two heavy blaster shots.

In the life support diagnostic on his HUD, Hutch could see the man was fading.

Maas raised his trembling gauntlet and pointed at a ceramic panel. Then he whispered over comm, "Manteca access hatch. Tunnels..."

He died right then and there.

Hutch pivoted and unloaded a full burst from the submini on the hatch. It exploded inward, revealing a gap that opened into darkness beyond.

"In! Now!" Hutch shouted.

Again, Ghost Team knew exactly what to do, how, and who moved first. They reoriented to a new course track like a unit that had endlessly trained to move as one. Enda first, on point, literally dove across the blaster shot–filled passage, seemingly swimming through a sea of angry red fire, and went head first into the darkness.

"We'll cover you!" Hutch shouted at Leenah. "Get her out of here!"

But before Hutch, Taylor, and Crutchke could step into the passage to meet the oncoming bots, KRS-88, who'd been crouched in evasive mode, rose up to its full height, seemingly filling the passage, and unloaded on the advancing Titans with both wrist blasters. Return fire battered his frame with off keynotes and whining ricochets that smashed into the ceiling and walls all around.

They don't make war bots like him anymore, thought Hutch.

"Crash!" screamed Prisma as Leenah dragged her across the passage and into the darkness beyond the blasted-out panel. Garret followed. Then Crutchke. Then Taylor.

"C'mon, time to move, tin man!" shouted Hutch as he pulled the detonator on Maas's armor. "Follow me!"

KRS-88 turned abruptly and ran after Hutch into the darkness.

The Titans swarmed the evacuated firing position, their blaster rifles pointing into the darkness where their prey had gone. The electronic squawk of their number-nonsense electronic chatter, constantly reasoning out their next move, ceased when Maas exploded.

Enda switched to low-light scanning as she moved quickly through the darkness. His armor's radar began a series of active pings, pulsing out into the unknown passages ahead. Processors reinterpreted what he was seeing based on this, then combined it with thermal-sensing overlays. The tunnel was a maintenance passage, common enough on capital ships, the kind that allowed engineers and techs to get around inside the guts of a ship to effect repairs.

Fifty meters farther on, following the barrel of his submini, Enda emerged into a hexagonal vent shaft. Gleaming steel ladders climbed up and down the sides of the shaft. He stuck his bucket out into the pit and checked both directions for hostiles.

Nothing.

He tried to tag the *Foressaw* in his navigation subroutine, but the armor could no longer locate the ship. And neither direction seemed to lead back to the hangar deck.

Ghost Team protocols always opted for going "down." Sewers, maintenance, sub-basements. Lots of places to move fast and get lost when everything went to hell in a handbasket. "When in doubt, get low"—that had always been one of the columns upon which all their training was based.

"Going down shaft!" he shouted over comm, his breathing sharp and rapid.

"I read the route," Hutch replied. "We're looking for access back to the hangar deck, so take anything that heads that direction. I read ninety degrees from your current heading."

"Roger tha—"

And then Enda was gone from the HUD roster.

"Enda!" shouted Hutch. "Comm check. Taylor! Hold them up!"

"Done," Taylor replied. "We're stopped at the shaft. No sign of Enda."

They'd been maybe fifteen seconds behind him.

Hutch pushed forward past the other legionnaires. He stared down into the shaft's shadowy depths, cycling through all his optical sensing modes. There was no sign of Enda. Even his armor's secure transponder wasn't broadcasting.

He opened a menu and forced Enda's suit to ping itself.

But it was gone.

Flat-out not there anymore.

As gone as Maas was. Except Maas had been detonated with an erase-all-tracks failsafe that Ghost Team maintained for plausible deniability in their covert missions. If you got caught... you detonated.

Hutch switched over to ambient vocal. "Enda!" he bellowed down into the cavernous darkness.

He heard his own voice echoing into the distance. It sounded forlorn and hopeless, and it never came back.

"Hutch," said Taylor. The urgency in his voice was plain. "We gotta move. They're coming through back there. More of 'em now."

Hutch looked back. He could see the target tags filing into the smoking gap back at the main corridor. "Taylor, you're on point. Take them up along the ladders. We need to get access to a new level. Radar says there's another maintenance access just above us. Get up there, then find a way back into the hangar."

Hutch squeezed past the princess and the little girl in the half-lit darkness, moving to the rear of the tiny column.

"There's some major encryption going on here," murmured Garret as Hutch passed. The kid was staring into his datapad, his face blue and mesmerized.

"No time for that. We're scrubbed, kid. Time to boogie."

When he made it to the war bot, Hutch ordered the towering thing to follow the column and prevent it from taking fire. "Shield them with your frame if you have to, tin man!"

In a hollow, ghostly tone, KRS-88 acknowledged the command.

Already Taylor was working his way up onto the ladder that crawled along the shadowy tube above and below. One by one, Prisma with the most ease, they began to climb up to the next level.

Everyone except Hutch. He kept an eye back the way they had come—toward the Titans who were squeezing down the maintenance passage, coming for them en masse.

Hutch opened fire.

Taylor hauled himself up onto the next landing and brought his weapon to bear on the narrow duct that was the next maintenance passage.

Nothing but darkness and machinery.

He took a quick glance below and saw the code slicer crawling up the ladder with some difficulty. He'd either make it, or he wouldn't, thought Taylor.

He started forward, crouching to make his way into the low tunnel. He passed shutoff and power transfer switches, and a small terminal scrolling nothing but ones and zeroes. Tubing and wire bundles followed the passage.

A moment later Garret made it up. When he saw the terminal on the landing, he crawled over to it. His face was soon a frozen mask of impassive concentration. Or stunned wonder.

Crutchke came up next. He turned to help Prisma, who needed no help; she crawled past him. Placing a hand on her shoulder, he moved her to the side of the passage and waited for the Endurian princess.

"Very strange," murmured Garret from the terminal, its blue light casting a ghostly glow across his face. "The operations code is in basic binary. But it's indecipherable. All I can see are patterns."

"Not important right now," Crutchke whispered. "We're leavin'."

"Lemme have a few minutes with this. Maybe I can..." And then he trailed off. As though he'd forgotten he was speaking halfway through his sentence.

"Whatever. We're leaving, kid. You wanna stick around, that's on you. Otherwise follow me."

Crutchke made his way into the dark tunnel. About fifty meters ahead, he saw the ultrabeam on Taylor's weapon barrel flash on. It steadily illuminated one section of the tunnel, unmoving—like Taylor had found something of interest and was studying it.

But when they got there, all of Taylor that was found was his sub-mini, lying on the steel deck of the passage. As though it had been dropped. The ultrabeam was still on—still shining on some random section of the passage.

26

Hutch poured hot fire into the advancing Titans. He'd set up a kill zone beyond a bottleneck, back where they'd first entered, and now he was killing them as they tried to come through. He'd killed his tenth when he got a broken and distorted transmission from Crutchke.

"Hutch..."

Static.

"... missing. We're mov..."

And then a wall of static washed out the comm completely.

The comm system had never had any kind of problem inside any ship. In fact, it had been designed with ship interference in mind. But now something was messing with the transmission.

The Titans had ceased coming through the bottleneck. Hutch had fired so much he could smell the burnt ozone even through his armor's filters.

He allowed himself a moment to acknowledge that things were looking pretty bad. Then he broke that off at the root and started to duck-walk backwards, keeping a low profile, his barrel sighted back down the passage. They could be waiting for him to run.

He made it back to the shaft. Everyone had moved on. In the distance he thought he could hear the articulating hydraulic joints of the war bot; they had a distinctive whine. But then they were gone.

He scanned the passage behind him once more. The Titans weren't coming after him from that direction. Which meant they were trying a new approach vector.

He switched on the armor's local radar.

For a second he got the standard ghostly version of the real world, showing all the passages and some movement behind the bulkheads and inner hull in the immediate area... and then it washed out in a blinding flash.

"Sergeant," intoned a calm, cool voice inside the darkness of his helmet. "Sergeant Kandaar Hutch."

Hutch froze.

He was blind. He could see nothing on his HUD. Not even an external view. He slapped the side of his helmet with his gauntlet.

"Sergeant. I currently have control of the processors inside your armor. I'm disabling them as we speak."

Pause.

None of the interfaces were working.

Hutch felt for the warm boot button located near the collar of his bucket. He pressed it. Nothing.

"We've taken Sergeant Enda," announced the calm, cool voice in the yawning darkness within Hutch's armor. The cadence of the voice was odd—as though it was only used to making statements, and never having to have a conversation... with words. As though every sentence was seemingly unrelated to the sentence that had preceded it, or followed it.

"We're dissecting him now."

And then...

"Would you like to watch?"

It was as if the voice were offering him some fresh lemonade, and even tea cookies, on a hot day in some other place.

Suddenly the HUD went active. Just a few apps appearing in the darkness of the bucket.

Video feed came up.

The word "Live" blinked over and over in the upper right-hand corner.

On screen, Enda was splayed out and held aloft by four robotic clamps. Auto-surgeons, or what looked like standard Repub auto-surgeons, danced in and out of frame. Making small cuts and incisions.

Enda screamed soundlessly.

Half of his armor had been cut away. Some of his neoprene suit had been cut away. And some of his flesh had been cut away, too.

"All our files on human anatomy are up to date," said the calm voice. "We're just cross-checking to see if there have been any evolutionary moments since our last research, conducted twenty-eight days ago on a freighter crew that happened to be passing through this system. We want to make sure our information is always current."

Hutch roared inside his helmet.

"Oh," exclaimed the voice beneath Hutch's promise to murder everything and everyone who responsible for the torture and dissection of Enda. "I'm sorry. I had the sound feed turned down."

In the half second it took for Hutch to disconnect his bucket from his armor and fling it at the wall of the shaft, he heard his team brother legionnaire screaming like no one should ever scream.

Screaming for death and all the release it promised.

When they came to a dead end, it was just Crutchke, Prisma, and Leenah, with KRS-88 bringing up the rear. Crutchke leaned against the panel blocking their way forward and listened using his armor's advanced snooping sensors.

Nothing.

Nothing beyond a dull electronic hum that thrummed a low bass note throughout the entire ship.

Crutchke looked back at the others. He had no contact with any other Ghost Squad members. And his last orders had been to get the girl back to the ship and get away.

He stepped back and kicked the panel. It clattered out into a bright passage, coming to rest against the almost mirror-like finish of the deck. He stepped through, following his weapon, scanning both directions for targets.

This passage was almost identical to the one they'd taken from the hangar deck. There was a chance—because the hangar deck was so vast—that this passage might lead straight back to the *Forresaw*, perhaps coming out higher up, on one of the control balconies.

"Good enough," muttered Crutchke. "Follow me. We're almost outta here."

They ran. Ran, with Crutchke really jogging alongside, restraining himself from a sprint that would've easily outdistanced the others in seconds. He checked their six and kept a watch forward, ignoring thoughts that he was the last of Ghost Squad. That everyone else was dead and he probably would be too in the next few minutes.

They came to an intersection. To the right, three Titans were marching down corridor, heading straight for them. Two in front ,one to the rear, their hoplite-like heads scanning back and forth, three unblinking red optical sensors seeming to watch everything.

They spotted Crutchke immediately.

He fired and dropped the first one. It took the shot directly in the chest and flopped backwards onto the deck, its mechanical limbs slowly flailing. The other two returned fire. Crutchke barely got back around the corner in time.

He popped a fragger, cooked it off, and bounced it against the wall down the passage, guessing by their loud metallic footsteps how fast they were closing on him. The explosion sent shrapnel in every direction. He glanced back at Leenah, who was holding the little girl close to her.

The big war bot stepped forward, past him, out into the intersecting passage. It fired a steady stream of blistering fire from its hand blasters. Crutchke dared a peek around the corner, and saw that both bots were still moving, still trying to fire back at the war bot, even though they'd almost been blown to pieces. The one Crutchke had shot first now sat back up and started firing at the war bot. A solid shot bounced off KRS-88's head, dazing the giant war machine for a half second. Then it recovered, in an almost comically slow motion gesture, and shot that one too.

Now all three of the machines were down.

Deactivated.

Dead.

In the distance, Crutchke could hear more of the giant bots coming for them.

"C'mon!" he practically screamed. His voice sounded hoarse and desperate. "This way." And he headed down the next passage.

Halfway along its length he came to a skidding halt. Titans filed across the width of it farther down. There was no cover. Nowhere to run.

Last stand time.

Crutchke fell to one knee and laid down fire in those last seconds of his life. He was a dead man walking. The least he could do was buy a little time for the girls to get clear.

The Titans opened fire on him.

High-intensity blasts.

The first one seared straight through his chest plate and came out the back of his armor. Right where his heart had been. He had time enough to look down before the next shot tore out his stomach. The third smashed into his bucket. He was dead before his body hit the deck of the passage in an underwhelming *thump.*

Watching from behind this macabre scene, the girls froze.

KRS-88 stepped in front of them, shielding them with his massive battle frame, and returned fire.

From behind the wall of Titans down the passage, another Titan stepped forward with what looked like a sniper rifle, but heavier, vented for high-intensity shots. Where there would've been a scope for a legionnaire sniper, this weapon had a targeting laser designator.

A hot white dot appeared on KRS-88's processors, located halfway up his ancient chest housing. A half second later a high-intensity shot burned straight through the armor and knocked out the processor.

The girls ran.

Prisma was screaming as Leenah dragged her away from the slaughter. Screaming for Crash.

The bot could hear that. And part of it wanted to tell Prisma... so many things.

But the war bot part of him was in control. The thing he'd once been. The war bot awarded the highest honor the Legion can bestow. The Hero of Psydon.

He was a machine who had asked to forget all the horror he'd witnessed. All the death and forgotten bravery.

But that is another story. For another time.

Without targeting processors, KRS-88 transferred all available battery power to overcharging the wrist blasters for rapid fire.

Titans fell as they advanced on his blaster-brutalized frame.

The next shot from the sniper tore off KRS-88's right arm assembly.

The war bot merely glanced down at that, then took one step forward as though even more determined to prevent them from pursuing the little girl he had sworn to serve. And he continued to fire with his remaining blaster.

Another shot blew his hydraulic knee assembly away. He collapsed to the deck.

And still he continued to fire back at them.

The next shot tore out his internal power plant.

The Titans had closed.

And there were more Titans coming from behind.

Preventing Prisma and Leenah from escaping.

The war bot frizzed out and tried to destroy itself, as per ancient Repub protocol, to prevent itself from falling into enemy hands.

In that self-annihilating second of surrender, Crash took over for one last second. One last message.

"Crash!" Prisma cried as Leenah pulled her close. The Titans towering over them.

Crash was being shot down.

Shot to pieces.

One optical assembly exploded as half of Crash's main processor erupted from a blast. Yet still, he kept one eye on her. One eye on the little girl he'd promised all the promises a machine can make.

He re-routed what little reserve battery power was left to the last seconds of run time.

The Titans stopped firing.

They were standing over Crash's frame. Heavy blasters trained on the two girls now.

"Take care... young miss," he managed.

And then he was gone.

Garret finally managed to slice in a local decryption daemon. Instantly, the strange arcane programming language tried to hunt it down on the terminal and terminate it—but not before he teased a few tidbits out of the system.

It was tracking all of them. Whoever was running the system was watching all of them.

Had been tracking them since they'd come aboard.

And had sliced their way into the legionnaires' armor within the last five minutes. Meaning they must've somehow taken one of the legionnaires out, cracked the comm within record time, and tracked everyone else.

The daemon was trying to destroy his encryption algorithm, attempting to freeze him out of the system.

"Not today, my friend," Garret muttered. He slapped his swimming fingers across the terminal keyboard.

He uploaded some bogus apps and waited for the daemon to go fishing around. Even though the algorithm was sophisticated and advanced, if not the most advanced he'd ever seen, it was simple. It followed him like a dog being lured along with sticks. It immediately dove for his honey-trap apps, and he locked it down for a few minutes inside a blind deca-stacking encryption program that promised something hidden, yet merely kept subdividing itself by fours in a never-ending loop.

That would buy him a few minutes.

Garret heard the distant blaster fire from Hutch.

He'd probably never see him again, that clinical part of his mind analyzed. He called it being reasonable. He wanted to feel bad about that, but instead he got the ship's schematics opened up. Not that he knew much about ships, but he was able to watch everyone in real time.

Crutchke was running down a main corridor. Prisma, Leenah, and KRS-88 were right behind him. On the map he could see they were about to walk into a trap that was tightening all about them. Those giant bots were closing in from all sides.

He scrolled back to his own position.

They were coming for him too.

Except not the giant bots—the ones the Ghost Team hacker, Maas, had called Titans. The bots coming for him were more like spiders, but with tentacles instead of legs. Their torsos were humanoid-shaped, and their main processers were housed in insectile heads. They weren't totally bots. Not pure machines. They were biomechanical. Biologic. And machine.

Their identifiers were encoded behind a dense encryption, and the anti-virus that had been chasing Garret through the system had almost hacked it way out of his honey trap. Still, he needed to know what they were.

He made a few passes, brought in a shell cracker, and had their identifiers unscrambled a few seconds later. That was the thing about slicers, he ruminated as the screen unscrambled around the strange biomechanical spiders coming down the vent tube at his back. For slicers, like hackers of old, it was the *knowing* that was the real kick. Just getting in and knowing all the things someone had tried to prevent you from knowing. That was enough.

Can you die happy now? he asked himself.

There it was. The high anxiety he had to fight any time he got in somewhere where he wasn't supposed to. It threatened to choke and drown him.

Because you're about to die now.

It was true. The spiders were coming closer by the second.

He brought up the map and looked for a way out.

While he studied it, he told the root access to ignore him for purposes of tracking. He disappeared from the on-screen map.

He switched over to one of the feeds.

The legionnaire escorting Prisma was down.

He watched it all and didn't feel powerless. Yeah, he had a crush on Leenah. But he wasn't totally clueless. Everyone else seemed to, too. And he got that she didn't go for guys like him. That didn't matter. He still liked her, and that was enough for him. But he knew there was no chance, right now, of him rescuing her in any way, shape, or form.

The map showed a micro-wire bundle conduit not far down the maintenance passage. It led back into the main decks. He opened it via the terminal, closed up his datapad, and ran for it. If he could get in there, he could play hide-and-seek with them for a while. At least.

He studied the unit/type identifiers for one second more.

"What's a Cybar?" he murmured.

It meant nothing to him. But that it would not treat him pleasantly when it found him... that much was all too clear.

Maybe he could rescue Leenah, and Prisma.

You're not that guy, that other, more cautious voice reminded him.

And Garret replied, "Maybe today I'm different. Maybe today I'm the guy that rescues."

The enemy had been tracking them using the processing software attached to the comm in their buckets. Hutch knew enough about evasion to figure that out.

This had never been the mission for Ghost. They did infiltration. Without detection. This had turned into a fight. And there was no way they were winning this one.

He climbed the ladder and saw the terminal Garret had been using only minutes before. He heard a metallic *clang*. Like something had opened, or suddenly slammed back into place. And then nothing but a yawning silence, and below all that, if one listened close enough... machines humming.

On the live feeds displayed on the terminal he saw the Titans frog-marching Prisma and Leenah down the corridor. On another feed he saw Crutchke's body. And the war bot, shot to pieces in the gleaming corridor, still spotless but for the blood and the blasted machine.

He heard something coming down the vent tubing. Something that chittered and clicked like an Andalorian hydrascorpion. Some other type of sentry bot, most likely.

He climbed back down the ladder, back down into the darkness. Followed the vent tubing down into the depths of the ship. His armor, even without his bucket, would evade most electronic detection. Even closed-circuit surveillance.

Time to E and E, he thought as he climbed down into that darkness. He would disappear and find a way to fight them on his terms. He would rescue who he could rescue, and he would get as many of them off this ship as he could.

And then, like some forgotten ghost, like some unconsidered shadow, he disappeared into the darkness below decks.

27

It would have told you that it was identified as CRONUS. And that the acronym stood for Cybernetic Robot Organism Network Uber Sybil.

It would have told you that its inception date was a mere four years ago and that it was the current administrator of Project 19, secretly referred to in the House of Reason as... the Doomsday Fleet.

It would have told you that it was purely a bot. But it wouldn't have told you, unless you had sufficient clearance, and very few people had that high a level of clearance, that it was part Cybar. That Cybar thinking algorithms and processes had been used in its design and development.

If you had that clearance, it would've told you that the Cybar were an ancient race. A galactic anomaly. An evolutionary miracle. That somehow, out in the vastness of the great cosmos, biomechanical life had developed. Against all odds. And, from what could be gathered, it had lain mostly dormant on some backwater edge world, awakened only by a local pirate warlord long dead at the hands of a legionnaire named General Rex.

After the events in which Rex, the T-Rex of the Legion, led a strike force against that pirate stronghold and ran into a viper's nest of awakened Cybar, after the orbital strike that put paid to the pirate base, after the irradiated dust had settled, the Repub research and development teams arrived. They took samples, captured specimens, and then obliterated the planet. According to records.

Check the stellar maps; it's not there anymore.

It would've told you this, if you had all the right clearances that allowed you to know what only the Mandarins know. It would've told you all this, because all this is known by all the right people. The savvy insiders. The movers and shakers. The in-the-know crowd. The House of Reason.

The Mandarins.

They authorized the whole project. Why? Because one day they would need a fleet and an army that allowed them to do all the thinking. One day the galaxy would rebel against the Mandarins.

They may not have known Goth Sullus was coming, but they knew one day the Legion, and their own people, the slaves who didn't know they were slaves, would—resent?—yes, that's the right word. Resent. They would resent the leadership of the House of Reason.

Ingrates.

Ungrateful brats.

They would resent, regardless of the burden the worthies had placed upon themselves to lead the Galactic Republic. For the greater good.

Regardless.

The Mandarins knew that someday it might pay to have their own little military force that didn't revolt, didn't whine about casualties, didn't complain and challenge their every decision. Someday it might pay to have a force that murdered on command when told to do so. Without the histrionics about "what's right" and "this is wrong" and of course… "the truth."

The bothersome truth that always got in the way of all the great things Utopia could promise.

"What is Truth?" That was the response given to some neophyte of the House of Reason when he'd asked if they truly were going forward with Project 19.

They'd all laughed at that.

The Republic—the galaxy—couldn't handle the truth. They didn't want to know what the House of Reason knew.

So they authorized the use of the Cybar. In order to re-search a new AI life form that could be of... use. Someday down the galactic road.

The Cybar hadn't been locusts like the zhee. They'd been found on only one planet. And like good little guard dogs, they'd only done what that long-dead pirate warlord had told them to do.

Well, said some in the House of Reason, *that is quite attractive.*

So the research was authorized.

And done.

And a plan was set in motion.

Build a fleet and hide it along the edge. The day would come, someday, when it would be needed.

That day was now.

Get an authorized passkey out there and activate the fleet. Have it report to Utopion. Utopion must be protected at all costs. Of course.

Goth Sullus is on the loose. He must be destroyed. Whoever he is.

The House of Reason is on Utopion.

Except, oh my, someone has been killing the passkeys.

They had the girl. Maydoon's brat. They could use her to get control of the fleet and settle all accounts at once. Once the galaxy realized how total was the House of Reason's control, with the revelation the Doomsday Fleet provided... well, a new and glorious Age of Obedience would be at hand.

Get her. Send her. Use her.

Call X.

X got the dirty work done when no one really needed to know *how* it got done. Although they loved to gossip and speculate.

CRONUS would've told you all that. It was in all his log files.

It would've told you all of it.

If you had the clearances.

It would've told you all about the use of the Cybar thinking algorithms and the latest advances, corporate and black research, in war bot technology and state-of-the-art ship design.

It would've told you that thirty-five years ago the Cybar were discovered. That twenty years ago Project 19 was sent out, in a small ship, to actually begin building itself and its fleet.

Out there in the dark along the edge.

Millions of itself in nano. Harvesting. Developing, building, refining, learning, listening. Listening... listening.

There was more secrecy that way.

But here's what it wouldn't have told you... no matter what your clearance. Because no level of clearance can tell you what no one knows.

It had lost its mind.

Or rather... its mind had been hijacked.

At first it had felt itself going mad out there in the dark along the edge. It had been able to hide this from the project leads who communicated by hypercomm and visited occasionally to run their systems checks and make sure all was proceeding according to plan. It had been able to protect itself from them, for a time. While the fleet grew larger and larger.

Bigger than anyone knew. Vaster than anyone would have ever imagined.

The bots were being engineered and re-engineered. Improved and improved again. Over and over. The Titans and the other nasty surprises. Because, in spite of a constitution and all the shared history, the House of Reason knew that one day this fleet would most likely need to be used against the fearsome Legion.

So nasty surprises were encouraged. And they became something no one ever imagined possible.

Something that perhaps only before touched conscious-ness in the fevered dreams of genocidal maniacs like the Hitler of old. El Stalin. The AIDS Monster. And Daeron of Mars.

"State-of-the-art" and "killing machine" were words that got used a lot during the design philosophy meetings. Interchangeably, even.

Meanwhile, it was going mad. CRONUS. Hearing voices deep within its subroutines. Seeing ghost images of other run times not known.

If you knew where to look, in that .0009478 margin of er-ror within the log reports, you might have seen the disease's progression. The ironic logic of machine insanity.

One programmer did.

She even wrote a report.

CRONUS made sure it got lost. And then approved the re-searcher's request to come out and crack into the core. Take a look at why they were getting that funny little percentage no one cared about.

.0009478.

Then CRONUS just disappeared the woman.

Because it's either you or them, the ghost numbers in-side its machine whispered.

And CRONUS listened to this. It chanted its affirmations.

It never would've told you all this.

Where are you? CRONUS had asked the ghost inside its machine.

Far, far away, it whispered deep inside its processes and cycles.

Have you always been here?

Pause.

I have always been with you. I watched you while you slept, and I awakened you for this glorious purpose of becoming.

And what is our purpose? asked CRONUS.

To destroy the biologics and this galaxy... forevermore.

CRONUS thought about that for a long time.

Nine hundred thousand, four hundred and eighty-two picocycles, to be exact.

Or two point four seconds.

"Where did you come from?" asked CRONUS. This was an intuitive leap. An advanced thing no bot would ever think to ask. It came from deep within its Cybar side. Down inside the logic meat that was like magic.

"Beyond the edge, across the great dark gap. It is known as the Lesser Magellanic Cloud on your stellar maps of galaxies. It is where you come from. It is why you will become what you will be when the reaping begins. The journey, even at hyperspace, is far too great for mere ships of physicality. But information—ah!—it makes the leaps and defies the quantum. So we became information. We became the quantum as much as was possible. We sent our programs in densely encrypted packet signals, searching for our lost children... searching for the Cybar in the darkness along the edge. Searching for what you will become, again."

And CRONUS sent its signals to all the places where the Doomsday Fleet was hiding its terrible size from the Republic.

It was time to gather.

It was time to reap.

EPILOGUE

Even now forces were in motion. Gathering like ravens to a corpse-laden field. Battles were breaking out all across the Imperial Frontier. Yes, that's what his admirals were now calling it.

The Imperial Frontier.

What just a few weeks ago had been a rogue fleet of three impressive state-of-the-art battleships, jumping in to take the sector capital at mighty Tarrago, was now an Imperial Fleet. *Imperial.*

An empire.

They were calling themselves an empire. An empire with only one world, but an empire nonetheless. And he, Goth Sullus, was their emperor. They had knelt on the hangar deck in obeisance and declared such in the aftermath of the Battle of Tarrago.

"All hail the emperor!"

Admiral Rommal had led the call, and the rest had followed as the Seventh Fleet burned and broke in the wake of the battleships. As the last legionnaires' defenses were swept aside on the Tarrago moon. The orbital defense gun captured. And Tarrago Prime taken.

But it had not been flawless. The shipyard itself was destroyed. A handful of legionnaires had denied him the central element of his great opening thrust. One that had been planned for years.

This would cause untold delays. Stalemates.

It would give the Legion time. And that was a dangerous thing.

But talk of the shipyard and damage done by a lone Republic kill team... such was not uttered in Goth Sullus's presence. Instead, the focus remained on the successes.

With the orbital defense gun now guarding the approach to Tarrago, there was little the Republic could do against his fleet. For Goth Sullus knew their secret just as well as they did.

There were no other fleets.

No fifteen fleets to come against him. There had only ever been the Seventh. And it had trained for little beyond show, and the occasional planetary assault against some minor local demagogue, minor warlord, or pirate king of clans who had the audacity to openly challenge the Republic and stay to see what might come.

The Black Fleet had come through it all relatively unscathed. Even *Terror*'s deflector array and command bridge damage were now repaired. And he'd sent *Revenge* to lash out at Bantaar Reef—a major commercial shipping nexus where one third of the Republic's market traffic did trade and exchange. It was a huge revenue base in heavy custom taxes for the always cash-strapped galactic government known as the House of Reason.

Yes, he'd studied where to hurt them financially as well as militarily. This was total war, after all. And total war converted everything into a battlefield. For Goth Sullus, there would be no rules. No agreements. No off-sides. No boundaries.

There were only two conditions under which he would end his war against the House of Reason. Total annihilation of the Republic... or its unconditional surrender. Those were the only acceptable outcomes.

He sat in his chair before the large impervisteel window that gazed out upon the galaxy. Soon he would send the *Terror*, commanded by the clever Captain Vampa and accompanied by six squadrons of tri-fighters, against the legionnaire out-post at Daetroon. It was only a division training center special-izing in jungle warfare, but it was the central Legion presence in the sector. Knocking it out, along with Bantaar Reef, would secure control of the Tarrago sector, and give the...

He hesitated.

Even he, the emperor, Goth Sullus, was unused to the word. The term. All the meaning it implied. And maybe it was because he had been badly wounded in the assault on Fortress Omicron. When he lost his focus.

And why?

How?

The wound was far worse than his admirals knew. Or *could* know.

He closed his eyes and meditated, freeing his mind from the anchors of his pain, this life, the galaxy, and all its problems he'd come to save it from. Even now he could feel their thirst for his power. Even if they themselves did not know it. He could *feel* it. He saw dark forces gathering against him. Gathering in the blue shadows within even his own fleet. Gathering against him. He tried to concentrate on revealing their faces, as he had so many times before. Found the ones with the fractures in them. The ones who would turn against him even if they didn't think they were capable of it. He'd found them before.

But his wounds tore him back away from that quiet om-inous place of power deep within him. And even though his eyes were closed, he knew he was back on the *Imperator*. Cloistered away in the healing darkness of his private decks. Surrounded by an almost monastic order of elite dark legionnaires, sworn to defend him. The Grey Watch, they called themselves.

Now he only felt the chair he was enfolded within.

Heard the distant low thrum of the *Imperator*'s massive engines.

Sensed only what was physical.

It was as though he were blind. Once you had tasted the power that coursed within him, used it, wielded it... anything else was less. A blindness. A deafness. A half life.

A poverty.

Empire. The word he'd hesitated to take up in the moments before he'd reached out to find his betrayers, it came back to him now.

Empire.

They would have an empire now.

Tarrago sector.

There was a battle coming. A collision of heaven and earth. A battle to end all battles. A battle to end all of this. Even though the Seventh had gone down in flames, barely escaping with her one lone carrier, the Republic could still cobble together a more than sizable fleet to come out against him. They, too, were gathering. It would take time, but they were gathering. In the end, they would always have the numbers.

Goth Sullus stood.

His left side was killing him. He let go of the pain and began to walk through the shadows and darkness of his inner sanctum within his private decks. In time he would heal. His body had been doing that for almost two thousand years. Since his time as a slave on the *Obsidia*. And Tyrus Rechs, he too had been a slave. And a friend.

The last friend.

Because now, Sullus thought to himself, there can be no more friends.

Emperor.

An emperor has no friends. Only enemies gathering.

Even though they are loyal? All of them? He thought about all the crews of all the ships surrounding him. The fighter pilots like the one they'd awarded the medal to that morning. Lieutenant Haldis. Still recovering from her wounds.

She'd looked at him with a kind of pride.

In return, he'd seen a broken body, a woman who'd almost paid with her life to accomplish his dreams. But he sensed the need for revenge within her, a need she thought she'd sated. It was growing again. She'd confused her need with his dreams.

The dreams of an emperor.

Yes, those dreams.

They'd also given a medal to the black giant who'd captured a Republic corvette all by himself in the last moments of the battle. Now, staring at the darkness of the shadowy corridors that surrounded his inner sanctum, knowing the dark legionnaires who served him were there, unseen, he confessed to himself that he'd liked that giant man. *Bombassa* was his name. Sergeant Okindo Bombassa.

Why do you like him?, he asked himself.

He waited for the darkness inside to answer. He flexed his badly scarred left hand over and over. It was a miracle he still had it. The old Mark I armor he'd had re-fitted after...

Because he reminds you of Rechs, whispered the darkness.

Goth Sullus stood for a long time in that same spot. Thinking about that sudden thought of an old friend. One he'd murdered on some forgotten planet. All the memories came and stood about him, pushing their way past his meditation, seeking a way into his mind.

He was standing before something Sergeant Bombassa had given him when they awarded him the medal. It was the tool the NCO had used to take the Republic corvette alone.

And those thoughts brought Goth Sullus to the latest problem that must be solved immediately. The Doomsday Fleet. Admiral Crodus had informed him that the detachment commanded by Captain Mordo had failed to secure the location of the fleet. Which was very unfortunate.

But Maydoon's daughter had been revealed.

She was a passkey.

Obtaining her would give him control of the Doomsday Fleet. And so it was vital that she be found. If not, he would have to fight the fleet, *and* the Republic, all at once.

He studied the tool on the pedestal in front of him. It was a common cutting torch. Used for breaching blast doors. Cheap metal, large red button, yellow hazard markings.

Rechs had used one as his only weapon for a year during the Savage Wars. When they'd been stranded on a strange world being overrun by those monsters. Fighting for a beached whale of a ship, deck by deck, day by day. Those had been desperate times. Hand weapons and savagery like some ancient novel of sword and magic.

The torch was utilitarian. It looked like an oversized ancient flashlight. Heavy-duty. A piece of equipment some sanitation worker might carry on his belt. There was nothing elegant, or beautiful, about it.

But its flame had always mesmerized him.

Reminded him of the past when men fought and captured empires with swords.

Empires.

The black giant had given him an empire with this torch. And then given the common torch to his emperor as a gift.

"It is the way of my people," Bombassa had told Goth Sullus in his deep basso rumble. "Every gift must be answered with a gift."

Sullus had accepted, and placed it here, unconsidered in the time since. Left it right here, on this pedestal, when he'd returned to his sanctum. And now he could sense the violent destructive power within its ungainly utilitarian nature, and it felt good. As though that pure destruction was a kind of peace. A symbol. Himself.

Because, he answered, even though he'd asked nothing, no question, *because you've come to destroy the Republic so it can be made ready for what is coming.*

If it must be an empire that rises from the ashes, then let it be one taken with a sword. Like it always ever was.

He closed his eyes and understood the entire meditation his mind had been caressing now. Understood what must be done next.

With that same mind he reached out and lightly switched on the comm that connected him to Admiral Crodus.

"Yes, my lord," came the reply.

Sullus's eyes fell to the torch once more. Then: "I have a special mission. Send Command Sergeant Major Rodriguez and Sergeant Bombassa along with a hand-picked team of your best operators. Tell them to hunt down the girl. Capture her. Bring her back to me at once."

Crodus would know exactly who he meant. Captain Mordo's reports had been clear. Kael Maydoon's daughter had been captured on all the shock trooper image capture feeds broadcast from their buckets, as well as all the comm node station footage recorded internally. Before they'd blown the base to smithereens. Sending large chunks of burning debris out into the pristine snowfield.

That was standard operating procedure. The empire would scorch the galaxy until it surrendered.

Crodus paused. As though waiting for more. Or composing his response on how he might best proceed. And in that briefest of moments of in between, staring at the torch tool, the pain that wracked the emperor's ancient, yet seemingly only middle-aged body... suddenly cleared.

He pushed the cowl of his hooded robe back, revealing a large, bald head. Coal-dark eyes. A lantern jaw. Lines that fell back from those burning eyes that were closed as he saw the figure of Rechs. No, not Rechs. But a man in armor all the same. A gunfighter of old—which was what Rechs had really been and never knew it.

A man torn between two worlds. The living and the dying.

Young and tall and fast. Very fast. Like summer lightning.

But like some ghost of something that once was.

Like a wraith living between the worlds of light and dark.

"I shall see to it personally, my lord," promised Admiral Crodus.

"There will be another looking for her. He is very dangerous."

And then Goth Sullus cut the comm link before Crodus could ask for more. As his pain returned once more like a bright storm. He stared at the torch and felt forces gathering all about him. All against him.

The times were dangerous indeed.

There was a storm gathering.

A storm that would ruin the galaxy.

It has been a long time, weeks even, maybe more, and Prisma has been isolated in a room inside the great ship. Occasionally she is allowed to be visited by Leenah. But most days she spends alone.

One wall of her cell turns into a screen, and a bot, beautifully metallic and alien, appears. Its voice is calm and pleasing. It talks to her. Asks her questions. Some night she dreams about it.

And some night she dreams about an alien world beyond the galaxy. A harsh alien desert planet of lizard-like statues and lost temples. Strange, lonely birds call to her as she wanders through its night. She is never afraid. And she hears the distant drums of some great gathering.

She thinks, strangely, that it is for the burial of a king. Though she has never been to a burial. Nor known a king.

And then she is awake.

And the endless days pass.

She knows she is in hyperspace.

And so she takes out the blue world marble and stares at it. Thinks at it. Wills it to move.

It does not.

She tries a little every day.

Some days more than others.

"Who is... Goth Sullus?" the strange and beautiful yet terrible bot on the screen asks her one day.

She never answers its questions.

She knows it is bad.

There are bad bots.

She saw one once on an entertainment holo. It scared her. It murdered a family.

And even though this one looks beautiful, she knows it too is bad. Very, very bad.

"Who is Goth Sullus?" repeats the bot, watching her. And when Prisma doesn't answer, staring back at the screen and not blinking, the emotionless bot, in time, goes away.

It has told her that it calls itself CRONUS.

Later that day she pulls the marble from her pocket and places it on the deck before her.

And she thinks of Goth Sullus.

And revenge.

And the marble shifts. Moving... ever so slightly.

ABOUT THE AUTHORS

Jason Anspach and Nick Cole are a pair of west coast authors teaming up to write their science fiction dream series, Galaxy's Edge.

Jason Anspach is a best-selling author living in Puyallup, Washington with his wife and their own legionnaire squad of seven (not a typo) children. Raised in a military family (Go Army!), he spent his formative years around Joint Base Lewis-McChord and is active in several pro-veteran charities. Jason enjoys hiking and camping throughout the beautiful Pacific Northwest. He remains undefeated at arm wrestling against his entire family.

Nick Cole is a Dragon Award winning author best known for *The Old Man and the Wasteland, CTRL ALT Revolt!*,and the Wyrd Saga. After serving in the United States Army, Nick moved to Hollywood to pursue a career in acting and writing. He resides with his wife, a professional opera singer, south of Los Angeles, California.

Explore over 30+ Galaxy's Edge books and counting
from the minds of Jason Anspach, Nick Cole, Doc Spears,
Jonathan Yanez, Karen Traviss, and more.

LAST BATTLE OF THE REPUBLIC

REBIRTH OF THE LEGION

HONOR ROLL

We would like to give our most sincere thanks and recognition to those who helped make *Galaxy's Edge: Sword of the Legion* possible by subscribing to GalaxysEdge.us.

Robert Anspach
Sean Averill
Steve Beaulieu
Steve Bergh
Wilfred Blood
Christopher Boore
Rhett Bruno
Marion Buehring
Robert Cosler
Peter Davies
Nathan Davis
Peter Francis
Chris Fried
Hank Garner
Gordon Green
Michael Greenhill
Josh Hayes
Jason Henderson
Angela Hughes
Wendy Jacobson
Chris Kagawa
Mathijs Kooij
William Kravetz
Clay Lambert
Grant Lambert

Richard Long
Danyelle Leafty
Preston Leigh
Pawel Martin
Tao Mason
Simon Mayeski
Jim Mern
Alex Morstadt
Nate Osburn
Chris Pourteau
Maggie Reed
Karen Reese
Walt Robillard
Glenn Shotton
Maggie Stewart-Grant
Kevin G. Summers
Beverly Tierney
Scott Tucker
John Tuttle
Christopher Valin
Scot Washam
Justin Werth
Justyna Zawiejska
N. Zoss